Dear Target Reader,

When I received the call sharing the extraordinary news that Target had selected *The Other Einstein* for its book club, it was a wonderful moment for me, to say the least. I have long been a Target Book Club reader, and I had to pinch myself thinking of *The Other Einstein* on those bookshelves! I can only hope that *The Other Einstein* inspires in you the same rich, nuanced thoughts and conversations that other Target Book Club picks have brought me and my own book club.

As you read the story of Mileva Marić, Albert Einstein's first wife and a physicist herself, will you marvel at a brilliant young woman who made an astonishing rise from the relative backwater of nineteenth-century Serbia, where it was illegal for girls to attend high school, to the all-male university physics classrooms of Switzerland? Will you discuss, even debate, the role Mileva played in the iconic scientist's discoveries, particularly since she was educated in the same classrooms as her famous husband, partnered with him regularly, and sat across the dinner table from him night after night during his most prolific period? Will you shake your heads in wonder and dismay as personal tragedy forces Mileva to consider marginalizing her academic ambitions and intellect in favor of Albert's ascent? Will you see yourselves, and others you know, in Mileva? Will you look at history and society through a new lens?

Oh, I hope so! Because if *The Other Einstein* sparks these sorts of discussions and prompts "aha" moments of affinity and clarity, then the book will have done the work I sent it out into the world to do. By excavating Mileva from the detritus of history—and sharing the story of a remarkable woman whose light has been lost in her husband's vast shadow—I have hoped to offer readers not only an important, timely story, but also a fresh perspective from which to view history and ourselves.

I am thrilled that *The Other Einstein* has the chance to be part of your Target Book Club conversations.

Marie Benedict

Marie Benedict

PRAISE FOR *THE OTHER EINSTEIN*

"Superb…the haunting story of Einstein's brilliant first wife who was lost in his shadow."

—Sue Monk Kidd, *New York Times* bestselling author of *The Invention of Wings*

"Beautifully written and filled with fascinating historical detail, *The Other Einstein* is a finely drawn portrait of not only what it was like to be a woman in love with physics at that time, but also what it was like to be a woman in love with the wrong man."

—Jillian Cantor, author of *Margot* and *The Hours Count*

"Marie Benedict brings us into the life and times of Mileva Marić Einstein, Albert's first wife. A brilliant mathematician in her own right, Mileva and Albert plan a life together of equal scholarship, but Albert's ambitions and Mileva's role as a wife and mother at the turn of the twentieth century make this an impossibility. Could the theory of relativity actually have been conceived by 'the other Einstein'? In this fascinating and thoughtful novel, we learn that this is more than possible."

—B. A. Shapiro, *New York Times* bestselling author of *The Art Forger* and *The Muralist*

"Convincingly resurrected by Marie Benedict, Mileva Marić Einstein is a crusading scientist undone by love. *The Other Einstein* is a fascinating glimpse into the failings of Albert Einstein as a husband and father. Mileva Marić fully deserves this welcome spotlight."

—Nuala O'Connor, author of *Miss Emily*

"*The Other Einstein* is phenomenal and heartbreaking, and phenomenally heartbreaking."

—Erika Robuck, national bestselling author of *Hemingway's Girl*

"Has the reader rooting for our heroine from the very first pages."

—Kathleen Tessaro, bestselling author of *Elegance* and *The Perfume Collector*

"An engaging and thought-provoking fictional telling of the poignant story of an overshadowed woman scientist."

—*Booklist*

"Intimate and immersive historical novel... Prepare to be moved by this provocative history of a woman whose experiences will resonate with today's readers."

—*Library Journal*, Editors' Pick

"An intriguing...reimagining of one of the strongest intellectual partnerships of the nineteenth century."

—*Kirkus Reviews*

"In her compelling novel...Benedict makes a strong case that the brilliant woman behind [Albert Einstein] was integral to his success, and creates a rich historical portrait in the process."

—*Publishers Weekly*

"A compelling read...[putting] Marić at the forefront of the narrative, letting her tell her own story."

—*Pittsburgh Post-Gazette*

THE OTHER EINSTEIN

a novel

MARIE BENEDICT

sourcebooks
landmark

Published by Sourcebooks Landmark, an imprint of Sourcebooks, Inc.
P.O. Box 4410, Naperville, Illinois 60567-4410
(630) 961-3900
Fax: (630) 961-2168
www.sourcebooks.com

Library of Congress has cataloged the hardcover edition as follows:

Names: Terrell, Heather, author.
Title: The other Einstein : a novel / Heather Terrell.
Description: Naperville, Illinois : Sourcebooks Landmark, [2016]
Identifiers: LCCN 2015046814 | (hardcover : acid-free paper)
Subjects: LCSH: Einstein-Marić, Mileva, 1875-1948--Fiction. | Einstein,
   Albert, 1879-1955--Marriage--Fiction. | Women
   physicists--Germany--Fiction. | GSAFD: Biographical fiction. | Historical
   fiction.
Classification: LCC PS3620.E75 O84 2016 | DDC 813/.6--dc23
LC record available at http://lccn.loc.gov/2015046814

Printed and bound in the United States of America.
VP 10 9 8 7 6 5 4 3 2 1

For Jim, Jack, and Ben

NORTH SEA

GERMANY

Paris

Heidelberg

Schaffhausen

Zürich

Stein am Rhein

Aarau

Sihl Valley

Basel

Mettmenstetten

SWITZERLAND

Bern

Engadine Valley

Lenk

Chiavenna

Cadenabbia

Lake Como

FRANCE

Como

ITALY

TYRRHENIAN SEA

PROLOGUE

August 4, 1948

62 Huttenstrasse
Zürich, Switzerland

The end is near. I feel it approaching like a dark, seductive shadow that will extinguish my remaining light. In these last minutes, I look back.

How did I lose my way? How did I lose Lieserl?

The darkness quickens. In the few moments I have left, like a meticulous archaeologist, I excavate the past for answers. I hope to learn, as I suggested long ago, if time is truly relative.

Mileva "Mitza" Marić Einstein

PART I

Every body perseveres in its state of rest, or of uniform motion in a right line, unless it is compelled to change that state by forces impressed thereon.

Sir Isaac Newton

CHAPTER 1

Morning
October 20, 1896
Zürich, Switzerland

I SMOOTHED THE WRINKLES ON MY FRESHLY PRESSED WHITE blouse, flattened the bow encircling my collar, and tucked back a stray hair into my tightly wound chignon. The humid walk through the foggy Zürich streets to the Swiss Federal Polytechnic campus played with my careful grooming. The stubborn refusal of my heavy, dark hair to stay fixed in place frustrated me. I wanted every detail of the day to be perfect.

Squaring my shoulders and willing myself to be just a little taller than my regrettably tiny frame, I placed my hand on the heavy brass handle to the classroom. Etched with a Greek key design worn down from the grip of generations of students, the knob dwarfed my small, almost childlike hand. I paused. *Turn the knob and push the door open,* I told myself. *You can do this. Crossing this threshold is nothing new. You have passed over the supposedly insurmountable divide between male and female in countless classrooms before. And always succeeded.*

Still, I hesitated. I knew all too well that, while the first step is the hardest, the second isn't much easier. In that moment, little more than a breath, I could almost hear Papa urging me on. "Be bold," Papa would whisper in our native, little-used Serbian tongue. "You are a *mudra glava*. A wise one. In your heart beats the blood of bandits, our brigand Slavic ancestors who used any means to get their due. Go get your due, Mitza. Go get your due."

I could never disappoint him.

I twisted the knob and swung the door wide open. Six faces stared back at me: five dark-suited students and one black-robed professor. Shock and some disdain registered on their pale faces. Nothing—not even rumors—had prepared these men for actually seeing a woman in their ranks. They almost looked silly with their eyes bulging and their jaws dropping, but I knew better than to laugh. I willed myself to pay their expressions no heed, to ignore the doughy faces of my fellow students, who were desperately trying to appear older than their eighteen years with their heavily waxed mustaches.

A determination to master physics and mathematics brought me to the Polytechnic, not a desire to make friends or please others. I reminded myself of this simple fact as I steeled myself to face my instructor.

Professor Heinrich Martin Weber and I looked at each other. Long-nosed, heavily browed, and meticulously bearded, the renowned physics professor's intimidating appearance matched his reputation.

I waited for him to speak. To do anything else would have been perceived as utter impertinence. I could not afford another such mark against my character, since my mere presence at the

Polytechnic was considered impertinent by many. I walked a fine line between my insistence on this untrodden path and the conformity still demanded of me.

"You are?" he asked as if he weren't expecting me, as if he'd never heard of me.

"Miss Mileva Marić, sir." I prayed my voice didn't quaver.

Very slowly, Weber consulted his class list. Of course, he knew precisely who I was. Since he served as head of the physics and mathematics program, and given that only four women had ever been admitted before me, I had to petition him directly to enter the first year of the four-year program, known as Section Six. He had approved my entrance himself! The consultation of the class list was a blatant and calculating move, telegraphing his opinion of me to the rest of the class. It gave them license to follow suit.

"The Miss Marić from Serbia or some Austro-Hungarian country of that sort?" he asked without glancing up, as if there could possibly be another Miss Marić in Section Six, one who hailed from a more respectable location. By his query, Weber made his views on Slavic eastern European peoples perfectly clear—that we, as dark foreigners, were somehow inferior to the Germanic peoples of defiantly neutral Switzerland. It was yet another preconception I would have to disprove in order to succeed. As if being the only woman in Section Six—only the fifth to *ever* be admitted into the physics and mathematics program—wasn't enough.

"Yes, sir."

"You may take your seat," he finally said and gestured toward the empty chair. It was my luck that the only remaining seat was the farthest away from his podium. "We have already begun."

Begun? The class was not designated to start for another fifteen minutes. Were my classmates told something I wasn't? Had they conspired to meet early? I wanted to ask but didn't. Argument would only fuel the fires against me. Anyway, it didn't matter. I would simply arrive fifteen minutes earlier tomorrow. And earlier and earlier every morning if I needed to. I would not miss a single word of Weber's lectures. He was wrong if he thought an early start would deter me. I was my father's daughter.

Nodding at Weber, I stared at the long walk from the door to my chair and, out of habit, calculated the number of steps it would take me to cross the room. How best to manage the distance? With my first step, I tried to keep my gait steady and hide my limp, but the drag of my lame foot echoed through the classroom. On impulse, I decided not to mask it at all. I displayed plainly for all my colleagues to see the deformity that marked me since birth.

Clomp and drag. Over and over. Eighteen times until I reached my chair. *Here I am, gentlemen*, I felt like I was saying with each lug of my lame foot. *Take a gander; get it over with.*

Perspiring from the effort, I realized the classroom was completely silent. They were waiting for me to settle, and perhaps embarrassed by my limp or my sex or both, they kept their eyes averted.

All except one.

To my right, a young man with an unruly mop of dark brown curls stared at me. Uncharacteristically, I met his gaze.

But even when I looked at him head-on, challenging him to mock me and my efforts, his half-lidded eyes did not look away. Instead, they crinkled at the corners as he smiled through the dark shadow cast by his mustache. A grin of great bemusement, even admiration.

Who did he think he was? What did he mean by that look?

I had no time to make sense of him as I sat down in my seat. Reaching into my bag, I withdrew paper, ink, and pen and readied for Weber's lecture. I would not let the bold, insouciant glance of a privileged classmate rattle me. I looked straight ahead at the instructor, still aware of my classmate's gaze upon me, but acted oblivious.

Weber, however, was not so single-minded. Or so forgiving. Staring at the young man, the professor cleared his throat, and when the young man still did not redirect his eyes toward the podium, he said, "I will have the attention of the entire classroom. This is your first and final warning, Mr. Einstein."

CHAPTER 2

Afternoon
October 20, 1896
Zürich, Switzerland

Entering the vestibule of the Engelbrecht Pension, I closed the door quietly behind me and handed my damp umbrella to the waiting maid. Laughter drifted into the entryway from the back parlor. I knew the girls were waiting for me there, but I didn't feel up to the well-intentioned interrogation just yet. I needed some time alone to think about my day, even if it was just a few minutes. Taking care to tread lightly, I started up the stairs to my room.

Creak. Damn that one loose step.

Charcoal-gray skirts swishing behind her, Helene emerged from the back parlor, a steaming cup of tea in her hand. "Mileva, we are waiting for you! Did you forget?" With her free hand, Helene took my hand in hers and pulled me to the back parlor, which we now referred to among ourselves as the gaming room. We felt entitled to name it, as no one used it but us.

I laughed. How would I have made it through these past months in Zürich without the girls? Milana, Ružica, and most of all Helene, a soul-sister of sorts with her sharp wit, kindly manner, and, oddly enough, a similar limp. Why had I waited even a day to let them into my life?

Several months ago, when Papa and I arrived in Zürich, I could not have imagined such friendships. A youth marked by friction from my classmates—alienation at best and mockery at worst—meant a life of solitude and scholarship for me. Or so I thought.

Stepping off the train after a jostling two-day journey from our home in Zagreb, Croatia, Papa and I were a bit wobbly. Smoke from the train billowed throughout Zürich's Hauptbahnhof, and I had to squint to make my way onto the platform. A satchel in each hand, one heavy with my favorite books, I teetered a bit as I wove through the crowded station, followed by Papa and a porter carrying our heavier bags. Papa rushed over to my side, trying to relieve me of one of my satchels.

"Papa, I can do it," I insisted as I tried to wriggle my hand out from under his grip. "You have bags of your own to carry and only two hands."

"Mitza, please let me help. I can handle another bag more easily than you." He chortled. "Not to mention that your mother would be horrified if I let you struggle through the Zürich train station."

Placing my bag down, I tried to extricate my hand from his. "Papa, I have to be able to do this alone. I'm going to be living in Zürich by myself after all."

He stared at me for a long moment, as if the reality of me living in Zürich without him just registered, as if we had not been working toward this goal since I was a little girl. Reluctantly, finger by finger, he released his hand. This was hard for him; I understood that. While I knew part of him relished my pursuit of a singular education, that my climb reminded him of his own hard-scrabble ascent from peasant to successful bureaucrat and landowner, I sometimes wondered whether he felt guilty and conflicted at propelling me along my own precarious journey. He'd focused on the prize of my university education for so long, I guessed that he hadn't actually envisioned saying good-bye and leaving me in this foreign place.

We exited the station and stepped into the busy evening streets of Zürich. Night was just beginning to fall, but the city wasn't dark. I caught Papa's eye, and we smiled at each other in amazement; we'd only ever seen a city lit by the usual dim, oil streetlamps. Electric lights illuminated the Zürich streets, and they were unexpectedly bright. In their glow, I could actually make out the finer details on the dresses of the ladies passing by us; their bustles were more elaborate than the restrained styles I'd seen in Zagreb.

The horses of a for-hire clarence cab clopped down the cobblestones of the Bahnhofstrasse on which we stood, and Papa summoned it. As the driver dismounted to load our luggage onto the back of the carriage, I wrapped my shawl around me for warmth in the cool evening air. The night before I left, Mama gifted me with the rose-embroidered shawl, tears welling in the corners of her eyes but never falling. Only later did I understand that the shawl was like her farewell embrace, something I could keep with me, since she had to stay behind in Zagreb with my younger sister, Zorka, and my little brother, Miloš.

Interrupting my thoughts, the driver asked, "Are you here to see the sights?"

"No," Papa answered for me with only a slight accent. He'd always been proud of his grammatically flawless German, the language spoken by those in power in Austro-Hungary. It was the first step upon which he began his climb, he used to say as he badgered us into practicing it. Puffing up his chest a little, he said, "We are here to register my daughter for the university."

The driver's eyebrows raised in surprise, but he otherwise kept his reaction private. "University, eh? Then I'm guessing you'll want the Engelbrecht Pension or one of the other pensions of Plattenstrasse," he said as he held the cab door open for us to enter.

Papa paused as he waited for me to settle in the carriage and then asked the driver, "How did you know our destination?"

"That's where I take many of the eastern European students to lodge."

Listening to Papa grunt in response as he slid into the cab alongside me, I realized that he didn't know how to read the driver's comment. Was it a slur about our eastern European heritage? We'd been told that, even though they adamantly maintained their independence and neutrality in the face of the relentless European empire building that surrounded them, the Swiss looked down upon those from the eastern reaches of the Austro-Hungarian Empire. And yet the Swiss were the most tolerant people in other ways; they had the most lenient university admissions for women, for example. It was a confusing contradiction.

Signaling to the horses, the driver cracked the whip in the

air, and the carriage rumbled down the Zürich street at a steady clip. Straining to see through the mud-splattered window, I saw an electric tram whiz by the carriage.

"Did you see that, Papa?" I asked. I'd read about trams but never witnessed one firsthand. The sight exhilarated me; it served as tangible evidence that the city was forward-thinking, at least in transportation. I could only hope that the way its citizens treated female students was also advanced to match the rumors we'd heard.

"I didn't see it, but I heard it. And felt it," Papa answered calmly with a squeeze of my hand. I knew he was excited too but wanted to appear worldly. Especially after the driver's comment.

I turned back to the open window. Steep green mountains framed the city, and I swear I smelled evergreens in the air. Surely, the mountains were too distant to share the fragrance of their abundant trees. Whatever the source, the Zürich air was far fresher than that of Zagreb, ever redolent of horse dung and burning crops. Perhaps the scent came from the crisp air blowing off Lake Zürich, which bordered the southern side of the city.

In the distance, at what appeared to be the base of the mountains, I glimpsed pale yellow buildings, constructed in a neoclassical style, set against the backdrop of church spires. The buildings looked remarkably like the sketches of the Polytechnic that I'd seen in my application papers but vaster and more imposing than I'd imagined. The Polytechnic was a new sort of college dedicated to producing teachers and professors for various math or scientific disciplines, and it was one of the few universities in Europe to grant women degrees. Although I'd dreamed of little else for years, it was hard to fathom that, in a few months' time, I'd actually be in attendance there.

The clarence cab lurched to a halt. The hatch door opened, and the driver announced our destination, "50 Plattenstrasse." Papa passed up some francs through the hatch, and the carriage door swung open.

As the driver unloaded our luggage, a servant from the Engelbrecht Pension hurried out the front door and down the entry steps to assist us with the smaller bags we were carrying by hand. From between the handsome columns framing the front door of the four-story brick town house, an attractive, well-dressed couple emerged.

"Mr. Marić?" the heavyset, older gentleman called out.

"Yes, you must be Mr. Engelbrecht," my father answered with a short bow and an outstretched hand. As the men exchanged introductions, the spry Mrs. Engelbrecht scuttled down the stairs to usher me into the building.

Formalities dispensed with, the Engelbrechts invited Papa and me to share in the tea and cakes that had been laid out in our honor. As we followed the Engelbrechts from the entryway into the parlor, I saw Papa cast an approving glance over the crystal chandelier hanging in the front parlor and the matching wall sconces. I could almost hear him think, *This place is respectable enough for my Mitza.*

To me, the pension seemed antiseptic and overly formal compared to home; the smells of the woods and the dust and the spicy cooking of home had been scrubbed away. Although we Serbs aspired to the Germanic order adopted by the Swiss,

I saw then that our attempts barely grazed the Swiss heights of cleaning perfection.

Over tea and cakes and pleasantries and under Papa's persistent questioning, the Engelbrechts explained the workings of their boardinghouse: the fixed schedule for meals, visitors, laundry, and room cleaning. Papa, the former military man, inquired about the security of the lodgers, and his shoulders softened with every favorable response and each assessment of the tufted blue fabric on the walls and the ornately carved chairs gathered around the wide marble fireplace. Still, his shoulders never fully slackened; Papa wanted a university education for me almost as much as I wanted it for myself, but the reality of farewell seemed harder for him than I'd ever imagined.

As I sipped my tea, I heard laughter. The laughter of girls.

Mrs. Engelbrecht noticed my reaction. "Ah, you hear our young ladies at a game of whist. May I introduce you to our other young lady boarders?"

Other lady boarders? I nodded, although I desperately wanted to shake my head no. My experiences with other young ladies generally ended poorly. Commonalities between myself and them were few at best. At worst, I had suffered meanness and degradation at the hands of my classmates, male and female, especially when they realized the scope of my ambitions.

Still, politeness demanded that we rise, and Mrs. Engelbrecht led us through the parlor into a smaller room, different from the parlor in its decor: brass chandelier and sconces instead of crystal, oaken panels instead of blue silken fabric on the walls, and a gaming table at its center. As we entered, I thought I heard the word *krpiti* and glanced over at Papa, who looked similarly surprised. It was a Serbian phrase we used when disappointed or losing, and I wondered who on earth would be using the word. Surely, we had misheard.

Around the table sat three girls, all about my age, with dark hair and thick brows not unlike my own. They were even dressed much the same, with stiff, white blouses topped with high lace collars and dark, simple skirts. Serious attire, not the frilly, fancifully decorated gowns of lemon yellow and frothy pink favored by many young women, including those I'd seen on the fashionable streets near the train station.

Looking up from their game, the girls quickly set their cards down and stood for the introduction. "Misses Ružica Dražić, Milana Bota, and Helene Kaufler, I would like you to meet our new boarder. This is Miss Mileva Marić."

As we curtsied to one another, Mrs. Engelbrecht continued, "Miss Marić is here to study mathematics and physics at the Swiss Federal Polytechnic. You will be in good company here, Miss Marić."

Mrs. Engelbrecht gestured first to a girl with wide cheekbones, a ready smile, and bronze eyes. She said, "Miss Dražić is here from Šabac to study political science at the University of Zürich."

Turning next to the girl with the darkest hair and heaviest brows, Mrs. Engelbrecht said, "This is Miss Bota. She left Kruševac behind to study psychology at the Polytechnic like yourself."

Placing her hand on the shoulder of the last girl, one with a halo of soft brown hair and kindly, gray-blue eyes framed by sloping eyebrows, Mrs. Engelbrecht said, "And this is our Miss

Kaufler, who traveled all the way from Vienna for her history degree, also at the Polytechnic."

I didn't know what to say. Fellow university students from eastern Austro-Hungarian provinces like my own? I had never dreamed that I wouldn't be unique. In Zagreb, every other girl near the age of twenty was married or readying for marriage by meeting suitable young men and practicing to run a household in their parents' home. Their educations stopped years before, if they ever went to formal schooling at all. I thought I'd always be the only eastern European female university student in a world of western men. Maybe the only girl at all.

Mrs. Engelbrecht looked at each of the girls and said, "We will leave you ladies to your whist while we finish our conversation. I hope that you will show Miss Marić around Zürich tomorrow?"

"Of course, Mrs. Engelbrecht," Miss Kaufler answered for all three girls with a warm smile. "Maybe Miss Marić will even join us in whist tomorrow evening. We could certainly use a fourth."

Miss Kaufler's smile seemed genuine, and I felt drawn to the cozy scene. Instinctively, I grinned back, but then I stopped. *Be careful*, I warned myself. *Remember the beastliness of other young ladies: the taunts, the name-calling, the kicks on the playground. The Polytechnic's mathematics and physics program lured you here, so you could follow the dream of becoming one of a very few female physics professors in Europe. You did not travel all this distance just to make a few friends, even if these girls are indeed what they seem.*

As we walked back to the front parlor, Papa linked his arm with mine and whispered, "They seem like remarkably nice girls, Mitza. They must be smart too, if they are here to study at the university. It might be the right time to find a female companion or two, since we've finally met a few that might be your intellectual equals. Some lucky girl should get to share in all the little jokes you usually save for me."

His voice sounded oddly hopeful, as if he were actually eager for me to reach out to the girls we'd just met. What was Papa saying? I was confused. After so many years professing that friends did not matter, that a husband was not important, that our family and education alone counted, was he giving me some sort of test? I wanted to show him that the usual desires of a young woman—friends, husband, children—didn't matter to me, as always. I wanted to pass this strange examination with the highest honors, just as I had all others.

"Papa, I promise you I'm here to learn, not to make friends," I said with a definitive nod. I hoped this would reassure him that the fate he foretold for me—even wished for me—all those years ago had become my own embraced destiny.

But Papa wasn't elated with my answer. In fact, his face darkened, with sadness or anger I couldn't tell at first. Had I not been emphatic enough? Was his message truly changing because these girls were so different from all the others I'd known?

He was uncharacteristically quiet for a minute. Finally, with a despondent note in his voice, he said, "I had hoped you could have both."

In the weeks that followed Papa's departure, I avoided the girls, keeping to my books and my room. But the Engelbrechts' schedule meant that I dined with them daily, and courtesy required that I politely converse over breakfast and dinner.

They constantly entreated me to join them in walks, lectures, café-house visits, theater, and concerts. They good-naturedly chided me for being too serious and too quiet and too studious, and they continued to invite me no matter how often I declined. The girls had persistence I'd never witnessed anywhere but within myself.

One early evening that summer, I was studying in my room in preparation for the courses beginning in October, as had become my custom. My special shawl was wrapped around my shoulders to ward off the chill endemic to the pension's bedrooms no matter how warm the weather. I was parsing through a text when I heard the girls downstairs begin to play a version of one of Bizet's *L'Arlésienne Suites*, fairly badly but with feeling. I knew the piece well; I used to perform it with my family. The familiar music made me feel melancholy, lonely instead of alone. Glancing over at my dusty tamburitza in the corner, I grabbed the little mandolin and walked downstairs. Standing in the entrance to the front parlor, I watched as the girls struggled with the piece.

As I leaned against the wall, tamburitza in hand, I suddenly felt foolish. Why should I expect them to accept me after I'd declined their invitations so frequently? I wanted to run back upstairs, but Helene noticed me and stopped playing.

With her characteristic warmth, she asked, "Will you join us, Miss Marić?" She glanced at Ružica and Milana in mock exasperation. "You can see that we can use whatever musical assistance you can offer."

I said yes. Within days, the girls catapulted me into a life I'd never experienced before. A life with like-minded friends. Papa had been wrong, and so had I. Friends did matter. Friends like these anyway, ones who were fiercely intelligent and similarly ambitious, who suffered through the same sort of ridicule and condemnation and survived, smiling.

These friends didn't take away my resolve to succeed as I'd feared. They made me stronger.

⌘

Now, months later, I plopped down into the empty chair as Ružica poured me a cup of tea. The smell of lemon wafted toward me, and with a self-pleased grin, Milana slid over a plate of my favorite lemon-balm cake; the girls must have specially requested it for me from Mrs. Engelbrecht. A special gesture for a special day.

"Thank you."

We sipped tea and nibbled on the cake. The girls were unusually quiet, although I could see from their faces and the glances they shot one another that it was a hard-won restraint. They were waiting for me to speak first, to offer up more than an appreciation for the treats.

But Ružica, the most high-spirited, couldn't wait. She had the most abundant persistence and the least patience and simply burst with her question. "How was the infamous Professor Weber?" she asked, eyebrows knit in a comic interpretation of the instructor, well-known for his formidable classroom style and equally formidable brilliance.

"As billed," I answered with a sigh and another bite of cake; it was a glorious mix of sweet and savory. I wiped away a crumb from the side of my mouth and explained, "He insisted on consulting his roster before he let me sit in the classroom. As if he didn't know I was entering his program. He admitted me himself!"

The girls giggled knowingly.

"And then he made a dig about me coming from Serbia."

The girls stopped laughing. Ružica and Milana had experienced similar humiliations, having come from far reaches of the Austro-Hungarian Empire themselves. Even Helene, who hailed from the more acceptable region of Austria, had suffered her own degradations from her Polytechnic professors because she was Jewish.

"Sounds like my first day in Professor Herzog's class," Helene said, and we nodded. We had heard Helene's tale of mortification in excruciating detail. After noting aloud that Helene's surname sounded Jewish, Professor Herzog spent a substantial part of his first Italian history lecture focusing on the Venetian ghettos where Jews were forced to live from the sixteenth to eighteenth century. We didn't think the professor's emphasis was a coincidence.

"It isn't enough we are but a few women in an ocean of men. The professors have to manufacture other flaws and highlight other differences," Ružica said.

"How are the other students?" Milana asked in a clear attempt to change the subject.

"The usual," I answered. The girls groaned in solidarity.

"Self-important?" Milana asked.

"Check," I said.

"Heavily mustached?" Ružica suggested with a giggle.

"Check."

"Overly confident?" Helene proposed.

"Double check."

"Any overt hostility?" Helene ventured, her voice more solemn and cautious. She was very protective, a sort of mother hen for the group. Especially for me. Ever since I told them about what had happened to me on my first day at the upper school in Zagreb, the Royal Classical High School, a story I'd shared with no one else, Helene was extra wary on my behalf. While none of the others had experienced such overt violence, they'd all felt the menace seething beneath the surface at one time or another.

"No, not yet anyway."

"That's good news," Ružica announced, ever optimistic. We accused her of fabricating silver linings in the blackest storms. She maintained that it was a necessary outlook for us and briskly recommended that we do the same.

"Sense any allies?" Milana tiptoed into more strategic territory. The physics curriculum required collaboration among the students on certain projects, and we had discussed strategies about this. What if no one was willing to partner with me?

"No," I answered automatically. But I paused, trying to follow Ružica's advice to think more optimistically. "Well, maybe. There was one student who smiled at me, maybe a little too long, but still, a genuine smile. No mockery. Einstein, I think is his name."

Helene's heavy eyebrows raised in concern. She was always on high alert for unwelcome romantic overtures. She believed them to be almost as much cause for concern as outright violence. Reaching for my hand, she warned, "Be careful."

I squeezed her hand back. "Don't worry, Helene. I'm always careful." When her expression failed to lighten, I teased, "Come on. You girls always accuse me of being *too* cautious, *too* private. Of only showing you three my true personality. Do you really think I wouldn't be careful with Mr. Einstein?"

Helene's worried look lifted, replaced by a smile.

I constantly astonished myself with these girls. Astonished that I had the words to express my long-buried stories. Astonished that I allowed them to see who I really was. And astonished that I was accepted regardless.

CHAPTER 3

April 22, 1897
Zürich, Switzerland

I NESTLED INTO MY LIBRARY CARREL. THE AIRY, WOOD-PANELED library at the Polytechnic was full almost to capacity, but still, the room was hushed. The students were quietly worshipping at the altar of one discipline or another, some studying biology or chemistry, others math, and still others physics like myself. Here, buffeted from the world by the carrel, barricaded in by my books, fortified by my own musings and theories, I could almost pretend that I was like every other student at the Polytechnic library.

Spread before me were my class notes, several required texts, and one article from my own collection. They all clamored for my attention, and as if I were selecting among beloved pets, I found it hard to choose to which I would devote my time. Newton or Descartes? Or perhaps one of the newer theorists? The air at the Polytechnic, indeed throughout Zürich itself, felt charged with talk of the latest developments in physics, and I felt like it was speaking directly to me. The world of physics was where I belonged. Embedded in its secretive rules about the workings of the world—hidden forces and unseen causal relationships so complex that I believed only God could have created them—were answers to the greatest questions about our existence. If only I could uncover them.

Occasionally, if I relaxed into my reading and calculations—instead of studying and working so earnestly—I could see the divine patterns I desperately sought. But only in the periphery of my sight. As soon as I turned my gaze directly upon the patterns, they shimmered away into nothingness. Perhaps I wasn't yet ready to view God's masterwork head-on. Perhaps in time, he would allow it.

I credited Papa for bringing me to this scintillating threshold of education and curiosity. My only regret was that he still worried about me here in Zürich, both in terms of my future prospects and the safety of my daily living. While I worked hard in my letters to convince him of the abundance of teaching positions for me when I finished, if research should not be my career, and the inviolability of my structured life at school and the pension, I sensed his anxiety through his endless questioning.

Interesting that Mama seemed more comfortable with my current path. After a lifetime bristling against her disapproval of my unorthodox need for education, once I settled into my life in Zürich, she seemed to surrender to my choice, particularly when I started to fill my letters to her with tales of my outings with Ružica, Milana, and Helene. In her responses, I saw that Mama delighted in these new friendships. My first friendships.

Mama's approval wasn't always so freely given. Until this recent rapprochement, my relationship with her was darkened by her worries over me, her lame, lonely, and unconventional child. And by the impact my thirst for education had on her own life.

On one brisk September afternoon in my birthplace of remote Titel, nearly seven years ago, she didn't bother to mask her opposition to my decidedly unfeminine path, even though Papa himself propelled it forward, and she rarely challenged him. We were on our pilgrimage to the cemetery where my older brother and sister were buried, the siblings who had died of infant illnesses years before my birth. The wind was fierce, whipping the kerchief around my head. I grabbed the black fabric and held it down tightly, imagining the cluck of Mama's disapproval should the kerchief fly off, leaving my head exposed while treading on sacred ground. The folds covered my ears, muffling the low, mournful moans of the wind. I was grateful for the quiet, although I knew the wind's keening befitted our destination.

I smelled *tamjan*, a sweet and pungent incense, wafting from our church as we passed, and fallen leaves crunched underfoot as I struggled to keep up with Mama's stride. The hill was rocky and hard for me to climb, which Mama knew well. But she wouldn't slow down. It was almost as if the arduousness of the walk to the cemetery was part of my penance. For surviving when my brother and sister did not. For living when childhood sicknesses claimed the others. And for inspiring Papa to accept the new governmental post in Zagreb, a larger city with better schooling for me, but a move that would take Mama farther away from the graves of her firstborn children.

"Are you coming, Mitza?" Mama called to me without

turning around. I reminded myself that her sternness didn't stem solely from her displeasure over the move to Zagreb. Strict discipline and high expectations were her daily prescription for righteous children; she often said, "The Proverbs say that 'The rod and reproof give wisdom, but a child left to himself brings shame to his mother.'"

"Yes, Mama," I called back.

Dressed in her usual mourning black and dark kerchief, worn in honor of my dead brother and sister, Mama walked ahead, looking like an ebony shadow against the gray autumnal sky. I was short of breath by the time I reached the summit, but I muffled my labored breathing. This was my duty.

Risking a cluck, I turned around; I loved the view from this vantage point. Titel spread out before us, and above the church spire, the vista of the town looked as though it clung to the banks of the Tisa. The dusty town was small, with only a town square, market, and a few governmental buildings at its center, but it was still beautiful.

But then I heard Mama lowering herself to the ground, and my guilt set in. This was no pleasure stroll; I should not be enjoying myself. This would be one of our last visits to the cemetery for a long time to come. Even Papa couldn't make me feel better about our move today.

I took my place at Mama's side before the gravestones. The pebbles dug into my knees, but I wanted to feel pain today. It seemed a reasonable sacrifice for the pain I was inflicting on Mama by sparking our move to Zagreb. Since I'd reach the limits of my local education, Papa wanted me to attend the Royal Classical High School in Zagreb. We wouldn't be returning to Titel with any frequency. I glanced over at her. Her brown eyes were shut, and without their flinty animation, she looked older than her thirty-odd years. The burden of loss and the weight of daily minutiae had aged her.

I made the sign of the cross, closed my eyes, and offered a silent prayer to the souls of my long-departed brother and sister. They had always served as my invisible companions, a replacement for the friends I never had. How different my life might have been had they lived. Maybe with an older brother and sister by my side, I would not have been so lonely, secretly longing to play with the girls in the schoolyard, even the ones who hurt me.

A shaft of sunlight passed over me, and I opened my eyes. The arched marble gravestones of my older brother and sister stared back at me. Their names—Milica Marić and Vukašin Marić—glistened in the sun as if they had just been chiseled, and I held back an impulse to run my finger along each of the letters.

Mama usually liked to keep our visits silent and reflective, but not that day. She reached for my hand and called out to the Virgin in our native, rarely used Serbian:

> *Bogorodice Djevo, radujsja*
> *Blagodatnaja Marije...*

Mama was so loud that she drowned out the wind and the rustling leaves. And she was swaying. I felt embarrassed by the strength of Mama's voice and her dramatic movements, especially when two mourners in the distance peered over at us.

Still, I chanted along. The words of the Hail Mary usually soothed me, but today, they felt unfamiliar. Almost thick on my tongue. Like a lie. Mama's utterances sounded different too, not like reverential worship but like a condemnation. Of me, certainly not of the Virgin.

I tried to focus on the wind, the crackling of the branches and leaves, the gallop of hooves as horses passed by, anything but the words coming from Mama's mouth. I did not need further reminders that so much rested on my success at the school in Zagreb. I had to succeed. Not just for myself and Mama and Papa but for my departed brother and sister too. Souls left behind.

⚬⚬⚬

I heard the scratch of fountain pens from other students working nearby in the library, but only one man captivated my attention. Philipp Lenard. I reached for the article by the noted German physicist and began reading. I should have been reading the texts of Hermann von Helmholtz and Ludwig Boltzmann, assigned by the professor, but I was drawn to Lenard's recent research on cathode rays and their properties. Using evacuated glass tubes, he bombarded the tubes' metallic electrodes with high-voltage electricity and then examined the rays. Lenard observed that, if the end of the tube opposite the negative charge was painted with a fluorescent material, a minuscule object within the tube began to glow and zigzag around the tube. This led him to believe that cathode rays were streams of negatively charged energetic particles; he dubbed them quanta of electricity. Putting down the article, I wondered how Lenard's research might impact the much-debated question about the nature and existence of atoms. Of what substance had God made the world? Could the answer to this question tell us more about mankind's purpose on God's earth? Sometimes, in the pages of my texts and in the glimmers of my musings, I sensed God's patterns unfolding in the physical laws of the universe that I was learning. These were the places I felt God, not in the pews of Mama's churches or in their cemeteries.

The clock in the university tower struck five. Could it really be so late? I hadn't even touched the day's assigned reading.

I craned my neck to glimpse out a well-positioned window. There was no shortage of spired clock towers in Zürich, and the clock hands I saw confirmed that it was five. Mrs. Engelbrecht was Teutonically firm with her pension dinner schedule, so I could not linger. Especially since the girls would be waiting, instruments in hand, for some predinner music. It was one of our little rituals, the one I loved best.

I organized my papers and began to slide them into my bag. Lenard's article sat on top of the pile, and a phrase caught my attention. I began reading again and became so engrossed that I jumped when I heard my name.

"Miss Marić, may I intrude on your thoughts?"

It was Mr. Einstein. His hair was wilder than ever, as if he had been running his fingers through his dark curls and willing them to stand on end. His shirt and jacket looked no better; they were rumpled almost beyond recognition. His disheveled appearance was at odds with the careful mien of the other students at the library. But unlike them, he was smiling.

"Yes, Mr. Einstein."

"I'm hoping that you can help me with a problem." He thrust a stack of papers into my hand.

"Me?" I asked without thinking and then chastised myself for my obvious surprise. *Act confident*, I told myself. *You are every bit as bright as the other students in Section Six. Why shouldn't a fellow classmate ask you for help?*

But it was too late. My self-doubt had already been revealed.

"Yes, you, Miss Marić. I think you're quite the smartest in our class—by far the best at maths—and those *Dummkopfs* over there"—he gestured to two of our classmates, Mr. Ehrat and Mr. Kollros, who stood between two book stacks, whispering and gesticulating wildly to one another—"have tried to help me and failed."

"Certainly," I answered. I was flattered by his assurances but still wary. If Helene were here, she would urge caution but also push me to forge a collegial alliance. Next term, I would need a lab partner, and he might be my only option. In the six months since I had entered the physics program and sat in class with the same five students every day, the others had shown only the basest civilities and an otherwise practiced indifference toward me. By his daily kindnesses in greeting me and occasionally inquiring into my thoughts on Professor Weber's lectures, Mr. Einstein had proven to be my sole hope.

"Let me see." I looked down at his papers.

He had passed me a nearly incomprehensible mess. Was this the kind of unorganized work that my fellow students were doing? If so, I did not have to worry about my own efforts. I glanced over his messy computations and quickly spotted the error. It was laziness, really, on his part. "Here, Mr. Einstein. If you switch these two numbers, I believe you will arrive at the proper solution."

"Ah, I see. Thank you for your assistance, Miss Marić."

"It's my pleasure." I nodded and turned back to the business of packing up my belongings.

I felt him peering over my shoulder. "Are you reading Lenard?" he asked, surprise evident in his voice.

"Yes," I answered, continuing to pack my bag.

"He isn't part of our curriculum."

"No, he isn't."

"I'm quite amazed, Miss Marić."

"Why is that, Mr. Einstein?" I turned to face him square on, daring him to challenge me. Did he think I couldn't handle Lenard, a text far more complicated than our basic physics curriculum? Because he was quite a bit taller than me, I was forced to look up. My short stature was a disadvantage that I had come to loathe as much as my limp.

"You seem the consummate student, Miss Marić. Always in attendance at class, following the rules, scrupulous in your note-taking, toiling for hours in the library instead of whiling them away in the cafés. And yet, you are a bohemian like me. I wouldn't have guessed."

"A bohemian? I don't catch your meaning." My words and tone were sharp. By calling me bohemian, a word I associated with the Austro-Hungarian region of Bohemia, was he insulting my heritage? From cracks made by Weber in class, Mr. Einstein knew I was Serbian, and the prejudice of the Germanic and western European people such as himself against easterners was well known. I had wondered about Mr. Einstein's own heritage, even though I knew he hailed from Berlin. With his dark hair and eyes and distinctive last name, he didn't look the traditional Germanic blond. Perhaps his family settled in Berlin from somewhere else?

He must have sensed my latent anger, because he rushed to clarify himself. "I use the word bohemian in the French manner, after the word *bohémien*. It means independent in your thinking. Progressive. Not so bourgeois as some of our classmates."

I did not know how to read this exchange. He didn't seem to be mocking me; in fact, I thought he was trying to compliment me with his strange bohemian label. I felt more uncomfortable by the minute.

Busying myself with the remaining sheaf of papers on the carrel's desk, I said, "I must go, Mr. Einstein. Mrs. Engelbrecht keeps to a strict schedule at her pension, and I mustn't be late for dinner. Good evening." I sealed my bag shut and curtsied in farewell.

"Good evening, Miss Marić," he answered with a bow, "and my gratitude for your help."

I passed through the arched oak door of the library and across its small stone courtyard out onto Rämistrasse, the busy street bordering the Polytechnic. This boulevard overflowed with boardinghouses, where Zürich's plentiful students slept at night, and cafés, where those same students debated great questions in the daylight hours not spent in class. From my furtive glances, it seemed that coffee and pipes were the primary fuel for these heated café conversations. But this was only a guess. I didn't dare join in at one of these tables, even though I once spied Mr. Einstein with a few friends at an outdoor table at Café Metropole, and he waved me over. I pretended not to see him; sightings of women alongside men for these free-spirited café exchanges were rare, and it was a line I couldn't yet bring myself to cross.

Night was falling over Rämistrasse, yet the street was bright with electric illumination. A fine mist began to form in the air, and I pulled up my hood to prevent the dampness from settling on my hair and clothes. The rain increased—unexpectedly, as the day had started bright and clear—and I found it harder to weave my way through the warren of Rämistrasse. I was by far the shortest person in the crowd. I was drenched, and the cobblestones were getting slippery. Dare I break my own rule and duck into one of the cafés until the weather broke?

Without warning, rain stopped pouring down on me. I glanced up, expecting to see a shaft of blue sky, but instead saw only black and rivers of water gushing down all around my sides.

Mr. Einstein was holding an umbrella over my head.

"You are dripping wet, Miss Marić," he said, his eyes full of their usual humor.

What was he doing here? He did not look ready to leave the library just moments ago. Was he following me?

"An unexpected deluge, Mr. Einstein. Many thanks for the umbrella, but I'm fine." It was imperative that I insist on self-sufficiency; I didn't want any of my classmates to see me as a helpless female, Mr. Einstein in particular. He wouldn't want me as a lab partner if he perceived me as weak, would he?

"After you saved me from the certain wrath of Professor Weber with your correction of my calculations, the least I can do is to escort you home in this rain." He smiled. "Since you seem to have forgotten your umbrella."

I wanted to object, but in truth, I needed the assistance.

Slick cobblestones were hazardous with my limp. Mr. Einstein placed his hand on my arm and held the umbrella high above my head. The gesture was perfectly gentlemanly if a bit bold. Feeling the pressure of his hand on my arm, I realized that, apart from Papa and a few of my uncles, I had never been so close to a grown man before. Even though multitudes of people packed the boulevard and we all wore burdensome layers of cloaks and scarves, I felt oddly exposed.

As we walked, Mr. Einstein launched into a spirited monologue about Maxwell's electromagnetic wave theory of light, tossing out some rather unusual thoughts about the relationship of light and radiation to matter. I piped in with a few comments that Mr. Einstein responded to with encouragement but otherwise stayed quiet, listening to his irrepressible chatter and evaluating his intellect and spirit.

We reached the Engelbrecht Pension, and he delivered me directly up the stairs to the covered front door. Relief flooded through me.

"Again, my thanks, Mr. Einstein. Your courtesy was unnecessary but much appreciated."

"My pleasure, Miss Marić. I'll see you in class tomorrow," he said and turned to leave.

A disjointed Vivaldi piece floated out of the slightly open parlor window and onto the street. Mr. Einstein started back up the front steps and peered through the window where the girls had gathered for a casual concert.

"By God, that's a lively group," he exclaimed. "I wish I'd brought my violin. Vivaldi is always better with strings. Do you play, Miss Marić?"

Brought his violin? How presumptuous of him. These were my friends and my sanctuary, and I did not invite him to join us. "Yes, I play the tamburitza and piano, and I sing. But it's no matter; the Engelbrechts are very strict about gentlemen callers."

"I could come as a classmate and fellow musician, not as a caller," he offered. "Would that appease them?"

I blushed. How stupid of me to imply he wanted to come as a caller. "Perhaps, Mr. Einstein. I would have to make inquiries." I hoped he understood that my demur was a gentle rejection.

He shook his head in appreciation. "You have astonished me today, Miss Marić. You are much more than just a brilliant mathematician and physicist. It seems you are a musician and bohemian too."

His smile was infectious. I could not help but return it.

He stared in amazement. "I do believe that's the first time I've seen you smile. It's quite fetching. I'd like to steal more of those smiles from your serious little mouth."

Flustered by his comment and uncertain how to reply, I turned and entered the pension.

CHAPTER 4

April 24, 1897
The Sihl Valley, Switzerland

FOR THE FIRST TIME SINCE WE DISEMBARKED THE TRAIN from Zürich and set out on the path through the Sihl Valley, our group was quiet. A hush settled over us, almost like we had entered a cathedral. In a way, that was what these primeval woods, the Sihlwald, felt like.

Ancient, giant trees flanked us, and we stepped over the corpses of their fallen brethren. The carpet of moss muffled the sound of our footsteps, making the croak of the frogs, the knocking of woodpeckers, and the song of the birds seem louder. I felt as though I had stepped into the primordial wilderness from one of the fairy tales that I loved growing up, and from their silence, I sensed that Milana, Ružica, and Helene felt the same awe.

"*Fagus sylvatica,*" Helene whispered, interrupting my thoughts. I did not understand the meaning of her vaguely Latin-sounding phrase, strange since I spoke or read German, French, Serbian, and Latin, two languages more than Helene. I wondered if she was speaking to me or to herself.

"Pardon me?"

"Sorry, it's the genus and species of this particular beech tree. My father and I used to go on long walks in the forest near our home in Vienna, and he had an affinity for the trees' Latin names." She twirled a fallen beech leaf between her fingers.

"The name is as beautiful as they are."

"Yes, I've always been partial to the name. It's quite lyrical. *Fagus sylvatica* can live for nearly three hundred years. If given enough space to grow, they can reach nearly thirty meters. Crowd them, and their growth is stunted," she said with an enigmatic smile.

I caught her unspoken meaning; in our own way, we were like *Fagus sylvatica*. I grinned back.

I glanced down at the hiking path. I was wary of my footing, even though I had not taken a misstep yet. I became so engrossed with the ground that I bumped into Milana, who had stopped suddenly. When I gazed over her shoulder to see what lay before us, I understood why.

We had reached the Albishorn, the peak of these woods, with its legendary vista. Spread before us was the vivid blue of Lake Zürich and the Sihl River, set off against white-capped mountains and rolling green hills dotted with farms. The blue of the Swiss waters was so much more brilliant than the muddy Danube of my youth; the Albishorn's accolades were well deserved, particularly since the air was filled with the crisp wonder of the mountains' ample evergreens.

I felt reborn here.

I took in a big breath of the invigorating air. I had done it. I had not been certain that I could manage this hike. I had never tried anything like it before. Only when the girls begged me to come—and Helene pointed out her own success on past Sihlwald hikes despite her limp—did I concede. Helene really left me with no excuse. Although her limp resulted from a childhood bout of tuberculosis in her hip and not a congenital hip defect like mine, her gait approximated my own. How could I claim that my disability prevented me from trying?

I had learned something new about myself. The unevenness of my legs was not as marked on uneven terrain. My disability was actually more pronounced on even ground. I could climb as well as any of the girls. What freedom.

I glanced over at Helene, and she smiled at me. I wondered if she had experienced the same self-doubts and the same revelation on this trail, even though she had hiked with her father growing up. When I smiled back, she reached for my hand and gave it a little squeeze. She released it only when she walked closer to the tip of the Albishorn for a better view.

The sun had set by the time we stumbled back into the Engelbrecht pension. The foyer seemed overstuffed and dim compared to the clear, bright, simple beauty of the wilderness, not to mention that it smelled cloyingly musty, no matter the cleaning lengths to which Mrs. Engelbrecht went. The maid helped us struggle out of our packs and rumpled coats, and we giggled with the effort.

"You girls are quite a sight!" Mrs. Engelbrecht said as she entered the foyer. The commotion had attracted her attention, and although she usually liked order and quiet in the pension, she could not help but laugh along with us.

"What a day we've had, Mrs. Engelbrecht!" Ružica said in her usual singsong.

"The Sihlwald was breathtaking as usual?"

"Oh yes," Milana answered for us all.

Mrs. Engelbrecht turned to me. "And you, Miss Marić? How did you find our jewel?" She had raved about the Sihlwald to me before our departure, reminisced about walks that she and Mr. Engelbrecht had taken there in the early days of their marriage.

The words to describe my experience did not come easily—for me, it was so much more than a mere hike—and I stammered. "It was so very…"

"So very…?" Mrs. Engelbrecht asked expectantly.

"Miss Marić adored it, Mrs. Engelbrecht." Helene came to my rescue. "Look, the Sihlwald rendered her speechless!"

Milana and Ružica chortled, and Mrs. Engelbrecht indulged us with another smile. "I'm delighted to hear it."

Mrs. Engelbrecht pointedly glanced up at the clock on the wall and then scanned us. "Perhaps you will want to freshen up before dinner? It will be served in fifteen minutes, and the windy boat ride across Lake Zürich has wreaked havoc on your hair. *Unordentliches Haar.*" She emphasized the unsightliness of our appearance.

Even though we were brilliant university students outside the Engelbrecht pension, within the pension doors, we were ladies who were expected to be respectable at all times. I patted my hair. I had carefully braided it this morning, then swept the heavy braids together on top of my head in a topknot, thinking it would withstand the hike and return boat trip, but I felt a mass of curly tendrils slipping out of the braids, knotting together in places.

"Yes, Mrs. Engelbrecht," Ružica said, answering for us all.

As we tromped upstairs to our rooms, I tried to untangle one particularly stubborn knot. No success. As Milana and Ružica tromped off to their respective rooms, Helene reached from behind me to help. I paused as she teased out the hairs.

"Do you want me to come to your room, and we can take turns with each other's hair? Otherwise, I'm not sure we will make dinner in fifteen minutes," she asked.

"Please."

After I unlocked my door, I grabbed two combs and some hairpins from my dressing table. We settled onto my creaky bed, and Helene began the painful business of fixing my hair. We visited each other's rooms often enough, but this was the first time I recalled ever working on each other's hair, although I'd spotted Ružica and Milana creating styles for each other often enough.

"Ow," I yelped.

"Sorry. There's nothing for this birds' nest other than a thorough combing. You'll have your revenge in a few minutes."

I laughed. "Thank you for encouraging me to come today, Helene."

"I'm so glad you did. Wasn't it wonderful?"

"Yes, it was. The view and the woods were magnificent. I never thought I could manage such a climb."

"That's ridiculous, Mileva. You were more than capable of that hike."

"I was worried about holding everyone back. You know, with my leg."

"For a brilliant girl who's had so much success in the class-room, you're awfully unsure of yourself elsewhere, Mileva. You did wonderfully today, and now you have no excuse not to join our hikes," Helene said.

A question about Helene had been haunting me since we met. "Your leg seems not to concern you at all. Don't you ever worry how people perceive you?"

Helene's heavy brows knitted in confusion. "Why should I? I mean, it's a nuisance—sometimes I'm a little unsteady on my feet, and I might not be the quickest in the bunch—but why should it affect how others see me?"

"Well, in Serbia, if a woman has a limp, she's not suitable for marriage."

Helene stopped brushing. "You're joking."

"No."

She placed the brush down on the bed, looked me in the face, and reached for my hand. "You're not in Serbia anymore, Mileva. You're in Switzerland, the most modern country in Europe, a place that would never adhere to such ridiculous, antiquated ideas. Even in my homeland of Austria, which seems like the hinterlands compared to progressive Zürich, such an idea would never be tolerated."

I nodded my head slowly. I knew she was right. Still, the notion of unmarriageability had been jangling around in my mind for so long, it almost seemed a part of who I was.

This perception started years before with an overheard conver-sation. I was seven, impatiently waiting after school on a cold

November day for Papa to return home. I had a surprise for him, one I hoped would make him smile.

Bored with pacing around the parlor, I grabbed a book off the shelf and sunk into Papa's armchair. Tucking my legs under me, I curled around the leather-bound, gold-embossed book, an exterior that belied the dog-eared, well-loved pages within. Although our family library contained many books—Papa believed that it was everyone's duty to become educated, even if his or her upbringing, like his own, did not provide a formal education—I returned to this collection of folk and fairy tales over and over. The stories were a bit simple for me at seven, but the book contained my favorite tale, "The Little Singing Frog."

I was halfway through the tale about a couple who prayed for a child and, when they received a frog daughter instead of a human girl, became embarrassed by her differences and hid her away. Just as I was about to read my favorite scene, where the prince hears the frog girl's singing and decides that he loves her despite her appearance, I erupted in a fit of laughter. Papa had snuck into the room and was tickling me.

I gave him a big hug, then excitedly stood up and pulled him across the room. I wanted to show him the ramps I'd built, based on the sketches I made in school earlier that day. "Papa, Papa, come see!"

Weaving through the fussy green velvet and walnut furniture to the one and only undecorated corner of the parlor, I led Papa to the experiment I had created, based on an earlier dinner conversation about Sir Isaac Newton. We talked about Newton at dinner often. I liked his idea that everything in the universe, from apples to planets, obeyed the same unchanging laws. Not laws made by people, but laws inherent in nature. I thought I might find God in such laws.

Papa and I had discussed Newton's writings about the force of objects in motion and the variables that affect them—more simply, why objects move the way they do. Newton intrigued me because I suspected he might help me understand why my leg dragged while other children's legs skipped lightly down the streets.

Our conversation had given me the idea. What if I made my own little experiment, exploring Newton's question about how increasing mass affects the force of objects in motion? Using strips of wood leaning on book stacks, I could create ramps with different inclines, and if I sent different-size marbles down those ramps, I would have a wealth of data to discuss with Papa. After school, I had begged the strips of wood off Jurgen, our house steward, and then leaned them against carefully stacked books, five books for each of the four ramps to be exact. Once I had tinkered with them for over an hour to ensure the inclines were exactly the same, I thought they were ready for Papa and me to perform the experiment.

"Come on, Papa," I implored, handing him a marble slightly larger than the one in my own hand. "Let's see how the *size* of the marbles affects their motion and speed."

Grinning at me, Papa ruffled my hair. "All right, my little bandit. An Isaac Newton experiment it is. Do you have your paper ready?"

"Ready," I said, and we knelt on the floor.

Papa lined up his marble on the ramp. After checking to make sure I did the same, he called out, "Go!"

For the next quarter hour, we released marbles down ramps and recorded the data. The minutes flew by in a blur. It was the time of day when I felt happiest. Papa really understood me. He was the only one.

Our housemaid, Danijela, interrupted us. "Mr. Marić, sir, Miss Mileva, dinner is served."

The peppery, meaty scent of my favorite *pljeskavica* wafted through the air, but still, I was disappointed. I had to share Papa over dinner. True, Papa and I dominated the dinnertime conversation—Mama barely spoke except to serve—but her presence dampened my enthusiasm and Papa's openness. Mama had so many expectations about who I should be, and none of them included a scientific little girl. *Why aren't you like the other girls?* she often asked me. Sometimes, she filled in the name of a specific Ruma child; there were any number of ordinary little girls in Ruma for her to pick from. She never explicitly filled in the question with the name of my late sister, but I knew that was implicit. Why wasn't I more like Milica might have been had she survived?

Often, in the darkness of my bedroom at night, in the silence of the hours after everyone had fallen into slumber, I wondered if I was making the wrong decision by pleasing Papa instead of Mama. I couldn't gratify both.

Despite their differences of opinion on my path, Papa would not brook any criticism of Mama, however slyly I made it. He defended her expectations as appropriate for a mother protecting her daughter. And I knew he was right. Mama loved me and wanted the best for me, even if her vision of the best didn't comport with my own.

Dinner ended after a stifled conversation about Newton. I was sent back to the parlor alone. Something was wrong between Mama and Papa, something unspoken but palpable. Mama would never openly disagree with Papa, certainly not in front of me, yet her manner—her unusually terse dinner prayer, her abrupt passing of plates, her failure to ask about the acceptability of the meal—spoke of defiance. To occupy myself until Papa returned, I reviewed the data we'd gathered and prepared for a second experiment to examine another one of Newton's theories. In order to measure the impact that friction has on the motion of identically sized marbles, I had asked Jurgen to prepare three strips of wood, each with varying degrees of roughness.

I thought about Papa's comment when I proposed this experiment: "Mitza, you are like the objects in one of Newton's investigations. You tirelessly maintain your velocity through life unless you are acted upon by an outside force. I hope no outside force ever changes your velocity."

Papa was funny.

As I created ramps using the different strips of wood, voices scratched at the edges of my consciousness. The maids were probably bickering again, a skirmish that resurfaced nearly every day as the dinner hour ended and the cleaning duties mounted. The voices escalated near the kitchen. What was going on? I had never known Danijela and Adrijana to be so loud before, so disrespectful. Nor had I ever known Mama to lose control of the kitchen. She was spare with her words but always firm. Curious, I strained my ears but could not make sense of the conversation.

I wanted to find out what was going on. Instead of nearing the kitchen through the parlor entrance, I crept down the servants' hallway. Here, the wood used for the dull floors was a rougher grade, and there were no pictures on the walls, unlike the rest of our house. In the area where we lived, the floors were polished to a high gleam and were covered with Turkish rugs, and the walls were crowded with still lifes of fruit and portraits of people we didn't know. Papa always said he wanted our house to be as fine as any home in the lauded city of Berlin.

No one expected me here. Trying to tread lightly—not easy in my heavy boots—I realized that the voices did not belong to Danijela and Adrijana. They belonged to Mama and Papa.

I had never heard Mama and Papa fight before. Soft-spoken and submissive everywhere but the kitchen—and even there, she was quietly adamant—Mama hardly even talked in Papa's presence. What horrible event had caused Mama to raise her voice?

Drawing closer to the kitchen door, I heard my name.

"Do not give the child false hope, Miloš. She is only seven years old. You spend too much time with her, encouraging her ideas and reading," Mama pleaded. "She is a gentle spirit, in need of our protection. We must prepare her for her *real* future. Here, at home."

"My hope in Mitza is not unfounded. No amount of time spent on her is too great. If anything, it is too little. Do I have to repeat what Miss Stanojević told me today? About Mitza's brilliance? About her genius with math and sciences? Her nimble way with other languages? Need I tell you again what I have long suspected?" Papa's voice was firm.

Surprisingly, Mama did not relent. "Miloš, she is a girl. What good does it do for you to teach her German and math? To do science experiments with her? Her place is in the home. And Mitza's home will be *this* home; her leg will make marriage—and children—impossible. Even the government recognizes this. Girls can't even attend high school."

"That may be true for ordinary girls. But it does not apply to a girl like Mitza."

"What do you mean, 'a girl like Mitza'?"

"You know what I mean."

Mama was quiet. I thought she had backed down, but then she spoke again.

"Do you mean a girl with a deformity?" Mama spat out the word.

I recoiled. Had Mama really just called my leg a deformity? Mama was always telling me how beautiful I was, how my limp was hardly noticeable. That no one really took account of the unevenness of my legs and hips. I had always known that this wasn't completely true—I could not ignore a lifetime of strangers' stares and schoolmates' teasing—but a deformity?

My father's tone was filled with fury. "Don't you dare call her leg a deformity! If anything, it is a gift. With a leg like that, no one will claim her in marriage. This gives her license to pursue the intellectual gifts God has given her. Her leg is a sign that she is destined for greater, better fates than a simple marriage."

"A sign? God-given gifts? Miloš, God would want us to protect her in this home. We must keep her expectations realistic so as not to crush her spirit." Mama paused, and Papa broke into the momentary silence.

"I want Mitza to be strong. I want her to walk by any *kli-pani* who mock her leg, confident that God gave her a special gift—her intelligence."

I felt like I was viewing myself for the first time. Mama and Papa perceived me much the same way the parents in "The Little Singing Frog" saw their daughter. I heard them say I was smart, but mostly, I sensed their shame. They wanted to hide me away everywhere but the classroom and our home. They didn't even think that I was worthy of marriage, something to which even the dullest farm girl could aspire.

Mama didn't answer, a long silence that signaled her return to submission. Papa spoke for them both, more calmly. "We will get her the education that her fine mind deserves. And I will teach her an iron will and the discipline of mind. It will be her armor."

Iron will? Discipline of mind? Armor? This was to be my future? No husband. No home of my own. No children. What about the hopeful ending of "The Little Singing Frog," where the prince sees the beauty within the frog daughter's ugly exterior and makes her his princess, clothing her in golden gowns the color of the sun? Was this not to be my fate? Didn't I deserve a prince of my own, no matter how horrible I was?

I ran out of the house, not bothering to mask the thuds of my ungainly hobble. Why should I? Mama and Papa had made clear that it was my limp that defined me.

⧼⧽

I had grown quiet, thinking about the past. Helene released my hand and took me by the shoulders. "You do see, don't you,

Mileva? That your limp does not make you unmarriageable? Or limit you in any other way? That you need not be tied to such old-fashioned beliefs?"

Looking into Helene's clear blue-gray eyes and hearing the conviction in her steady voice, I agreed with her. For the first time in my life, I believed that—maybe, just maybe—my limp was irrelevant. To who I was, to who I could become.

"Yes," I answered with a voice as steady as Helene's own.

Helene let go of my shoulders, picked up the brush, and resumed the painful work of untangling my hair. "Good. Anyway, why should we even worry about marriage? Even if you wanted to get married, why would you? Look at our group—me, you, Ružica, and Milana. We will be four professional women with busy lives of our own, here in Switzerland with its tolerance of women, intelligence, and ethnic peoples. We will have one another and our work; we need not follow the traditional path."

I considered this for a moment. Her statement seemed almost revolutionary—a bit like Mr. Einstein's description of a bohemian—even though it was a future we had all been marching toward. "You're right. Why should we? What's the point of marriage these days? Maybe it's something we don't need anymore."

"That's the spirit, Mileva. What fun we'll have! By day, we will work as historians or physicists or teachers, and by night and weekends, we will play our concerts and go for hikes."

I imagined the idyllic life Helene described. Was it possible? Could I really have a happy future full of meaningful work and friendships?

Helene continued, "Shall we make a pact? To a future together?"

"To a future together."

As we shook hands on our pact, I said, "Helene, please call me Mitza. It's the name used by my family and everyone who knows me well. And you know me better than almost anyone."

Helene smiled and said, "I'd be honored, Mitza."

Laughing over the day, we finished with each other's hair and readied for dinner. Unruly hair addressed and arms linked, Helene and I strode down the stairs. Deep in an animated debate about which of the rotating courses of entrees would be served that evening—I craved the creamy white wine and veal dish *Zürcher Geschnetzeltes*, and Helene was longing for something simpler—we were late in noticing Mrs. Engelbrecht standing at the bottom of the staircase, waiting for us. Or, rather, me.

"Miss Marić," she called up, her displeasure evident, "it seems you have a caller."

The sound of a throat clearing came from behind Mrs. Engelbrecht, and a figure stepped out from her silhouette. "Pardon me, ma'am, but I am a classmate, not a caller."

It was Mr. Einstein. Violin case in hand.

He had not waited to be asked.

CHAPTER 5

May 4, 1897
Zürich, Switzerland

GENTLEMEN, GENTLEMEN. IS THERE NOT A SINGLE ONE among you who knows the answer to my query?" Professor Weber strutted across the front of the classroom, delighting in our ignorance. Why a teacher derived such glee from his students' failures was incomprehensible and disturbing to me. Being called a gentleman did not trouble me nearly as much. Months ago, I had become inured to Weber's regular slights, whether they be remarks about eastern Europeans or his insistence on referring to me as a man. I only wished Weber's lectures were like those of other professors, like oysters cracked open to reveal the most lustrous of pearls.

I knew the answer to Weber's question, but, as usual, I hesitated to raise my hand. I glanced around, hoping someone else would answer, but every one of my classmates—including Mr. Einstein—had his arm glued to his desk. Why wasn't anyone raising his hand? Perhaps the unseasonable heat was making them languorous. Unexpectedly hot for spring, even the opening of the classroom windows did not stir a breeze, and I saw Mr. Ehrat and Mr. Kollros pushing the limpid air around with makeshift fans. Perspiration beaded on my forehead, and I noticed that my classmates' suit jackets were stained with sweat.

Why was it so hard to raise my hand? I'd done it several times before, although not easily. I shook my head slightly as a recollection took hold of me. I was seventeen, and I had just left my first physics class at the all-male Royal Classical High School in Zagreb, where Papa managed to get me admitted after my time in Novi Sad, despite a law prohibiting Austro-Hungarian girls from attending high school, by applying successfully to the authorities for an exemption. Relieved and thrilled with my first day—where I ventured to answer the instructor's question and got it correct—I floated out of my classroom. I had waited until the room nearly cleared so the hallway was empty. A man came behind me suddenly and pushed me down another more dimly lit hallway. Was he in such a rush that he didn't see me?

"Sir, sir," I called out over my shoulder, but he didn't stop pushing me down the ever-darkening corridor. There was no one around to hear my pleas. What was going on?

I struggled to turn around but couldn't. The man was over a foot taller than me. He shoved me against the wall—my face smashed against it and away from his, so I could not identify him later—and held me down tightly. My arms burned.

"You think you're so smart. Showing off with that answer." He seethed, spit from his angry words spraying my one exposed cheek. "You should not even be allowed in our class. There's a law against it." He gave me a final shove into the wall and then ran off.

I stayed frozen, still facing the wall, until I heard his last footstep. Only then did I turn around, shaking uncontrollably.

I had not expected an eager welcome from my fellow students, but I had not expected this either. Leaning against the wall, I began to cry, something I had promised myself I would never do at school. Wiping away my tears and the attacker's spittle from my cheeks, I realized that I was going to have to tamp down my intelligence and keep my smarts quiet too. Or risk everything.

Weber interrupted my unpleasant memory with chiding. "Tsk, tsk. I am very disappointed that not one of you has your hand raised. We have been leading up to this question for the *entire* class. Doesn't anyone know the answer?"

Remembering my conversation with Helene from a month ago, I decided to stop my past from paralyzing me. I took a deep breath and raised my hand. Weber stepped down from the podium and walked toward my seat. What sort of ignominy would he make me suffer if I was wrong? What would my classmates do if I was correct?

"Ah, it's you, Miss Marić," he said as if surprised. As if he didn't know whose desk he was walking toward. As if I hadn't already demonstrated my intellect to him. This feigned astonishment was just another way he humiliated me. And tested me.

"The answer to your question is one percent," I said. I felt more heat rise in my cheeks and wished I hadn't opened my mouth.

"I'm sorry, can you repeat that a little louder, so we can all share in your wisdom?" Wisdom. It sounded as if Weber was mocking me. Had I gotten the answer wrong? Was he reveling in my failure?

I cleared my throat and said, in the strongest voice I could muster, "Given the context of your question, the closest we can come to stating the time necessary to cool the earth is by one percent."

"Correct," Weber admitted with not a small amount of surprise and disappointment. "For those of you who could not hear it, Miss Marić has arrived at the correct answer. By one percent. Please mark it down."

Murmurs built around me. At first, I could not hear any of the comments clearly, but then I teased a few pointed remarks out of the chatter. I heard "she got it" and "nice work" among the phrases. These compliments were a first; I had answered a couple of Weber's questions correctly before without a single reaction. Most likely, today, my classmates were merely delighted that someone got the better of Weber.

As class came to an end, I stood and began to pack my satchel. Mr. Einstein walked the few steps over toward my desk. "Most impressive, Miss Marić."

"Thank you, Mr. Einstein." I answered quietly with a nod. "But I'm certain any one of our classmates could have done just as well." I resumed my packing, wondering why I felt the need to diminish my accomplishments.

"You do yourself a disservice, Miss Marić. I can assure you that none of us other fellows knew the answer." His voice dropped to a whisper. "Or else we wouldn't have allowed Weber to badger us for so insufferably long."

An irrepressible smile crept upon my face at Mr. Einstein's audacity in criticizing Weber while he was standing right there at the podium.

"There it is, Miss Marić. That elusive smile. I believe I've only seen it twice before."

"Is that so?" I glanced up at him. I didn't want to encourage his silly banter—especially in the presence of my classmates and Weber, who I wanted to think of me seriously—but I did not want to be rude.

He met my gaze. "Oh yes, I've been keeping careful—and quite scientific—notes about your smiles. A few evenings ago, when you were kind enough to allow me to play music with you and your friends, I spied one. But that wasn't the first. No, the first smile took place on the steps of your pension. That day I walked you home in the rain."

I didn't know how to respond. He seemed serious, not at all his usual bemused self. And that very fact made me apprehensive. Was it possible that he was making some sort of overture toward me? I had no experience with such things, and other than Helene's occasional warnings, I had no way to assess his comments.

Out of nerves or discomfort, I started walking toward the classroom door. The rustle of papers behind me and the fast clip of shoes told me that Mr. Einstein was racing to follow me. "Will you ladies be playing this evening?" he asked once he reached my side.

Ah, perhaps he simply sought musical companionship. Maybe his statements had not been flirtatious at all. A strange mix of disappointment and relief washed over me. This startled me. Was there some part of me that sought his attentions?

"It is our custom to play before dinner," I answered.

"Do you have a piece selected?"

"I believe Miss Kaufler chose Bach's Violin Concerto in A Minor."

"Ah, that is a beautiful piece." He hummed a few bars of the music. "May I join you again?"

"I didn't think that you waited for an invitation." I surprised myself with my saucy retort. Despite my conflicted feelings and my attempts to steer the conversation back to a more appropriate course, I could not resist the jab at Mr. Einstein's disregard of normal protocol over a week ago when he arrived uninvited to the pension after our Sihlwald outing.

While he waited in the parlor for us to finish dinner, Milana and Ružica bombarded me with questions about Mr. Einstein, expressing their dismay at his presumptuousness, while Helene simply listened, her eyes wary. We agreed to let him join us for music, but the wariness lingered throughout our disjointed playing of a Mozart sonata. Since I did not think of the evening as a success, I was bewildered that he was inquiring about another such night.

He snorted in surprise then chuckled. "I suppose that is well deserved, Miss Marić. But then, I already warned you that I am a bohemian."

Mr. Einstein followed me as I walked through the hallways toward the back entrance of the school building. Given that my nerves were already a bit jangled, I wanted to avoid the clamor of Rämistrasse. He pushed open the heavy doors, and we passed from the dim school hallways into the bright daylight of the terrace on the back side of the building. I squinted into the light, and the mountainous backdrop of Zürich, dotted equally with ancient church steeples and modern-day office structures, came into view.

As we crossed the terrace, out of habit, I counted its right angles and calculated the symmetry of its design. I'd begun this ritual as a way of distracting myself from the derogatory whispers I sometimes overheard from male students and teachers— even their sisters, mothers, and girlfriends—as they too walked across the terrace. The criticisms about the inappropriateness of a woman student, the snickers about my limp, the ugly remarks about my dark looks and serious face—I didn't want my confidence in the classroom to be tainted by their commentaries.

"You are so quiet, Miss Marić."

"I am often accused of such, Mr. Einstein. Unfortunately, unlike a typical lady, I have no gift for small chatter."

"Unusually quiet, I mean. As if an important theory has taken hold. What thought has captured your formidable mind?"

"In truth?"

"Always the truth."

"I was assessing the colonnades and geometric layout of the square. I've realized that they have an almost exact bilateral, axial reflection, symmetry."

"Is that all?" he asked with a smirk.

"Not quite," I retorted. If Mr. Einstein did not play by the rules of social niceties, why should I? It was a relief, so I explained my actual thoughts. "Over the past few months, I've noted the parallels between artistic symmetry and the concept of symmetry as it plays out in physics."

"What have you concluded?"

"I've determined that a follower of Plato would say that the square's beauty is solely attributable to its symmetry." I didn't mention how this conclusion saddened me; imbedded into the theories of the studies I love best, math and physics, was the ideal of symmetry, a standard that I myself, with my irregular legs, could never achieve.

He stopped walking. "Impressive. What else have you noticed about this square, which I stroll by obliviously each day?"

I gestured around the square to the abundant spires. "Well, I've noted that Zürich seems to sprout church towers rather than trees. Bordering this square alone, we have the Fraumünster, Grossmünster, and St. Peter's."

He stared at me. "You were right, Miss Marić, about not being a typical lady. In fact, you are a most extraordinary young woman."

After this roundabout perambulation, Mr. Einstein made a turn leading toward Rämistrasse. I paused, not wanting to go that way. I craved instead the peace of a stroll through quiet residential neighborhoods on my way back to the pension. I wondered if he would follow, unsure whether I wanted his company. I enjoyed my conversations with Mr. Einstein, but I worried that he might follow me all the way back to the pension, and that might incur the girls' acrimony again over his uninvited presence.

"Mr. Einstein! Mr. Einstein!" A voice called out from a café across the street on Rämistrasse. "I say, you are late for our meeting! As usual!"

The voice came from a sidewalk café table. Glancing over, I spotted a dark-haired, olive-complected gentleman waving his hands in our direction. I did not recognize him from the Polytechnic.

Mr. Einstein waved to his friend, then turned back toward me. "Will you join me and my friend for a coffee, Miss Marić?"

"My studies beckon, Mr. Einstein. I must go."

"Please, I should so like you to meet Mr. Michele Besso. Even though he graduated from the Polytechnic as an engineer and not a physicist, he's introduced me to many new physics theorists, like Ernst Mach. He is very likable and intrigued by many of the same big, modern ideas as you and I."

I was flattered. Mr. Einstein seemed to believe that I could hold my own in a scientific discussion with his friend. Not many other men in Zürich would make such an offer. Part of me wanted to say yes, to accept his invitation, to sit across a café table from my classmate and discuss the thorny big questions that physics raised. Secretly, I longed to participate in the fervent conversations happening on the streets of Zürich and in its cafés. Instead of just watching.

But part of me was scared. Scared of the confusing nature of Mr. Einstein's attention, and scared of stepping over the invisible divide and taking the risks that came with becoming the person I dreamed of being.

"Thank you, but I can't, Mr. Einstein. My apologies."

"Another time, perhaps?"

"Perhaps." I took my leave and began walking in the direction of the Engelbrecht Pension.

I heard his voice piping up in the mounting distance. "Until then, we shall have music!"

Feeling very bold—more like a fellow scholar instead of a lady—I called back over my shoulder. "I don't recall extending an invitation!"

Laughter came from Mr. Einstein. "As you yourself said, I have never waited for invitations!"

CHAPTER 6

June 9 and 16, 1897
Zürich, Switzerland

Rᴜžɪᴄᴀ ᴀɴᴅ I ᴇxɪᴛᴇᴅ ᴛʜᴇ Cᴏɴᴅɪᴛᴏʀᴇɪ Sᴄʜᴏʙᴇʀ ᴀɴᴅ walked arm in arm down Napfgasse. The afternoon sun was soft and hazy, lighting the buildings from behind and creating a lambent glow on all the shop fronts we passed. We both sighed in satisfaction.

"That was delicious," Ružica said. Last night after dinner, she and I had made plans to try the coffee, hot chocolate, and *patisseries* at Conditorei Schober. The famous confectionary was located in between the University of Zürich, where Ružica studied, and the Polytechnic, and we had been fantasizing about the café's delights since we learned of its existence from Mrs. Engelbrecht. Helene and Milana declined to join us for our outing; not only did they prefer savories to sweets, but they also weren't inclined toward the frivolous adventures that Ružica sought out. I'd surprised myself by agreeing to join her.

"I can still taste the caramel and walnuts from my torte," I said about my selection, a delicious shortbread confection with decadent filling.

"And I can still taste the marzipan and crème from the *Sardegnatorte*," Ružica countered.

"I shouldn't have had that second *Milchkaffee*," I said, referring to the rich, milky coffee I adored. "I'm so full that I might need to unlace my corset when we get back to the pension."

We giggled at the notion of appearing for one of Mrs. Engelbrecht's dinner with undone corsets.

"You think you need to unlace your corset? What about me? I'm the one who ordered the second dessert. But I couldn't resist the look of the *Luxemburgerli*," Ružica said. The exquisite macaroon-style confections came in a variety of flavors, and Ružica claimed they were so airy and light they simply melted on her tongue. "Maybe it's a good thing that there's nothing like Conditorei Schober at home in Šabac. I would have arrived here in Zürich for my studies quite the dumpling."

Laughing again, we strolled down the Napfgasse, admiring the newfangled ladies' suits that the affluent Zürich women had begun to wear. We approved of the fresh style of the fitted jacket over the trumpetlike skirt shape but decided that the cinched nature of the jacket on top of the mandatory corsets would make us uncomfortable for long hours of studying. No, we would remain with the more practical full-sleeved blouses tucked into bell-shaped skirts, always in somber colors to ensure that we were taken seriously by our professors and classmates.

After fifteen minutes of chatter, we lapsed into companionable silence, enjoying the rare unstructured moments. I thought, not for the first time, how unexpected my life in Zürich was.

When I set out from Zagreb, I never could have imagined that I'd be sauntering down a boulevard, arm in arm with a girlfriend, after enjoying afternoon tea together in a fanciful café. Chatting about fashion, nonetheless.

"Let's walk over to Rämistrasse," Ružica suddenly said.

"What?" I asked, certain that I hadn't heard her correctly.

"Rämistrasse. Isn't that the street with all those cafés that Mr. Einstein frequents with his friends?"

"Yes, but—"

"Didn't Mr. Einstein invite us to join him and his friends when he was at the pension playing Bach with us last night?"

"Yes, but I don't think it's a good idea, Ružica."

"Come on, Mileva, what are you afraid of?" Ružica taunted and began pulling me in the direction of Rämistrasse. "We won't seek him out or anything so inappropriate. We will simply walk down the street like any other passerby, and if Mr. Einstein and his friends should happen to spot us, then so be it."

I could have insisted that we return to the pension. I could have spun around in the other direction and marched off. But in truth, I yearned to join in the café culture all around me. Ružica was the external source of confidence I needed to take that step.

Emboldened, I nodded in agreement. Still arm in arm, an arrangement that grew harder as the streets grew more crowded, we took a few lefts and rights before reaching Rämistrasse. As if we had planned it but without a word between us, we slowed our pace and ambled down the boulevard.

My grip on Ružica's arm grew tighter as we neared Café Metropole, a favorite of Mr. Einstein's. I didn't dare turn my head to the right to see if he or his friends sat in the coveted outside tables. I noticed that, despite all her bravado, Ružica didn't shift her glance either.

"Miss Marić! Miss Dražić!" I heard a voice call out. I knew precisely who it was: Mr. Einstein.

Ružica continued apace, and at first, I wasn't certain that she had heard the call. But then she shot me a furtive glance, and I realized that she was pretending not to hear. To force Mr. Einstein to seek us out again. I had no experience with guile, so I took Ružica's lead and kept strolling. Only when Mr. Einstein cried out our names again and Ružica glanced in the direction of his voice did I allow my eyes to follow.

Mr. Einstein nearly sprinted across the boulevard from Café Metropole to the sidewalk upon which we stood. "Ladies," he yelled, "what a delightful surprise! I insist that you join me and my friends. We are deep in debate over J. J. Thomson's demonstration that cathode rays contained particles called electrons, and we could use some fresh opinions."

Releasing our grip on each other, Ružica and I followed Mr. Einstein to the café. The tables were packed elbow-to-elbow with male students, and we wove through the throngs to reach Mr. Einstein's group of three jammed into a back corner. How had he seen us from this awkward vantage point? His gaze must have been fixed on the street.

Two gentlemen rose and stood alongside Mr. Einstein for the introductions. I realized that I knew one of the men quite well, by sight at least. It was Mr. Grossman, one of my five other classmates. Other than general greetings and necessary classroom exchanges, he and I had never really spoken. The other man was the Mr. Besso that Mr. Einstein had mentioned to me. Dark-haired with brown eyes bearing a humorous spark, he smiled easily.

The men busied themselves borrowing the few free chairs from other café patrons and arranging them around the table for us. As we settled into our seats, Mr. Besso offered to pour us some coffee and order some pastries.

Ružica and I glanced at each other and burst into laughter at the mere thought of another morsel of food or drink. With quizzical expressions, the men stared at us, forcing me to explain. "We just came from Conditorei Schober."

"Ah," Mr. Grossman said knowingly, "I completely understand. My mother visited from Geneva last week, and we spent a long afternoon there. I don't think I ate for two days afterward." These words were the most Mr. Grossman had spoken to me since we became classmates and were most agreeable. For the first time, I wondered whether the fault in our communication was mine.

The men launched back into their discussion of J. J. Thomson's experiment, and Ružica and I grew quiet. This situation was new to me. Should we voice opinions, I wondered, or wait until asked. I worried that Mr. Grossman and Mr. Besso would misinterpret my shyness for sullenness or ignorance, but I didn't want to be overbold either.

"Miss Marić, what do you think?" Mr. Einstein asked, as if he could hear my thoughts aloud.

With his encouragement and invitation, I said, "I wonder whether the particles Mr. Thomson found with his cathode rays might be the key to understanding matter."

The men were quiet, and immediately, I recoiled. Had I said too much? Had I said something stupid?

"Well said," Mr. Besso said.

Mr. Grossman nodded along. "I quite agree."

The three men catapulted back into the debate about the existence of atoms that had obviously started before Ružica and I arrived, and I grew silent again. But not for long. When the next break in the conversation occurred, I began to interject my opinions. Once it became evident that I would not recede into my shell like a mollusk, the others sought out my thoughts as we moved into a discussion about experiments from around Europe, in particular Wilhelm Röntgen's discovery of X-rays. Even though I tried to solicit from her a political science perspective on these developments, Ružica remained uncharacteristically quiet throughout. Did the company of Mr. Einstein and his friends disappoint? Had she hoped for a more traditionally structured exchange, with the regular pleasantries instead of this scientific conversation?

Perhaps this adventure had not developed precisely as Ružica hoped, but for me, this inclusion, this discussion, Mr. Einstein's confidence in me, made me feel alive, as electric as the currents running throughout Zürich. I tried not to think what Mr. Einstein's encouragement might mean beyond this.

⊘

"Is that you, Mileva? You missed the Mozart!" I heard Milana call out from the gaming room.

Oh no. The Mozart. Two times this week alone, I had missed my musical appointments with the girls. My cheeks were now flushed with more than exhilaration over my afternoon at Café Metropole.

I crept into the back parlor, not bothering to hide my nervousness over their reception or my own sheepishness at my behavior. Why should I? I deserved blame; these girls had offered me affection and emotional shelter in a new place, and I could not even keep my meetings with them. At the first distraction, I was off. I was a poor friend indeed.

Ružica, Milana, and Helene sat around the gaming table, china tea cups emptied and instruments strewn about. The musical interlude was plainly finished—or perhaps never even begun due to my absence—and undoubtedly they were stewing over me. For once, their expressions matched the sternness of their attire.

"It wasn't the same without you on tamburitza," Ružica scolded, but I could see the affection and teasing behind her disappointment. She would be hard-pressed to berate me further; after all, she was the one who had practically dragged me into the coffeehouse culture, even though she'd declined to join in our discussions since. Too scientific, she'd labeled them.

"Yes, Mileva," Milana concurred, "the piece sounded hollow. Rather thin."

Helene said nothing. Her silence was worse than any overt condemnation. It was like the flash of lightning before the thunderclap.

"Where were you?" Milana asked me.

Before I could respond, Helene shot me an indignant glance. The resentment and ill will that began the first night Mr. Einstein played with us was obviously festering. On the evening of his first visit, Helene greeted him with a disgruntled, "Who simply appears on a classmate's doorstep uninvited?" When Milana and Ružica included him in our Bach concerto, despite Helene's obvious displeasure, Helene stopped our playing several times to criticize his technique, an unusual act for usually kind Helene. This behavior had continued on the three other times he had joined us—without notice or explicit invitation—for our nightly music.

Helene finally unleashed her thunder. "Let me hazard a guess. You were discussing science at Café Metropole. With Mr. Einstein and his friends."

I did not answer. Helene was right, and the girls knew it. I had no justifiable excuse. What could I say? How could I explain to the girls how exhilarated I felt at the Café Metropole? What would it mean about how I felt with them? Especially when I'd repeatedly chosen Mr. Einstein and his café friends over our musical interludes.

Tears welled in the corners of my eyes; I was angry at myself. Nothing was worth the disappointment of these girls. They had rekindled my dreams of a fulfilling future, and together, we had fashioned a refuge from the world, where we could be our true intellectual yet sometimes silly selves. Mr. Einstein, for all his insinuation into my life over the past two months, for all the excitement I felt around him, was not deserving.

I gingerly sat down on the one empty chair, wiping a tear away. "I can offer nothing but my apology."

Ružica and Milana reached across the table to clasp my hand. "Of course, Mileva," Milana offered, and Ružica nodded.

Helene did not move. "I sincerely hope this will not become a pattern, Mitza. We count on you."

Her words were about more than the failed concerts or her feelings about my actions. They were a sort of ultimatum. Helene was offering me another chance, but only if I committed to making our group paramount. To keeping our pact.

I reached across the table to take her hand. "I promise you that forgetting about our plans and staying too long at Café Metropole will not become a pattern."

She smiled that same warm, inviting grin from our first encounter. An audible sigh of relief passed over the gaming room.

"Anyway, what could be the possible lure of Mr. Einstein other than a boring old physics discussion?" Milana offered a bit of levity. "Certainly not his wild hair."

We burst into laughter. Mr. Einstein's unruly curls were fast becoming legendary among us. In the carefully coiffed world of Zürich, Mr. Einstein's hairdo had no equal. It was as if he did not even own a comb.

"Certainly, she is not lured by his fastidious dress," Ružica chimed in. "Did you see his rumpled suit jacket when he was last here? For the Bach? It looked as if he stored his clothes on the floor."

Our laughter deepened, and suddenly everyone wanted a shot at Mr. Einstein. Even Helene.

"And then there's his pipe! Does he think that it adds years to those pudgy childish cheeks? Or makes him look professorial?" She did a wicked imitation of Mr. Einstein loading tobacco into his yard-long pipe and puffing on it thoughtfully.

Just as we squealed at the impersonation, the dinner bell rang. Composing ourselves, we rose for the meal.

Later that evening, back in my room, I wrapped around my shoulders the rose-embroidered shawl Mama had given me. The June night was pleasantly cool, and though I could have warmed my room by keeping the window closed, I needed the fresh air on my face. I had mountains of homework, physics chapters to read, and mathematical calculations to make. I longed for a bracing *Milchkaffee*, but none was to be found at the pension.

I heard a knock on my door and jumped. No one ever came to my room at this hour. I cracked my door open a sliver so I could see who it was.

Helene stood in the hallway.

"Please come in." I hurried to welcome her.

Gesturing for her to settle at the foot of my bed, the only place to sit other than my single desk chair, I felt anxious. Was she here to discuss Café Metropole? I thought the issue had been resolved. The lighthearted mood from the gaming room had carried on throughout dinner.

"Do you remember the first time you realized that you were different from other girls? Smarter perhaps?" Helene asked.

I nodded, although her question surprised me. I remembered well the day in Miss Stanojević's class when I realized I wasn't like everyone else. I was seven years old, and I was terribly bored. The other students—all girls—looked flummoxed by the teacher's explanation of the basic principles of multiplication, an easy concept I had taught myself by the age of four. I had the vague sense that I could make the girls understand. If only I could take Miss Stanojević's place at the chalkboard, I believed I could show the girls the ease of the numbers, the effortless way one could see through and around them, combining them in endless groups and making elegant connections. But I didn't dare. A student at the chalkboard would be unprecedented in the *Volksschule*. Order and strata reigned in all regions of the Austro-Hungarian Empire, no matter how remote. Instead of getting up and taking charge of the chalkboard as I wanted, I had stared down at the ugly black boots Mama made me wear each day—in the hopes that they'd lessen my limp—and compared them unfavorably to the delicate, ivory lace-up shoes that my classmate, the sweet, blond-ringleted Maria, always wore.

"Can you tell me about it?" Helene asked.

I told her about that day as a frustrated seven-year-old.

"Did you ever act on your suspicion that you were a better math teacher than Miss Stanojević?" She laughed.

"Actually, yes." It felt strange to be sharing this incident.

"What happened?"

"For some reason, the teacher was called away from the classroom. She was gone a long time, and the girls began to chatter and wander away from their seats. Seriously disobeying the class rules, of course."

"Of course."

"One of the girls, Agata I think her name was, walked over to me. I wondered what she wanted. It wasn't like I was friends with her or any of the other girls for that matter. I thought maybe she was going to make fun of me, you know?"

"I do know."

"Instead, she leaned over my desk and asked me to explain multiplication to her. So using my own methodology, I started to explain Miss Stanojević's lesson. As I talked, more and more girls drifted over to my desk, until nearly the whole classroom was gathered around me. Finally, even though it was risky, I limped up to the chalkboard. I did it to help them as much as to help myself. If I made the lesson easy for all of them, then maybe Miss Stanojević would be able to move on to something more interesting. Like division."

"What was the methodology you showed them?"

"Instead of reviewing the tables Miss Stanojević had written on the board, I took a single equation: six times three. I told the girls not to memorize the equation but to think of it using addition, which they'd already started to understand. I explained that all six times three really meant was this: to add the number six three times. When I heard 'eighteen' called out a few times, I realized that I helped at least a couple of my classmates."

"So that was the moment."

"Actually, the moment came just after that. I turned away from the chalkboard and saw that Miss Stanojević had returned. She stood in the doorway with another teacher, Miss Kleine, at her side. Their jaws had dropped at the sight of a student at the chalkboard."

We giggled, thinking of the bold little Mileva and her scandalized teacher.

"I froze, thinking that my knuckles would be rapped for my audacity. But incredibly, after the longest minute of my young life, Miss Stanojević smiled. She turned to Miss Kleine, and after they conferred for a moment, she said, 'Well done, Miss Marić. Will you kindly show us that lesson again?'" I paused. "That's when I knew."

"Knew that you were different? More clever?"

"Knew that my life wouldn't be like the other girls'." My voice dropped to a whisper. "The girls made sure that I understood that too, that I would never be one of them."

I told Helene my secret story. How, later that same day, when I was walking home from school and carefully avoiding the scrubby field where the students played, Radmila, one of my classmates, walked over and invited me to join their games for the very first time. Even though I was suspicious and I wanted to look into Radmila's muddy brown eyes and decline, part of me wanted a friend. So I said yes. The girls, who had already linked hands in a circle, opened their closed ranks to admit me and Radmila to their game. I joined in the games' rhythmic swaying and silly chants, bobbing to and fro on the waves of the children's hands, dust swirling around us. Then, suddenly, the rules changed. The pace increased furiously, and I was whipped around wildly. When my legs buckled beneath me, the children dragged me around the circle, chanting all the while. They then released my hands, tossed me in the circle's center, dusty and bruised, and stood by laughing while I struggled to stand. Crying, I pushed myself to standing and hobbled down the dusty road toward home. I didn't care if they laughed as I lurched down the road; they had already cut into me as deeply as they could go. Humiliation for my audacity in leading the classroom and for being different had been their goal all along.

"My own story is much the same," Helene whispered.

Reaching over to embrace me, she said, "Mitza, I wish I'd known you all my life."

"Me too, Helene."

"I apologize for being so hard on you today and for my obvious distrust of Mr. Einstein. I know I encouraged you to form an alliance with him initially, but I didn't realize he'd be so, well, presumptuous and unorthodox. It's taken me so long to find others like myself. I find it difficult—and I overreact—when it seems they are drifting away, particularly to someone I'm not certain deserves them."

Squeezing her tight, I said, "I'm sorry, Helene. I wasn't drifting away from you. By spending time with Mr. Einstein and his scientist friends, I actually thought I was moving closer to the professional goals we talk about so often. The men speak of nothing but the latest scientific developments at the café, advancements of which I would otherwise be unaware."

She grew quiet. "I didn't realize. I thought you were being lured by the 'bohemian' ways he's always talking about. By him, not science."

I rushed to correct her. "No, Helene. The time I spend with him is more in the manner of a colleague. I glean much from him professionally at school and at Café Metropole, no matter how frivolously he acts here." But as I said these words to Helene, I realized they were not entirely true. My feelings were more complex; I felt alive in Mr. Einstein's company, understood and accepted. The sensation was unique and unsettling.

Reassuring myself as much as her, I said, "But it is of no further consequence. Your good opinion means the world to me. Above all else."

CHAPTER 7

July 30 and 31, 1897
Zürich, Switzerland, and the Sihl Valley

EVEN THOUGH HELENE NEVER REALLY CAME TO ACCEPT Mr. Einstein in those final weeks of the term, she did soften toward him after our conversation. Whether it was the reaffirming of our pact or our mischievous remarks about his grooming, her concerns about him seemed diffused. She no longer viewed him as a threat to our little rituals, even though he was persistently, abundantly, present.

This benefited me as well, as my assurances and mild mockery of Mr. Einstein helped keep him in perspective. It reminded me that he was merely a kindred lover of physics and a classmate—and a rather silly, certainly ridiculous-looking one. I believed that I could quell any feelings toward him. I felt well-armed to politely stamp out any inkling of an overture that he might spring upon me. Not that anything other than frivolous banter and hints had been forthcoming.

The evening after the last arduous day of the Section Six first-year finals—for which I'd studied harder than anything ever before—Mr. Einstein appeared on the Engelbrecht

Pension doorstep, violin in hand, as had become his habit. This was no surprise. He had not been specifically invited, but then, he never was. His violin playing was so full of virtuosic feeling that the girls grew to welcome him, even though they never quite got accustomed to his lack of explicit invitation.

A night of Antonio Vivaldi's *The Four Seasons* had been planned, a nod to the changing of our own season. Mr. Einstein's playing was especially heartfelt that evening. We paused in satisfaction after the last bars sounded, and in that moment of quiet contentment, he sprung.

"Miss Kaufler, you ladies have spoken of this magical Sihlwald forest for months now," Mr. Einstein said.

"Yes, we have, Mr. Einstein," Helene answered.

"I distinctly recall you mentioning the vista from the top of the Albis hills, Miss Kaufler."

"I have indeed." She nodded in our direction, continuing the pleasant exchange with a description of the Albishorn. She seemed to find it innocuous, although I could see where Mr. Einstein was headed.

"If I may be so bold, I should very much like to be included in the Sihlwald outing you ladies have planned for tomorrow morning."

The four of us had decided upon a final outing to mark the end of term. We had taken longer and longer trips since our initial Sihlwald excursion, and after much discussion, we had agreed that we should end the term as we began—with a trip to the Sihlwald.

Even though Mr. Einstein's intentions seemed plain to me,

Helene seemed surprised. She stammered in reply, "Well, Mr. Einstein, you see... Um, this outing... I believe it was designed to be a farewell excursion for just the four of us."

Undeterred, Mr. Einstein pushed on in his humorous yet determined way. "Am I to be deprived of both the natural beauty of the Sihlwald forest and the pleasure of your companies this final Saturday before the holiday, Miss Kaufler? It will be months before we meet again."

His boldness, brash even for him, unsettled her further. "You see, um, I cannot... The decision is not mine alone."

He looked directly at me, his brown eyes pleading. My stomach fluttered a little as his eyes moved on to Ružica and Milana. "What say you, ladies?"

He was shameless. How could we, well-bred, sheltered girls reared to be polite, say anything but yes?

⁓

Packs on our backs—full of hiking gear, lunches foisted upon us by the eager Mrs. Engelbrecht, and maps of the forest—we stood on the platform for the train. I kept checking the station clock. Mr. Einstein was horribly late.

"Where is he?" Ružica tapped her foot impatiently. She'd asked this question no less than eight times.

"I say we get on board," Milana suggested. "The train departs in two minutes."

Glancing up at the station clock yet again, I felt conflicted. I wanted Mr. Einstein to join us but didn't want my insistence on waiting to cause a delay in our trip. Not wanting to appear too eager, I said, "Milana is right. We can't wait any longer.

Anyway, Mr. Einstein is notoriously late. Who knows when he will show up?"

Helene nodded in agreement, and we got on board. Settling into an empty compartment—we had our choice as the train was sparsely populated at this early Saturday hour—we loaded our packs into the overhead racks. Just as we sat down on the worn upholstered benches, the train whistle blew, and we started to move.

A reprieve. I sighed. Perhaps it was best that I wouldn't see Mr. Einstein until next term, in three months' time. His constant presence lately had only heightened my bewilderment. *Yes*, I thought, *this is precisely what I need.* The beginning of the summer holiday without him was a good portend.

"Oh my," Milana said as she looked out the compartment window.

"What is it?" Ružica asked.

Milana didn't answer. She just pointed out the window, as if the sight could only be seen, not described.

Craning my neck to see over Helene's head, I saw two men running through the station toward our train. Even through the thick glass, I could hear them yelling, "Hold the train!"

I strained my eyes to see if either was Mr. Einstein. Curly mop of hair. Untucked shirt. All his hallmarks certainly, not the usual careful ablutions of Swiss men. But he was meant to come alone, and there was another man in tow. Maybe it wasn't him. My stomach churned with mixed emotions.

The chug of the train slowed a bit, and the two men leaped on board. A moment later, the compartment door burst open. There was Mr. Einstein, beaming. "I made it!" Bowing at us, he gestured behind him. "Ladies, may I introduce my friend, Michele Besso, whom Miss Marić and Miss Dražić already know from Café Metropole. He is an engineer and graduate of the Polytechnic."

I nodded in acknowledgment; I had shared many conversations with Mr. Besso about Ernst Mach, a physicist he admired. At Café Metropole, I enjoyed talking with the soft-spoken Mr. Besso, but I wondered how the girls would perceive him. Certainly Ružica had not engaged much with him that first afternoon at the café.

"Welcome, gentlemen," I said.

Without waiting for my leave, and without offering an excuse for having brought an extra guest, Mr. Einstein plopped down on the bench next to me. His leg brushed up against the folds of my skirt, and I realized that we had never sat side by side before. Wooden student chairs, spindly iron café seats, and the Engelbrechts' ornate parlor chairs had been our perches. It felt too close, especially when I'd just decided the trip was better without him.

Mr. Besso was more circumspect. "May I?" he asked Ružica before sitting down.

As our unexpected guest exchanged pleasantries with Ružica, Milana, and Helene, I turned to Mr. Einstein. His face was very near mine, so close I could smell coffee and chocolate and tobacco on his breath.

"You made quite an entrance," I said with a half laugh as I slid the tiniest bit away from him.

"A day so fine deserves a grand gesture," he pronounced, sweeping his hand to the vivid blue skies visible from the window.

"Ah, so that was the reason for the sprint through the station and the calls to the stationmaster?" I asked with a sly grin. I guessed at the reason for his lateness—he had overslept, as the gentlemen often teased him about at Café Metropole—and it had nothing to do with the day's grandness. It wasn't exactly a ladylike comment, but then, I didn't want him to think of me as simply a lady. I wanted him to think of me as a scholar and an equal, and the comment was the sort one of his café friends might make.

He laughed and then lowered his voice to a whisper, "How I love to see that smile."

With a show of politeness, Mr. Besso interrupted us with a question, and soon, we were all discussing our excursion. Neither Mr. Einstein nor Mr. Besso had ever ventured into the Sihlwald before, and each of us ladies had a favorite aspect to share. In this companionable fashion, the ride passed quickly.

The first hours of the hike passed similarly, the thick canopy of the forest keeping us delightfully cool as we climbed. Enormous deciduous trees (of which only Helene knew the proper name) towered over us, and vast fallen trunks sometimes blocked our passage. Verdant foliage and mountain flowers abounded, and from their exclamations over the zealous forest growth, Mr. Einstein and Mr. Besso were suitably impressed with the sights. The girls were pleased by their reaction and grew even more animated in pointing out the silvery beech trees and the occasional purple bloom of alpine rock jasmine. We wanted everyone to love the Sihlwald as much as we did.

I kept pace with the girls as well as with Mr. Einstein and

Mr. Besso as we trudged up ever-steeper hills. No one paid my limp any heed, and I didn't need to either. The epithets of my younger days in Serbia felt like an ancient bad dream, one that the bright Sihlwald light washed away.

It seemed we all felt freer. I heard Ružica tell Mr. Besso one of her silly jokes, the sort she usually reserved for our games of whist and that made us groan and then begrudgingly giggle. Helene actually laughed at one of Mr. Einstein's quips. And when Milana pestered me for one of my imitations of Mrs. Engelbrecht, I complied. By the time we reached the Albishorn, we were all in good humor.

But then the majesty of the view took hold. The vaulting peaks of surrounding mountains capped by clouds and azure skies competed with the wide, navy swath of the lake and river. We were small against the vastness of nature. Even Mr. Einstein, ever garrulous, grew quiet.

Breaking the silence, Mr. Besso pulled a bottle of wine from his pack. "By way of thanks for your hospitality today, ladies."

Mr. Einstein good-naturedly chuffed him on the shoulder. "Good show, Michele."

We sat down to enjoy Mr. Besso's generosity. One after the other, we took swigs from the bottle; glasses had been impossible to bring in his pack, he explained with an apology. No one minded.

"I hate to say it, but if we're going to make the last train back to Zürich, we should head back now," Helene said.

"It's hard to leave, isn't it?" Milana asked, linking her arm with Helene's. I understood that she was speaking about much more than the Albishorn. This moment in time, shimmering and blissful, was hard to relinquish. Would another so perfect come again?

As I began to rise with the rest of the group, I felt a hand on my arm. Looking over, I saw it was Mr. Einstein. "Please stay a minute," he whispered.

I paused. What exactly did Mr. Einstein want? He certainly wouldn't seek out a quiet moment to discuss our physics exam. Deep within, in the secrecy of my thoughts, I sensed that—with all his hints and banter and encouragement—he had been building to this moment, but I still couldn't believe that he harbored romantic thoughts about me. I knew I should decline, insist that we follow the group. Hadn't I been steeling myself against this precise event? But I had to know what he was going to say.

Mr. Einstein waited. Only once I nodded did he announce to the others, "I would like a moment more. Why don't you go on, and we will catch up?"

The others headed toward the dirt path down the mountain, but Helene hesitated. Her eyebrows knitted into a familiar expression of wariness. "Are you certain, Mitza?"

I nodded. I didn't trust myself to speak.

"All right then. But don't take more than a minute, Mr. Einstein. We have a train to catch."

"Of course, Miss Kaufler."

Staring at me pointedly, she said, "You will keep him on course, won't you, Mitza?"

I nodded again.

Once the others passed out of sight, Mr. Einstein pulled me down gently to sit next to him on a fallen tree trunk. The vista spread out at our feet, and while I knew I should be enjoying the view, glazed with the soft pink of the setting sun, I was uncomfortably nervous instead.

"It is breathtaking, isn't it?" he asked.

"It is." My voice sounded shaky. I hoped he didn't notice.

He turned to face me. "Miss Marić, for some time now, I've been having feelings for you. The sort of feelings one doesn't have toward a classmate—"

I heard him speaking as if in a dream. While I had suspected this—even longed for it, if I was honest with myself, despite everything I professed to the girls—now that he was actually uttering the words, I was overwhelmed.

Pushing off the log, I tried to stand. "Mr. Einstein, I think we should return to the path—"

He touched my arm and gently pulled me back down onto the log.

He took my hands in his. Leaning toward me, he placed his lips upon mine. They were unexpectedly soft and full. Before I had the space or time to think, he kissed me. For a minute, I surrendered to the softness of his lips on mine and allowed myself to kiss him back. Heat rose to my cheeks as I felt the touch of his fingers on my back.

Izgoobio sam sye. These were the only words I could think of to describe how I felt at that moment. Roughly translated from the Serbian, they meant lost. Lost as in directions, lost from myself, lost to him.

Parting briefly, he looked into my eyes. I found it hard to catch my breath. "You astonish me once again, Miss Marić."

As he touched my cheek, I hungered for another kiss. The

intensity of my longing startled me. I calmed myself, took a deep breath, and said, "Mr. Einstein, I can't pretend your feelings are unreciprocated. However, I can't allow them to derail me from my course. Sacrifices have been made, and I've worked hard to proceed down this path. Romance and professions don't mix. For women, anyway."

His bushy eyebrows raised, and his mouth—those soft lips—formed a surprised circle. Obviously, he had expected compliance, not this resistance.

"No, Miss Marić. Surely bohemians such as ourselves— separate and apart from others with our vision and all our cultural and personal differences—can have both." His words pulled at me. How I wished his bohemian vision was indeed possible.

Forcing myself to be strong, I said, "Please do not take offense, Mr. Einstein, but I can't proceed with this any further. I may share your bohemian beliefs and your sense that we're different, but I have to push my own feelings aside for the sake of my professional goals."

Brushing off the bark and crushed leaves from my skirts, I started toward the path. "Are you coming?"

He stood and walked toward me. Clasping my hands in his, he said, "Never before have I been so certain of someone or something as I am of you. I will wait, Miss Marić. Until you are ready."

CHAPTER 8

August 29, 1897, and October 21, 1897
Kać, Serbia, and Heidelberg, Germany

T HE PAPER, CURLED AND WORN, FLUTTERED DOWN TO THE
floor. I watched as it spiraled languidly in the tepid breeze
that had drifted in through the bell tower's slat windows. The
book by Professor Philipp Lenard had been open to the same
page for over an hour, and I had not read a single word.

I reached down to pick the paper up from the scuffed
wooden floor. I sat in the vaulted bell tower of the Spire, our
summer house in Kać, where we decamped for the warm
months. This place, nicknamed for the two towers that adorned
each end of the Tyrolian-style villa and the central tower at its
center, had been my family's summer respite since I was a child.
No matter where we moved for Papa's governmental jobs or
my schooling—in turn, the eastern Austro-Hungarian towns
of Ruma, Novi Sad, Sremska Mitrovica, and then Zagreb—the
Spire was the one location I could always call home.

I'd spent my childhood summers in the bell tower of the
Spire, watching from its windows the shifting rural landscape of
sunflower and corn fields and reading piles of books. It was my

hideout, my dreamscape, the place where I read fairy tales as a child and began fantasizing about a life as a scientist. Currently, it was the place where I hid from everyone.

I stared at the paper in my hand. Scribbled across the surface was Mr. Einstein's address in his sprawling handwriting, as bold as his personality. He had hastily pressed it into my hand as we exchanged farewells the evening of the Sihlwald trip with an earnest request that I write him over the holiday. I used this flimsy slip as a bookmark so I would have an excuse to carry it with me everywhere. Although I refused to part with the address, I promised myself that I would not use it to write him. I adhered to this vow, even when full-blown conversations with him about physics and math appeared in my head. I knew that, if I wrote him, I would be continuing the nascent relationship that started in the Sihlwald, and this would make near-impossible the sort of career for which I'd worked so long, with Papa's unwavering support. I knew of no professional woman who was also married, so why should I begin with Mr. Einstein something that I could never finish? For consolation, I clung to the picture that Helene and I had painted of a single career life, abundant in culture and friendships.

Gazing out the window, I studied the fertile, sunflower-dotted plains of Kać. This part of the Vojvodina region, which stretched north from the Danube, had historically been the site of violent struggle between the Austro-Hungarian Empire to the west and the Ottoman Empire to the east and now faced tensions within its artificially created Austro-Hungarian borders from strife between the ethnically Germanic rulers and native Slav population. I had hoped that the familiar landscape, comfortable smells and phrases, and the warmth of my family would help me forget that moment in the Sihlwald with Mr. Einstein. Instead, I felt as torn as the countryside I inhabited, divided by my emotions and my promises.

The clomp of heavy steps reverberated through the thin bell tower walls. No one but barrel-chested, solid Papa had such a leaden footfall.

I pretended not to hear him. Not because I didn't want to see Papa, but because I wanted him to think I still had the capacity to become engrossed in a book, something I'd been unable to do in four weeks. Lying down on the threadbare chaise that Mama had relegated to this little-seen section of the Spire and curling around the book, I feigned total engagement.

His footsteps grew louder and closer, but I still didn't look up. I'd been famous for my ability to block out any disturbances in years past, but ignoring Papa's tickling fingers was a different matter. Within seconds, Papa tickled me in all my vulnerable spots, and I screeched with laughter.

"Papa," I screamed in mock-horror, pushing his hands away. "I'm almost twenty-one! Too old for tickles! Anyway, I'm reading."

He picked up my book, carefully marking my page. "Hmm, Lenard. It seems to me that you were reading the very same page of this very same book when I saw you last night."

My cheeks flushed. He sat down next to me.

"Mitza, you are not yourself. You are quiet, even with me. You don't spend any time downstairs with Mama or Zorka and little Miloš. I know that your brother and sister are younger than you, but you used to take them out for picnics at least."

Papa's words made me feel guilty. Several times every summer, I would pack up a picnic lunch for me, Zorka, and Miloš, and we would traipse into the fields. There, amid the sunflowers and under the warm summer skies, I would read my favorite childhood tales to them, even "The Little Singing Frog." I hadn't arranged even one of these outings this summer. I considered telling Papa that I'd stopped because, at fourteen and twelve, Zorka and Miloš were getting too old for such escapades, but I thought better of it. Papa would sniff out the lie in an instant.

He glanced down at my book again and then studied my eyes. "You're not even really reading or studying. Is everything all right?"

"Yes, Papa," I said, trying to stop my eyes from welling with tears.

"I don't know, Mitza. You didn't even seem excited about your grades when they arrived last week. You scored an average of four point five on your courses. Out of six, by God. That's cause for celebration, but you hardly raised a glass with us."

The secret about Mr. Einstein had been burning inside me since I returned home. On many occasions, I had wanted to confess it to Papa. He had been my confidant for as long as I could remember. But something held me back. My fear of disappointing him, perhaps, after the great lengths to which he'd gone to secure my education. My worries about eradicating his image of me as the brilliant, solitary scientist, maybe. How could I tell him about Mr. Einstein?

"I'm fine, Papa." Even as the words left my mouth, I knew they sounded false.

He pulled me to sitting, held onto my shoulders, and gently turned me to face him. He knew I could not lie to him or even omit a single aspect of the truth when looking at him straight in the eyes. "What is going on, Mitza?"

The tears I'd dammed up for four weeks broke through the barrier. Crying so hard that my chest heaved, Papa simply waited until I told him everything.

When my breathing finally slowed and the tears stopped, Papa still didn't speak. I glanced up, terrified that he was angry with me. That I'd failed this test, one far more important than my exams.

Tears were streaming down his face. "My poor Mitza. Why must your road be so hard?"

How could my invincible Papa be crying? How could this conundrum perplex him to tears? He was the one we turned to—indeed, governmental officials of all stations turned to—when we faced an insurmountable problem. Reaching into my pocket for the lace handkerchief that I always kept there, I wiped his eyes and cheeks. "You're not mad, Papa?" I was thankful, at least, that he wasn't angry at me.

"Of course not, my sweet girl. I wish more than anything in the world that your path was an easy one, that you could have everything your heart desires. But brilliance brings burdens, doesn't it?"

"I suppose," I said, disappointed that this might be Papa's advice. For my entire life, I'd heard his admonitions that I had a responsibility to nurture my intellect. Even though I knew it was unreasonable—impossible even—I'd hoped he could fix this problem of Mr. Einstein like he had so many others.

"Do you want to continue on your course of studies? Would you still like to be a professor of physics?"

But what of Mr. Einstein? I thought to myself. Instead, I willed myself to say what was expected. "Yes, Papa. That's what I've always wanted. What we've always discussed."

"Do you think it's prudent to return to the Polytechnic next term where Mr. Einstein exerts so powerful a presence? Perhaps a term away at another university might give you perspective. You could return the following term, once you've achieved a certain objectivity about Mr. Einstein."

A term away. My heart clenched at the thought of a longer separation from Mr. Einstein than three months, but the more I considered Papa's proposal, the more relief coursed through me. I wouldn't have to face Mr. Einstein, with his eager expression and hangdog eyes so capable of swaying me, for the next few months. The time away might work the necessary magic.

My gaze settled on the Lenard book I'd been carrying around with me for days. "Papa, I think I know just the place."

In early October, just before my arrival at Heidelberg University, a near impenetrable fog descended on the Neckar River valley in southeast Germany that the university called home. The fog showed no sign of lifting in the days after I settled into the Hotel Ritter, where I'd stay for the term. While the physics classes I was permitted to audit were indeed world-class, led by such renowned professors as Lenard himself, I could see nothing of the rumored loveliness of the buildings and setting of the ancient Heidelberg University through its heavy veil. In fact, laden with dense mist, the forest and river surrounding the university only served to remind me, by despairing comparison, of the gleaming beauty of the Sihlwald. Indeed, sometimes I felt as though the fog had affixed to my mood, so gloomy did I feel.

Loneliness outweighed any incandescence of thought brought about by Lenard's kinetic theory of gases and his experiments on the speed at which oxygen molecules travel. I missed the companionship, laughter, and compassion of Ružica, Milana, and Helene most of all, even though I hid my feelings in cheery letters to them, simulating excitement about my lectures. And in the dark hours alone in my hotel room, if I allowed myself to be honest, I missed Mr. Einstein too. But my malaise was so deep that I wondered whether missing my friends and Mr. Einstein were the sole sources of my despair.

One afternoon in late October, I returned from classes to find a letter from Helene waiting for me at the front desk of the hotel. Clutching it in my hands, I took the stairs by two, no mean feat with my leg, so that I could read Helene's letter all the more quickly. Slicing through the envelope with my razor-sharp letter opener, I devoured Helene's words. There, amid chatter about her studies and pension gossip, I read, "I thought Heidelberg did not allow women to matriculate. A family friend from Vienna tried to study psychology there, and she had to obtain permission from the professor on a course by course basis just to attend lectures! No credit for coursework allowed. Won't this decision put you behind a term?"

I slowly laid her letter down on my spindly hotel desk, better suited for the morning correspondence-writing of a lady than the heavy coursework of a student. In her usual shrewd way, Helene laid her finger on the source of my unease. My ill mood did not emanate solely from the fog or even my loneliness but on the burden that this term away might place upon my career path. What if this break from my schoolwork at the Polytechnic set me back in my studies? What if I barricaded myself away from Mr. Einstein's affections so that I could secure my career only to damage my career in the process? What if I returned, hampered by this Heidelberg term, and succumbed to Mr. Einstein anyway?

Helene's letter set me ablaze with determination to make this term in Heidelberg fulfill its purpose. I would simultaneously do my Heidelberg and Polytechnic courses so as not to fall behind. And I would make my intentions perfectly clear to Mr. Einstein.

I decided that I'd finally respond to the letter Mr. Einstein sent me three weeks into my stay at Heidelberg. He had ascertained my whereabouts from the girls, since I never wrote him over the summer. In its scrawled pages, it contained details of the Weber lectures I missed, descriptions of talks by Professors Hurwitz, Herzog, and Fiedler, and some remarks about the requisite number theory course. Even though I scoured every line, it bore no comment or reference, obvious or covert, of our moment in the Sihlwald. Nothing. Yet within each line, I sensed the words unsaid.

My fingers had itched with the desire to write back in the weeks since he wrote it, but now I was glad that I'd resisted.

I was ready to make myself perfectly clear. I wrote, "You instructed me not to write you unless I had absolutely nothing to do, and my days in Heidelberg have been hectic until this very moment."

After chattering on about the magnificent lectures I'd heard, echoing much the same verbiage I had sent to Helene, I ended the missive with what I hoped was a clear message. I referenced a bit of gossip he'd shared in his letter—that a mathematics classmate had left the Polytechnic program to become a forester because he'd been spurned by a Zürich sweetheart—and said, "How peculiar! In these bohemian days, where there are so many paths available other than that of the bourgeois, the notion of love itself seems so pointless."

I prayed my letter was unambiguous. Should I return, romance between us was not to be part of the equation.

No reply arrived from Mr. Einstein. Not in November. Or December. Or January. His silence told me that he had received my message. It was safe to return to Zürich.

PART II

The alteration of motion is ever proportional to the motive force impressed; and is made in the direction of the right line in which that force is impressed.

Sir Isaac Newton

CHAPTER 9

April 12, 1898
Zürich, Switzerland

DUSTED WITH AN EARLY SPRING SNOW AND TOPPED WITH
the icy spires of its clock towers, resembling the ivory
marzipan peaks of the desserts I'd seen at the Conditorei
Schober, Zürich welcomed me back. The girls and I quickly
settled into our routines. Meals, whist, tea, music. But as the
days marched toward the purpose of my return—matriculation
back into the Polytechnic—I felt nothing but dread.

Mr. Einstein's failure to respond to my letter had initially filled me with relief; it gave me license to reignite my
Polytechnic studies without fear of his romantic interest. As our
reunion drew nearer, however, the reality of his silence struck
me. I would be sitting beside Mr. Einstein in classrooms for
the next two and a half years, the duration of our program. But
what would I face from him? Disdain because of my rejection?
Rumor-mongering among our classmates over our sole kiss?
Would our previous friendship be my undoing? My reputation
as a serious student was everything. Women scientists didn't get
second chances.

As the days mounted, so did the apprehension that my return to Zürich was anything but wise.

On the first day of term, I delayed entering the classroom until the last possible second. When I heard the scrape of chairs pulling under desks, I knew I could wait no longer. Finally pushing open the door, I saw that my same seat was empty. The other chairs and desks were occupied by the familiar five students who had filled Section Six my first year; no other student had been added during the winter term that I'd missed, and no one else had dropped out. Had my seat been waiting for me all this time? It looked as forlorn as I felt. As I limped over to it, careful to fix my gaze on the desk and nothing else, I felt Mr. Einstein's dark brown eyes on me.

After I took my seat, I kept my eyes solely on Professor Weber. Initially, he played at my invisibility, and then suddenly, he said, "I see that Miss Marić has decided to rejoin us from the hinterlands of Heidelberg. While she undoubtedly witnessed some intriguing experiments during her sabbatical, I wonder if she can keep pace with the critical concepts that you all have been mastering in the first term of this year, the year of my cornerstone physics class, the foundation of your physics degrees." He then launched into his lecture.

My cheeks hot with shame at Weber's troubling comments, I scribbled down notes as quickly as he could speak. Weber's message was plain. My term in Heidelberg was ill-perceived, by Weber and God knows who else, and Weber would not be lenient with me. I reminded myself that I was making the right choice to return to Section Six, to reclaim my path to a physics professorship in spite of Mr. Einstein. I could not let Weber or anyone else at the Polytechnic see me as soft. I had worked hard—harder than any of my classmates, and certainly harder than Mr. Einstein—to reach this point, to examine the questions that philosophers have asked since time immemorial, the questions that the great scientific minds of our day were poised to answer: the nature of reality, space, time, and its contents. I wanted to scrutinize Newton's principles—the laws of action and reaction, force and acceleration and gravitation—and study them in light of the latest investigations into atoms and mechanics to see if any single theory existed that could explain the seemingly endless variety of natural phenomena and chaos. I hungered to examine the newer ideas about heat, thermo-dynamics, gases, and electricity, as well as their mathematical underpinnings; numbers were the architecture of an enormous physical system integral to everything. This was God's secret language, I was certain. This was my religion, I was on a crusade, and crusaders couldn't afford frailty. Feeling Mr. Einstein's eyes on me, I reminded myself that crusaders couldn't afford romance either.

"Gentlemen, that will suffice for today. Tonight, I want you to revisit Helmholtz. I will weave his theories into those we explored today." Weber pronounced this with an acid glare as he exited the classroom, robes trailing. Other than his obvious disgust with me, who knew what else we had done to warrant his wrath? There were a myriad of ways that we, once again, proved ourselves unworthy of him, he who had studied under the great physics masters Gustav Kirchhoff and Hermann von Helmholtz.

Chatter only started once Weber's departure was certain.

Messrs. Ehrat and Kollros offered me a pleasant welcome back, and Mr. Grossman bowed toward me. I returned their kind words and gestures with a quick curtsy, but then I sensed Mr. Einstein's approach. I scrambled to pack my bag and wrap my coat around me. I couldn't bear to have this awkward moment in front of my classmates. My reputation and my tenuous relationship with them wouldn't survive it.

Clomp, drag. The sound of my uneven footfalls echoed throughout the otherwise empty corridor outside Weber's classroom. I thought I'd escaped, but then I heard the race of footsteps behind me. I knew it was him.

"I see you are angry with me," he said.

I didn't answer. I didn't even stop walking. My emotions were fluctuating so wildly, I was afraid to speak.

"Your anger is understandable. I never wrote you back. That failure is rude and inexcusable," he offered.

I slowed my pace but still didn't respond.

"I'm not certain what else to do but to apologize and ask for your forgiveness." He paused.

I stopped and considered my response. He didn't seem angry at my rejection. Was I angry at him? Was he really offering a simple apology and requesting nothing more? Seeing him again, I felt myself slipping into old feelings of tenderness, warmth, even surrender. Was a simple apology—and nothing more—what I wanted? I wasn't sure, but I could not go back; I had sacrificed an entire term to secure an independent path and had made promises to Papa. I must pretend what I did not feel.

"Of course I forgive you for not writing me back." I sounded flat and formal. *Come on*, I told myself. *Be the old teasing Mitza*

with him. You want the relationship to return to normal, don't you?
Act as if it already had. With a taunting voice, I said, "After all,
you've forgiven me for leaving, haven't you?"

His face broke open in a wide grin, his eyes crinkling at the
corners. "I'm so relieved, Miss Marić. You departed so quickly,
and I was afraid—" He stopped himself. I knew he was about
to refer to our kiss. Thinking better of it, he said, "I'm sure you
won't regret your decision to return, even if we don't have such
esteemed professors on our faculty as you did at Heidelberg. No
Lenards here."

He asked if he could escort me to the library, and I agreed.
As we walked across the plaza, he regaled me with stories of
heated debates at the Café Metropole, hikes he had tackled in
the mountain ranges outside Zürich, and sails he and his friends
had launched on Lake Zürich. The stories were so smooth and
rehearsed, they seemed crafted just for retelling to me.

"You must sail with me and Mr. Besso when the weather
breaks. Perhaps your lady friends from the Engelbrecht Pension
might like to join? They are an adventurous group," he said as
we entered the library.

"You've painted such a dangerous picture, I'm not at all certain that we'd be safe," I jested.

A librarian passed by and glared at us, and two students
looked annoyed at our loud chatter, so we quickly quieted and
settled into adjoining carrels. Reaching into his messy bag, he
pulled out a stack of notebooks. Typically, he only carried one
notebook to class. He must have planned on delivering this pile
to me today.

Handing them to me, he whispered, "Everything you need

to catch up on your studies can be found in these notebooks. They contain notes from Hurwitz's lectures on differential equations and calculus. I think I captured Herzog's talks about the strength of materials. I tried to get every scrap of Weber's lectures on the qualities of heat. Oh, and I didn't forget Fiedler's lectures on projective geometry and number theory."

I felt sick as I flipped through the notebooks. I had tried to keep up while in Heidelberg, but had I really missed this much? How could I possibly catch up? Not only had I missed half of Weber's linchpin physics class, but I'd missed these other foundational classes. I needed to become proficient in this material before I could begin to comprehend my current and future courses. For the first time, I understood how stupid I'd been to go to Heidelberg. How, in trying to be strong and not let a man swerve me from my path, I'd actually let a man dictate my course.

I gave Mr. Einstein a wan smile, but my distress must have been evident. He stopped rattling off the theories I'd need to learn and the calculations I'd need to master and studied my expression, glimpsing outside himself for a rare moment. He placed his hand on my upper arm in a cautious gesture of reassurance. "Miss Marić, you will be fine. I will help you."

Taking a deep breath, I said, "Thank you, Mr. Einstein. You've been extremely generous and kind in assembling these notebooks for me. Especially given the way I left and our—"

He gently shook his head. With a solemn tone I'd never heard from him before, he said, "We need not speak of it. You know how I feel, and you have made your position clear. I will happily abide by your wishes to secure your ongoing friendship. I would not jeopardize that for anything."

"Thank you," I whispered, more ambivalent than ever.

His hand moved up and down my arm in a gentle caress. "Please know that I will be waiting. Should you ever change your mind."

As I tried to process his words, he dropped his hand, and his mischievous smile returned. "Now, let's get back to work, you little escapee."

CHAPTER 10

June 8, 1898
Zürich, Switzerland

How can he ignore the latest theorists? It is unconscionable for a man of science," Mr. Einstein exclaimed to me and Messrs. Grossman, Ehrat, and Kollros over coffee at the Café Metropole. As I listened to him, I thought how, in many ways, my days were passing precisely as they had before I left for Heidelberg. Or better. Just as Mr. Einstein had promised.

I glanced around the table at my Section Six classmates as Mr. Einstein continued his rant. We'd formed the habit of going to our favorite coffeehouse every Friday after last class, and my classmates had revealed themselves to be far more approachable and welcoming than I assumed. And more human as well. I learned that Mr. Ehrat was a worrier who kept his place at university only through sheer hard work. Mr. Kollros, who hailed from a French village, was cut from much the same cloth as Mr. Ehrat, only with a strong French accent. Only Mr. Grossman, from an old, aristocratic Swiss family, was naturally gifted, especially in the area of mathematics.

In between sips of coffee or drags on their pipes and cigars, everyone expressed their frustration with Professor Weber's stubborn adherence to only classical physicists' theories and refusal to pursue the latest ideas. Mr. Einstein's face alone displayed actual anger. Once Mr. Einstein had become certain that Weber wasn't going to cover any more recent material beyond theories created by his beloved teacher Helmholtz, including contemporary topics like statistical mechanics or electromagnetic waves, he had grown furious.

As Mr. Einstein postulated on Weber's failings, I glanced at the clock. We had to leave that minute or risk missing our concert date with the girls, and I would not break my commitments to them, as Mr. Einstein well knew. I shot Mr. Einstein a look and then directed his attention to the time. He sprang up.

The puddles splashed as we attempted to hurry down the streets. Light rainfall, jostling umbrellas, and laughter slowed our journey to the pension. Still, we managed to arrive only two minutes late, but when we glanced around the parlor, breathing hard from our exertions, it was empty.

"Helene? Milana? Where are you?" I called out. Were they in their rooms awaiting us? I couldn't believe that our slight delay would have caused them to stomp off. "Ružica?"

"What is all this noise about, Miss Marić?" Mrs. Engelbrecht asked, emerging from the kitchen with a crisp green-and-white tea towel in her hands. She loathed an excess of boisterousness at the pension.

I curtsied, and Mr. Einstein bowed. "I'm sorry, Mrs. Engelbrecht. I was just looking for Misses Kaufler, Dražić, and

Bota. We had an appointment to play some music, and Mr. Einstein was going to join us. Are they in their rooms?"

She sniffed, a signal of her disapproval. "No, Miss Marić. Misses Dražić and Bota stepped out for a brief walk, and Miss Kaufler is in the back parlor with"—another sniff—"a caller."

A caller? I almost laughed at the ridiculousness of Mrs. Engelbrecht's choice of words. Maybe Helene had a male visitor, perhaps a classmate or a male relative, but she certainly didn't have a caller. That was part of our pact.

I heard a rustle of noise from the gaming room, and Helene called out, "Is that you, Mitza?"

"It's me," I answered as quietly as possible under Mrs. Engelbrecht's warning glare.

Helene stepped out into the entryway, a wide grin on her face. "I'm so glad you're back. There's someone I want you to meet."

As she pulled me toward the gaming room, she noticed Mr. Einstein behind me and paused. "Ah, Mr. Einstein, you are here as well."

"I believe my violin was needed for the Beethoven?" he offered.

"Oh the concerto!" She clapped her hand to her mouth. "I had completely forgotten. My apologies to you both. I'll have to apologize to Milana and Ružica as well. Are they with you?"

"They went out for a walk," I said.

"Oh no. At this hour? They must be furious with me."

"Please don't worry, Helene. I've missed our musical gatherings many times. And I've been forgiven," I said, reminding her of her own mercy. To lessen her worry, I changed the subject. "You mentioned that you had someone to introduce to us?"

"Ah, yes." The smile returned. Maybe it was one of her cousins, of whom she often spoke so fondly.

Pulling me into the gaming room, Helene gestured to a dark-haired gentlemen overwhelming one of the spindly chairs that encircled the gaming table with his girth. The portly man rose to greet us.

He bowed to Mr. Einstein, who had followed me into the room, and then to me and said in heavily accented German, "Milivoje Savić, pleased to meet you."

After Mr. Einstein and I introduced ourselves, Helene chimed in, her voice a melody of delight. "Mr. Savić and I were just talking about you, Mitza. I told him that my closest friend was from Serbia."

I softened at being called Helene's closest friend, but her compliment did nothing to lessen my concern about Mr. Savić. Who was he, and why was Helene fussing over him? I had never heard a word about him before, and she didn't describe him as a relative or classmate. Was he truly a caller, as Mrs. Engelbrecht said? From the way Helene was acting, giggling like a schoolgirl and bustling around him, I could almost believe it.

"Mr. Savić is a chemical engineer, here in Zürich on behalf of a textile factory in Užice to observe practices at other factories. He is Serbian too," she said, as if his background and connection to Serbia explained everything.

I didn't know what to say. I was confounded by this gentleman and the reaction he elicited from my stalwart Helene. Even Mr. Einstein was uncharacteristically quiet as he absorbed the situation.

In the silence, Helene fumbled to fill the void. "I-I thought you two might have a lot in common, Mitza."

I found my tongue and gave him the customary Serbian welcome. "*Dobrodošao*. It's nice to meet a fellow Serbian here in Zürich, Mr. Savić."

"*Hvala*."

Helene and Mr. Savić turned back toward each other and referenced a previous, unfinished conversation. I waited to be included, but my presence seemed unnecessary, even unwanted.

"We will take our leave," I said to interrupt their quiet chatter. "Mr. Einstein and I have some studying to attend to."

Helene glanced at us as if she just remembered that we were still there. "Yes, your work! Miss Marić is here in Zürich studying physics, Mr. Savić. As is Mr. Einstein."

Mr. Savić raised a curious eyebrow. "Physics? That's most impressive, Miss Marić."

My antipathy toward him was allayed a bit by his response; most men recoiled at the thought of a woman physicist. I wanted Mr. Savić to know that Helene was equally formidable.

"Not as impressive as Miss Kaufler's knowledge of history, Mr. Savić, I assure you."

Mr. Savić looked into Helene's eyes. "I'm hoping to learn precisely how extensive Miss Kaufler's knowledge of history is."

Helene beamed at Mr. Savić, and in the quiet that filled the room to bursting, Mr. Einstein and I took our leave. As we stepped into the entryway, he whispered to me, "That Savić fellow has a thick Serbian accent. I could barely understand his German. Yours is so flawless. I always meant to ask how you manage it."

"Papa insisted that we speak German at home. It's the Austro-Hungarian Empire's language of success, after all. We only spoke Serbian to Mama and the servants," I whispered back, but my voice was flat. What had I just witnessed?

Just as Mr. Einstein and I crossed the threshold of the parlor, Helene reappeared and grabbed my arm. I gestured for Mr. Einstein to enter the parlor without me.

"I wanted to make sure you weren't angry with me." Her eyes were pleading.

"For forgetting about our little recital? That's silly. I told you already, I'm not mad at all."

She exhaled. "Good. I couldn't stand it if you were annoyed with me." I sensed she was worried about far more than the recital.

"Shouldn't you return to—" Did I dare say "your caller"? I wanted to know exactly who this man was, but my boldness dissolved when I saw the concerned look in her eyes. "Mr. Savić?"

"Mr. Savić?" Wonder shone in her eyes. "I guess I should return, shouldn't I?"

"How did you become acquainted with him?"

"Mr. Savić stopped by the pension yesterday. You see, his family is closely acquainted with my aunt, and she suggested that he pay a call. Our conversation was so easy and full of commonalities, well, when he asked if he could visit again today, I agreed." A smile never left her lips.

"You didn't mention him yesterday."

"I suppose I didn't know until today that he was worth mentioning." She paused, and the smile slipped away. She realized what she had unwittingly admitted.

"Is he a caller, Helene?" I needed to know. What would happen to our pact if she were to fall in love with Mr. Savić?

"I don't know, Mitza. I-I don't want to break our pact, but—" She stammered and then stopped.

"But what?"

"Will you allow me the latitude to find out what Mr. Savić means to me?" Her tone and her eyes were imploring.

My stomach lurched. I'd been hoping for a scoffing laugh. It seemed that I could only hope her time with Mr. Savić was fleeting. Or that he would leave town soon.

I wanted to scream no. I wanted to shake her and remind her of our shared vision of a full professional life without the need for a husband. But what could I say other than yes? "Of course, Helene."

"Thank you for understanding. I guess I should return."

Helene's skirts trailed behind her as she reentered the gaming room. I watched until the last scallop of her hem disappeared, as if we'd just said farewell. Because, in a way, we had.

I walked back into the parlor. The room appeared exactly the same as always. There were the rose damask chairs my father and I sat upon when we first arrived at the pension; there was the piano where Milana worked so diligently on her melodies; there were the embroidered armchairs where Helene and I always sat, our instruments in hand. I could almost hear the sweet strains of Mozart, Bach, Beethoven, and Vivaldi wafting in the air. Yet, on some level, the parlor was altogether changed, as if an enormous eraser had wiped clean the cherished memories and the plans this room contained.

The future had been cracked wide open.

CHAPTER 11

December 8, 1899
Zürich, Switzerland

M R. EINSTEIN RAN HIS BOW ACROSS THE VIOLIN STRINGS. The movement was slow, almost languorous, but the music was big and filled the room. Closing my eyes, I could very nearly envision rich, imperceptible waves reverberating the sound around the parlor, almost like the invisible X-rays recently discovered. And I could also imagine the notes washing over me like a caress.

My cheeks flushed red. Was it the music I imagined caressing me or Mr. Einstein's hands?

Turning away from Mr. Einstein and his violin, I settled more comfortably onto the piano bench and faced the keys. Even though I could no longer see him cradle his violin, his music moved me. Not because his playing was virtuosic but because it overflowed with emotion.

I shook my head to clear it. My cue to begin playing would happen in a few bars, and I didn't want to miss it because I was daydreaming about Mr. Einstein. For months, indeed for over a year, I had spent too many minutes of every day fighting against such impulses to surrender over a few lines of luxurious music.

Suppressed over the past year, my feelings for Mr. Einstein hadn't disappeared. If anything, they had grown. Sometimes, I wondered whether maintaining my friendship with Mr. Einstein was folly, whether it ignited emotions I should be dampening. But I had chosen my physics path, and he sat firmly upon it, I reminded myself for the hundredth time that day alone. I couldn't very well ignore him; after all, he was my lab partner.

My fingers hovered over the piano keys, ready for my moment, when shrill voices echoed throughout the house. The noise startled us both, and Mr. Einstein stopped playing.

"You silly. That's my umbrella!" a female voice shrieked playfully.

"Truly? It looks exactly like my own!" another answered back.

The voices belonged to Ružica and Milana.

I stood up from the piano. The girls had finally arrived, forty minutes past the time we usually played music before dinner. More and more frequently, Ružica and Milana claimed they couldn't make these previously sacrosanct appointments. Their excuses ranged from study sessions at school to late afternoon lectures to simply forgetting, but a clear pattern had emerged. If Helene couldn't make the musical gathering, a more frequent occurrence these days as her relationship with Mr. Savić deepened, or if Mr. Einstein was in attendance, then Ružica and Milana were unavailable.

Smoothing my skirt and taking a calming breath—I didn't

want to push the girls further away with my disappointment—I poked my head out of the parlor. "Hello, girls! Mr. Einstein and I were just beginning to play and hoping that you'd arrive soon. Care to play?"

Milana shot Ružica an inscrutable look. What did she mean by it? Once, I'd been able to read those glances as easily as I could read Papa's, but now they were as incomprehensible to me as hieroglyphics. Had Helene been the glue holding our formerly merry band together? If so, bit by bit, the adhesive joining Ružica, Milana, and me together was dissolving, leaving us as distant friends and dining companions. Even when I sat across from them at meals, I missed them.

Milana spoke for both of them. "That is such a kind offer, Mileva, but Ružica and I were just lamenting the amount of work we have. I think we'll retire to our rooms before the dinner bell rings."

"Yes, Mileva. Not all of us can function on as little sleep as you," Ružica said with a kindly wink. I was notorious for studying all night with my window open to keep me awake. Of the two, Ružica had remained the friendlier.

Giving me the politest of smiles, the sort normally reserved for maidenly aunts, not bosom friends, they trudged up the stairs to their rooms. I returned to the parlor, hurt and angry. Mr. Einstein and I had returned to the pension from our weekly Café Metropole coffee with our classmates instead of taking a stroll with them explicitly to meet the girls. And this was the treatment I received? What had I done to bear the brunt of such rejection, however kindly delivered?

I returned to the parlor from the entryway and plopped back

down at the piano. My fingers found the keyboard, and with Mr.
Einstein staring at me, I pounded out the music I was meant to
play before the girls' loud interruption. All my anger poured into
those notes, until slowly, the fury drained from me, and my fingers desultorily plonked out the last bars.

"The girls are too busy to play with us," Mr. Einstein said.
He had been listening. To the girls. To me.

"Yes," I said distractedly. "So they say."

Why had Ružica and Milana decided to exclude me from
all but the necessary interactions? I couldn't fathom what I
might have done to cause their behavior. After all, my relationship with Helene remained strong despite the time she spent
with Mr. Savić. Their affair had been a blow to me, but I could
not object when I saw the happiness lighting up Helene's face.

I stopped playing altogether. Perhaps the reason behind
Ružica and Milana's distance wasn't me. Perhaps it was Mr.
Einstein. With Helene gone so frequently, he had become
more of a presence. Did Ružica and Milana object to him? His
unkemptness, his familiarity, his jokes, his constant presence at
the pension, his strangeness? These were some of the irrever-
ent qualities I liked about him, the differences that drew us
together. Was I paying for his perceived sins?

"What's wrong?" he asked me.

"Nothing," I answered distractedly.

"Miss Marić, you and I have been friends for too long for lies."

He was wrong about that. In every interaction I had with
him, every day, I lied to him with my words and my body. I
fabricated the false persona of Mileva Marić, only classmate
and friend. And I lied to myself, reassuring myself that, if I just

pretended long enough not to care about him, it would become the truth.

I was sick of pretending.

I glanced over at him. Mr. Einstein sat on the settee by the fire, his usual spot, and was tuning his violin. I watched as he gently cradled the violin's neck and turned the tuning pegs, puffing his pipe all the while. As the pipe smoke rose and he twanged the strings, I realized that my feelings about him had grown much deeper since Heidelberg. Why was I clinging to falsehoods? For Papa? For my promises to Helene that she herself had broken? Aside from Papa, Helene had been the most instrumental person in my decision to walk away from Mr. Einstein's overtures, and I had lost her to Mr. Savić. Had I sacrificed Mr. Einstein—and the possibility of a love I never thought I'd have—for nothing in return? For a lonely life of work as my sole calling? Certainly, Ružica and Milana were not going to be my consolation prize for Helene or Mr. Einstein. I used to think of the solitary scientific life somewhat romantically, but not anymore.

This time would not be like the Sihlwald forest. I would not be caught unaware. I would not walk away. I would seize this chance with both my hands and fashion the life of *my* dreams.

Mr. Einstein stopped working on his violin and looked up at me. I walked over to him and sat on the chair next to his. I leaned toward him, bringing my face so close to his I could feel his breath on my cheeks and his mustache on my lips. He didn't move. My stomach fluttered. Was it too late?

"Are you certain, Miss Marić?" he whispered. I could feel his breath on my skin.

"I think so," I stammered. I was terrified.

He gripped my forearms with his hands. "Miss Marić, I am madly in love with you. I promise that my love will never impede your profession. In fact, my love will only propel you forward in your work. Together, we will become the ideal bohemian couple—equal in love and work."

"Truly?" I asked, my voice quivering. Could Mr. Einstein and I have the life I hadn't even dared to dream about? Perhaps even richer?

"Truly."

"Then I am certain," I said breathily.

He placed his lips on mine as gently as he had cradled his beloved violin. They were as soft and full as I remembered. I moved my lips against his, and we kissed.

Izgoobio sam sye. I was lost.

CHAPTER 12

February 12, 1900
Zürich, Switzerland

I PROMISE HE WILL BE IN CLASS TOMORROW, PROFESSOR Weber." I implored Weber to forgive Albert his absence, his third that week alone.

"It would be easier to overlook this, Miss Marić, if I believed he was ill. But if you will recall, he missed class last week due to an alleged bout of gout, and yet, I spotted him at a café on Rämistrasse when I walked home for the evening. He was well enough for cafés but not for classrooms." The nostrils of Weber's long nose flared, and I realized my begging had little chance of success.

"You have my word, Professor Weber. And you have no cause to doubt my word, do you?"

Weber exhaled, more the bray of an angry mule than a sigh. "Why do you persist on his behalf, Miss Marić? He is just your lab partner, not your ward. Mr. Einstein is clever, but he believes that no one can teach him anything. Professor Pernet is far more incensed at Mr. Einstein's behavior than I am."

Even if I wasn't successful in my pleas, at least I'd learned that our ruse was working; Weber believed that Albert and I were only classmates. We had tried to keep our relationship quiet from our fellow students and friends as well, limiting our public affections to sideward glances or the odd brush of hands under a table at Café Metropole. I wanted none of the change in treatment from my classmates and Albert's friends that so often happened when one morphed from colleague to loved one. As if one's intellect disappeared in the transition. I suspected that Mr. Grossman knew—I'd accidentally brushed up against his hand once instead of Albert's—but his attitude toward me remained unchanged.

By his question, I sensed an opening in Weber's unusually impenetrable exterior. I decided to take a chance at angering him and pushed a little further. "Please, Professor Weber."

"All right, Miss Marić. But this is purely on the strength of your solid reputation. You are the student with promise; your intellect and hard work will take you far. You even overcame the strange decision to spend a term at Heidelberg. I have hopes for your future."

Feeling relief at Weber's decision about Albert and some surprise at his rare compliment, especially given that, behind the scenes a year and a half later, I still struggled to overcome my Heidelberg decision, I started to thank him. But then I realized he wasn't finished.

"You warn Mr. Einstein that, if he fails to attend class tomorrow, he risks not only his own standing but yours as well."

"My little Dollie," Albert drawled as I walked into the Engelbrecht Pension parlor; he adored calling me Dollie, the diminutive of *Doxerl* or *little doll*. He looked comfortable, sunk into the settee, a book on his knee and his pipe in the corner of his mouth. Waiting for me.

I didn't answer him with his companion nickname of Johnnie, the diminutive of Jonzerl. In fact, I didn't feel like responding to him at all.

I was frustrated that I'd had to endanger my own reputation because Albert had begun to skip Weber's classes in order to study independently. Albert believed that together, he and I could solve major scientific riddles—but only if I went to class and took copious notes on Weber's traditional topics while Albert stayed behind and caught up on newer physicists like Boltzmann and Helmholtz. Albert's scheme involved our collaboration and sharing of old and new theories, and we were currently exploring the nature of light and electromagnetism. I'd been an enthusiastic participant in this experiment as a modern, bohemian couple, even though it meant I stayed up into the night undertaking this double duty when I already had the extra work stemming from my time away in Heidelberg. Until now.

Putting down our shared copy of the textbook by physicist Paul Drude, Albert reached for my hand. Pressing it to his cheek, he cooed, "So cold this little paw. I shall warm it for you."

I still didn't say anything. When he gently tried to pull me down onto the cushion next to him, I stayed standing.

"How did it go with Weber, Dollie?"

Usually, I loved the way my nickname sounded with his

accent. Today, the very word "Dollie" grated. I felt more like a puppet than a beloved doll.

"Not so well, Albert. Weber only agreed to admit you back into class tomorrow if I would stake my reputation on it. So I did."

He released my hand and stood up to face me. "I've asked too much of you, Dollie. I'm sorry."

"Really, Albert, one of us must receive a degree if your bohemian plans for us are to come true. How will we support ourselves otherwise? Neither one of us will be fit to teach physics if you fail because you've abandoned class and I fail because I've promised you would attend." I admonished him, but it was hard to stay firm when he offered apologies and implored me with his eyes. I was weak. And he knew it.

"Come here, Dollie."

I took one small, stingy step in his direction, refusing to look into his persuasive eyes again.

"Closer, please," he said.

I craned my neck to see if anyone was in the entryway. It would be the end of my standing at the pension if anyone spotted us in such close proximity. Physical contact was the worst violation of Mrs. Engelbrecht's house rules.

I took another step, and he drew me tightly to him. Whispering in my ear, he said, "You are so good to your Johnnie. I promise never to ask so much of you again."

Shivers traveled up and down my spine. I leaned toward him. Just as our lips brushed together for a kiss, the front door slammed, and we jumped apart. Ružica and Milana poked their heads into the parlor, checking to see if it was free. Once they saw that we occupied it, they very politely but coldly took their leave and headed into the gaming room. Only Helene brought us together these days, and she was in Serbia meeting Mr. Savić's family. They had just gotten engaged.

Albert knew how Ružica and Milana's treatment upset me. He grabbed my hand. "Don't you worry, Dollie. They are just jealous. Helene has Mr. Savić, and you have me. They have only each other."

I squeezed his hand back. "I'm sure that's all it is, Johnnie." I didn't dare tell him that I'd long suspected that he was the problem.

"More time for our studies, Dollie. Think on the bright side."

We sat down side by side on the settee, legs near but not touching, and exchanged notes. He clucked over Weber's lectures, and I marveled over Drude's descriptions of the various theories of light. Drude explained that embedded in the debate about the nature of light was a debate about the nature of the invisible void of the universe; this played to my privately held view that the secrets of God lurked in the corners of science, a belief at which Albert would certainly scoff but which I felt certain. Was light made up of tiny particles, or ether, as Newton suggested, or was light a kind of shifting in the plenum, an invisible fluid surrounding us, as René Descartes believed? Or, in an idea by James Clerk Maxwell that transfixed us, was light really a dance of electric and magnetic fields intertwined? And could this notion—that light rays were electromagnetic oscillations—be proven by mathematical equations? We turned this theory of electromagnetism round and round and, on my recommendation, decided to drill down into it with doubt and mathematical analysis. Our credo was to trust simplicity above all else and eschew archaic complicated ideas when necessary. Something of which I had to remind Albert, with his tendency toward tangents, constantly.

The dinner bell rang. I heard it but wanted one more moment with Drude. I flipped to the last page of the textbook, wanting to check on a reference, when a single piece of paper floated to the floor. As I reached down to pick it up, I noticed a distinct floral scent. Looking more closely, I saw not Albert's messy scrawl but unfamiliar handwriting.

Who wrote this sweet-scented letter that Albert carefully folded and kept in the back of Drude? My stomach lurching, I flipped it over. I saw a distinctly feminine script. I prayed that it was from his teenage sister Maja, the only one of his immediate family who still championed our relationship. Not his mother.

Last fall, Albert's parents, Pauline and Hermann, had visited Zürich as part of their roundabout trip to deliver Maja to Aarau, Switzerland, where she'd be studying and living with the Winterlers, longtime family friends. Immediately, I connected with the sweet, bright Maja. She reminded me of my own sister Zorka, and we found many commonalities of which to speak.

The same ease of manner did not apply to Albert's quiet, imposing father or his firm, opinionated, and perfectly bourgeois mother. When Albert presented me to them over afternoon tea at a local café with a sweeping gesture and a slightly naughty smile that made me blush, his mother assessed me head to toe with flinty gray eyes that matched her demeanor, not to mention her striped gray dress. Under her unflinching gaze, I felt small and dark and ugly.

At first she was silent, and I glanced over at Albert's father, assuming she was waiting for him to address me as protocol usually required. But I soon realized that, while he appeared formidable with his carefully waxed mustache and pince-nez, Mrs. Einstein was in control. Perhaps Mr. Einstein's string of failed businesses lessened his standing with his wife, or perhaps it was simply the natural order of their relationship.

"So this is the famous Miss Marić," Mrs. Einstein finally said. To Albert, not me. It was as if I weren't even in the room.

"It is indeed," Albert said.

I could hear the smile in Albert's voice, and it relaxed me enough to say, "It is a pleasure to finally meet you, Mrs. Einstein. Your son speaks of you fondly and often."

Acknowledging the compliment with a nod in Albert's general direction, she then turned her steely eyes back upon me and addressed me for the first time. "Your people come from"— she paused dramatically as if it pained her to even mention the name of my hometown—"Novi Sad, is it?"

"Yes, that is where I grew up—for part of the time, at least. And where my parents still live for part of the year," I answered, forcing a smile upon my face.

A long pause ensued before she spoke next. "I understand you are as intellectual as my Albert."

This was no compliment, and I didn't know how to respond. Albert had led me to believe that his mother, though irritatingly bourgeois in her concerns and ideals, was otherwise perfectly innocuous. By her last remark, I saw immediately that this was untrue. She exerted an insidious power over her family, and she planned on utilizing it with Albert about me. This would not bode well, as her dissatisfaction with me was unconcealed.

What had I done to make her dislike me? Was it that I wasn't Jewish? Albert had described his upbringing as largely secular, so I doubted that was the sole reason. Was it that I was a university student and not a more traditional young woman, readying herself for marriage? That couldn't be the case; Albert's parents planned for Maja to receive a university education as well. Perhaps she simply loathed me for being eastern European.

I played with a few responses to her comments, but it occurred to me that nothing I could say would appease her. She was predetermined to dislike me. So I settled on the truth. "If you mean that I am serious about my studies, Mrs. Einstein, that is indeed true."

Albert, finally realizing that our exchange was bordering on disastrous, intervened. He offered, "Miss Marić keeps me on track, Mama."

When his mother failed to take his pretty bait, Albert changed the subject altogether to Aarau and the Winterlers. While Albert, his mother, and sister gossiped, Mr. Einstein gestured for me to sit down and offered to pour me tea. As we sipped from our steaming cups and pretended to listen to the others, his natural cheerfulness slipped through his wife's barricade, and we shared a few pleasant words. But Mrs. Einstein was quick to exact a penance upon him for his kindness with a scathing look.

I tried not to think about this unpleasant exchange with Albert's mother as I flipped over the letter to search for its author's name. At first, I felt relief. The author wasn't his mother. But then I realized that it wasn't Maja either. It was someone named Julia Niggli.

> *Your invitation to help you idle away the hours is most enticing. I should like to visit you in Mettmenstetten if you plan on being there with your family in late August. Please send word if you do.*
>
> *Affectionate greetings,*
> *Julia Niggli*

As I turned the page over to read the front, Albert asked, "What brilliant theory of Drude's has you so captivated?"

"It isn't Drude that has me captivated, Albert."

"No?"

"No. It's Julia Niggli."

He said nothing, but his cheeks flamed.

I shoved the letter into his hand. "I'm quite familiar with how you idle away the hours, and I shudder to think of you sharing them with Julia Niggli, whoever she is. How do you explain this?"

Glancing over the front of the page, he handed me back the letter. "Look on the front, Dollie. What date do you see there?"

"August 3, 1899." I shook my head, sickened at the date. "Around the same time that you were writing *me* notes from Aarau, while I was at the Spire in Kać." I remembered well those notes from Albert. In fact, I had even memorized some of them. Last summer, I'd been trapped in the Spire while scarlet fever plagued the countryside, and Albert's love letters had been my solace.

"Exactly. I was in Aarau and Mettmenstetten last summer with my family who, you know well, were very aware of my relationship with you. My mother and my sister, Maja, even wrote notes to you in the postscript of my letters, for heaven's sake. Miss Niggli was a family friend with whom I played violin a few times. Nothing more."

His explanation was credible, but my suspicions were not fully allayed. "Why did you continue to correspond?"

"Because she was searching for a governess position, and my aunt was looking for a governess. I placed them in contact."

I suddenly felt ridiculous. Why would I doubt my Johnnie? He had never shown me anything but devotion, even when I pushed him away for so long. My true concerns about him had nothing to do with his love for me, only his obstinacy with Weber and his future employment prospects. I started to apologize when he interrupted me.

"No, Dollie. You have nothing to be sorry for. I would act the same if I found a note from another gentleman in your textbook. Jealousy is a hard, unpredictable business, even if you trust your beloved implicitly. Please know that last summer, spent in the philistine, empty world of my family and their vapid friends, like Miss Niggli, made my appreciation for you grow."

"You swear?"

"Yes, Dollie."

"Even when your parents urge you to leave your dark foreigner and find a more suitable girl?" Once Albert's mother realized that our relationship was not fleeting and she met me this past fall, the kind but very distant greetings I'd received in her letters last summer had turned into strident admonitions about Albert settling on a more "appropriate" partner this winter. His mother's efforts created a knot in my stomach that hadn't untangled. Only Maja still sent salutations in the letters Albert wrote me when we were apart. "Perhaps one like this Julia Niggli?"

"Dollie, my parents never pushed Miss Niggli or any other girl on me, no matter their misgivings about your bookish ways. They know better. They know I love only you."

I smiled at him for a long moment. By the time I broke our gaze, I was looking into the indignant face of Mrs. Engelbrecht.

"Ah, Miss Marić. I should have known you were ensconced in the parlor with Mr. Einstein. It explains why you did not respond to the dinner bell." I had rarely seen her so angry. But then, I'd utterly upended her order. "Misses Dražić and Bota await."

"My apologies, Mrs. Engelbrecht. I will head to the dining room directly." I curtsied, nodded to Albert, and hurried away. "Good evening, Mr. Einstein."

As I left them behind in the parlor, I heard Mrs. Engelbrecht speaking to Albert. "You have become quite a fixture here, Mr. Einstein. I might have to begin charging you for the many hours you've spent in my parlor."

Mrs. Engelbrecht didn't sound as though she was making polite chatter. I paused to listen to their exchange.

It took Albert a long minute to respond. "I am sorry if I've upset you, Mrs. Engelbrecht. I always make certain to leave before dinner commences or visit only after dinner is over, as are your house rules."

"You are always careful to obey the letter of the law, Mr. Einstein, but I fear you have no intention of obeying the spirit of it." Her voice grew harder and colder; she nearly seethed. "Take heed to obey the law in its entirety as it pertains to Miss Marić. She is in my charge, and I am a watchful crow."

CHAPTER 13

July 27, 1900, and August 10, 1900
Zürich, Switzerland, and Kać, Serbia

T HE STEAM FROM THE TRAIN BILLOWED THROUGHOUT the station. For a brief second, it filled the air between me and Albert, and I lost sight of him. I felt his hand reach for mine, and we giggled at the impossibility of being invisible to one another while standing only inches apart.

The thick puffs of smoke slowly cleared from the air, revealing him in stages. The thicket of chocolate-colored curls on his head first. The mustache hiding full lips next. And finally, his deep brown eyes, beseeching me for insights, kisses, promises, everything, and nothing. I would miss those looks in the days to come.

"It will only be two short months, my beloved sorceress," he said.

Beloved sorceress, little escapee, ragamuffin. I had become much more than just Dollie. Albert had a host of names for the bohemian intellect he believed me to be. He adored that I was different from all the other women he knew, particularly the ones with whom he'd be spending the next two months:

his sister, mother, aunt, and their insipid cronies. I had tried my hardest to become his ideal, no matter the toll it took on my studies.

"I know, Johnnie. They will be busy ones for me, so hopefully, they will pass quickly. But still..."

Albert could afford to lounge these summer months away. By cramming with the notes I'd taken during all the classes he'd skipped, he had passed the oral final examination for his diploma; only his dissertation remained, should he choose to finalize it. But not me. The term in Heidelberg—which now seemed so silly, running from the inevitable—combined with all our extra, noncurricular research projects meant that I was one step behind him. He could move forward, look for work, or research more deeply the subjects we worked on together, while I needed to take my final exams next July when they were next offered. To make the extra time worthwhile, I had decided that I would spend the upcoming year not only studying for my exams but also working on my dissertation with Professor Weber. That way, when I finished, I would have both my physics degree and my doctorate.

"But still..." He echoed my lamentation but didn't need to say anything more. That morning, he had listed all the things he'd miss while we were apart. The long afternoons in our quest to understand the rules of the universe. The stolen kisses and hugs when we were certain the omnipresent Mrs. Engelbrecht was occupied.

The summer months would be busy but hard for me. While he'd be hiking with his family in the picturesque towns of Sarnen and Obwalden, I'd be squirreled away studying at the Spire in Kać with only Papa, Mama, Zorka, and Miloš for sporadic company. Funny how the place I used to love above all else had become a lonely exile. My future was standing before me, and I hated to leave his side even for an instant.

The train released another pillar of steam, and we lost sight of each other a final time. I felt Albert's arms around my waist, and in the momentary veil of fog, he kissed me. Longing surged through me, and I thought of all the nights we exercised such restraint.

"How did I get so lucky as to find you? A being as bold and intelligent and single-minded as myself," he whispered into my ear.

I felt his hand at my back, guiding me toward the steps to my train car. I hurried to my seat, so I could get one last glimpse of him from the window. There he stood, looking sad and forlorn on the platform, bags piled all around him. His train would not leave for another three hours, but he insisted on coming to the station with me and waiting. Zürich, he said, held nothing for him without me.

"Miss Marić, dinner is served." Our new kitchen servant, Ana, called up the stairs to the attic, where I'd been holed up for the better part of three weeks. I knew the servants thought I was strange to be reading instead of socializing or strolling like the other ladies. I saw their sidelong looks at the tomes I read and the time I spent alone.

"I'll be right down," I called back.

I wanted a few more minutes with the letter I'd just received from Albert. I knew my parents would ask about him, and Zorka and Miloš were sure to tease me. I needed to be calm and unruffled to withstand the assault of my brother and sister and deflect Zorka with questions about school and Miloš with queries about his favorite games. I couldn't risk bursting into tears when they asked me about it.

Had Albert really written such upsetting lines? Didn't he know that it would torture me to know every detail of his mother's dramatic reaction when he told her we planned to get married? The image of his mother throwing herself down on her bed, crying hysterically at the news, and then hurling insults about me—that I would destroy his life and that I was entirely unsuitable for him—was almost unbearable. I knew now his parents wanted a Jewish wife for him or, at the very least, a Germanic one who would coddle him like his mother always had, but I didn't think either one of us expected this sort of tantrum. Her prejudices against me were many: my Orthodox Christian upbringing, my intellect, my Slavic heritage, my age, and my limp. Everything I suspected the first night I met her and more.

The most painful accusation, however, was her allegation that I might be pregnant. What type of girl did she think I was, and what sort of family did she think I came from? Even if we had wanted to consummate our feelings, Mrs. Engelbrecht circled us like a hawk; intimacy was an impossibility. Albert and I had naively believed that finding jobs would be the biggest obstacle to our union.

How would Albert and I ever overcome these sort of hysterical, illogical objections?

Tears welled up in my eyes. Would his mother's prejudices and hysteria drive us apart? Surely, Albert wouldn't allow that to happen. I consoled myself with his report that he remained stalwart about our plans in the face of his mother's onslaught. And that he loved me and missed me. He was still my Johnnie. We would find a way.

Taking a bracing breath, I went down the winding stairs from the attic. I settled into my place at the table next to Papa and said grace along with everyone else. As we sat back to allow Ana to fill our plates with *ćevapi*, I expected a battery of questions and a good dose of jibes, just like every other time I'd received a letter from Albert. But strangely, no one said a word. Had they not noticed the letter's arrival?

We passed the dinner hour in unusual, uncomfortable silence. Had something happened? I couldn't stand the quiet scrape of the forks on plates and the clink of the spoons, so I busied myself talking with Zorka about her plans for next term. A good but not stellar student, she had aspirations of studying abroad. Papa had been encouraging her to stay with me in Zürich and take a term at the Higher Daughter School to prepare her for the Matura exam. I wondered if this was Papa's way of observing and protecting me from afar. His worry over my studies and Albert pervaded all our exchanges these days.

The very minute Papa finished his last bite of the sweet dessert *gibanica*, Mama ushered Zorka and Miloš out of the room with her. Papa and I were left alone.

I stood to take my leave as well, but Papa said, "Please stay, Mitza. Sit with me awhile."

I sat back down in my chair, waiting as he lit his pipe and blew a few smoke rings up toward the ceiling.

"I saw that you had a letter from your Mr. Einstein today," he said.

He *had* noticed. If he knew, then certainly the others did too. Why hadn't anyone said anything?

"Yes, Papa," I answered quietly, waiting to see where Papa would lead.

"He is busy securing work, I gather?"

"His search will begin in the fall when he returns to Zürich. For now, he is on vacation in Switzerland with his family."

"Vacation? Why the wait, Mileva? A man who wants to marry must have employment."

Ah, so this was to be the direction of this conversation. My parents had never met Albert; they never came to Zürich, and Albert had never visited Kać, although I had invited him this summer and the preceding one. Albert had always declined, pleading the need to appease his parents with the summer holidays while still dependent upon them. And I'd never pushed. My parents distrusted Albert; it was not the Serbian way for a suitor to keep his distance.

Although I could understand Papa's concern—I would have been shocked if he felt otherwise—I sidestepped his question. Albert and I spoke of marriage often enough, but I knew he needed to ask Papa's permission for Papa to take him seriously. I'd said as much to Albert, who maintained that he needed a job before requesting my hand.

"Mr. Einstein believes that the opportunities will be more plentiful in the fall. Most academics are on holiday now."

"So he will keep you waiting then?" Papa pretended that he was asking a question, but he was casting judgment. He had never gotten over the fact that I'd succumbed to Albert after making the sacrifice of the term in Heidelberg, and of course, he was extremely protective of me in general. Not to mention that, as a Jewish foreigner, Albert was very mysterious to Papa.

Was Papa right? Was Albert keeping me at bay while he pursued life at his own pace? I'd always placed such faith in Albert to lead us through this bohemian wilderness. I knew he wanted me to be strong and independent, and it always seemed so weak and dependent to beg for commitment. I did my best to play the part Albert cast for me.

"I will hardly be waiting, Papa. I have to study for my final exams to take next summer, and I have my dissertation to work on as well."

"Then you two have discussed future plans?"

"Yes, Papa," I said with what I hoped sounded like conviction. Albert spoke often of our days after university—indeed, he had just declared me to be his future wife to his mother—but no fixed plans ever came from Albert's lips. Regardless, I needed Papa's backing, particularly in light of Albert's mother's recent histrionic opposition.

Papa's eyes and tone softened. He leaned toward me and took my hands in his. They looked tiny compared to the meaty strength of his fist. "I want to make certain that his intentions are honorable. It's my job to protect you."

With those words, Papa took me back to the time I overheard the conversation between Mama and Papa about my limp and my "unmarriageability." Suddenly, I felt rage.

"Is it so hard for you to believe that someone loves me, Papa? That someone might want to marry me, even with my deformity?"

Mouth agape and eyes wide, he looked aghast at my volume and my words. I had never spoken to him this way before. "Oh, Mitza, that's not what I—"

"Really? I know you and Mama think of me as 'deformed.' Unworthy of love. That's why you've always encouraged my studies. You assumed I'd live my life alone."

By emphasizing that hateful word—"deformed"—I wanted him to know that I'd overheard him and Mama all those years ago. I wanted him to comprehend that, no matter how hard I'd tried to bury their beliefs and embrace the modern views prevailing in Zürich, their label had never truly left me.

Tears trickled down his cheeks, and I knew he understood. "Oh, Mitza, I'm so sorry. I love you, my little Mitza, more than anyone in the world. My pride in you and your accomplishments fuels my days. I know you are capable of anything and that your limp would never stand in your way—in work or love. I was wrong to try to shield you from the world, to think that your limp somehow made you weaker or more vulnerable. Or less lovable."

I almost cried. Seeing tears in my stoic Papa's eyes and hearing the kindness in his words, I nearly buckled with the exhaustion of always acting so strong and of always needing to prove myself worthy. I wanted to fold into his arms and be little Mitza again instead of the strong and independent person I'd had to become.

Instead, I stiffened my spine and clenched his hand in a

gesture of confidence. After all these professions of strength, it was hardly the time to show weakness. "It's all right, Papa. I understand now."

He wrapped me in a hug. From deep within his arms, I heard him ask, "Is it wrong to want the best for you, Mitza? To want a husband for you who will appreciate and protect and love you as I do?"

I peeked up. "No, Papa, of course not. But please understand that Mr. Einstein will be that husband."

With his finger, Papa tilted up my chin so he could see my eyes. "Are you sure?"

I met his gaze square on. "Yes." And then I smiled. "Papa, he too encourages me to be a *mudra glava*."

CHAPTER 14

February 4, 1901
Zürich, Switzerland

T HE FANCIFUL DUSTING OF SNOW OVER THE SPIRES OF
 Zürich did nothing to lighten Albert's mood. Even when I
speculated that we might just have enough snowfall by the next
morning for a sled ride on the Uetliberg, Albert only grunted.
Nothing I could offer, not even the gifts of nature itself, could
rouse him from his dark humor.

"I know Weber is to blame for this," he grumbled again,
puffing on his pipe and sipping from the weak coffee they
served at the Café Sprüngli, known primarily for its bakery.
I longed for the rich *Milchkaffee* from Café Metropole, but
Albert found it too perilous to visit our usual haunt, because
we might run into one of our old classmates and we'd have to
talk jobs. Which Albert didn't yet have. "He must have sent
scathing reports about me to the universities with positions. I
should have never asked him for recommendations. He agreed
only to blackball me."

"I know you believe so," I said again. What else could I say?

Albert would tolerate no soothing or encouraging words. I had already tried.

"Why else would I have a pile of rejection letters sitting here before me? When every other one of our classmates has been working in their new positions for months?" Albert asked. I'd heard one variation or another on this diatribe for weeks if not the months to which he'd just referred.

Like a deck of cards, he spread the rejection letters out across the café table. But this was no game—this was our future splayed out before us. With my degree in the balance until I sat for the exams in July, we were entirely dependent on Albert's ability to secure work so we could make plans to marry.

"I can think of no other explanation other than Weber," I said, even though I only half believed this sentiment. Professor Weber's dislike of Albert was real enough, but I didn't think that his refusal to pen glowing recommendations for Albert was the sole reason for his rejections. Most of our classmates— indeed, most Polytechnic graduates, not only those with physics degrees—secured their positions through the advocacy of professors and alumni, and none of the other professors seemed inclined to extend themselves for Albert either. His flagrant flouting of classroom attendance rules and his brashness with the professors when he actually chose to make an appearance made him unpopular among our instructors.

"Maybe if you speak to Weber on my behalf again? See if he would send along more flattering letters?" he asked, reaching for my hand. Weber and I were in weekly contact with the work on my dissertation.

"Johnnie, you know I would do anything for you. But I

don't think we should risk it." Albert knew well that I couldn't cajole Weber on his behalf anymore for positive recommendations that he didn't want to give. Weber was in control of my professional destiny too, so I had to keep relations civil. Reminding him of any continued ties to Albert was sure to undercut my hard-won good standing and my ability to pass the finals this summer, particularly since Weber was the head of the panel that judged the rather subjective oral exams. And if Albert couldn't secure a post, I was determined to become employed. I needed to remove at least one of his parents' many objections to our union.

Sighing heavily, Albert dropped my hand and returned to puffing on his pipe. I knew better than to try to tease him out of this state. When he first began to receive rejections, he treated it like a joke, even a source of bohemian pride. But when the pile increased and he'd been turned down for physics professor assistantships at the University of Göttingen, the Istituto Tecnico Superiore di Milano, the Leipzig University, the University of Bologna, the University of Pisa, and the Technical College in Stuttgart, among many others, it was no longer funny.

"The German schools are rife with anti-Semitism. That may well be another factor." He offered another explanation, one he'd only hinted at before. He liked to think of himself as nonreligious, regardless of his heritage, even though he knew others didn't share this notion.

I nodded, for again, this was accurate. Anti-Semitism was rampant throughout Germanic educational institutions. Still, it didn't explain his string of Italian rejections, but I wouldn't dare point out this inconsistency.

The usual amused crinkle disappeared from around his eyes. An uncomfortable silence settled on the table. Uncomfortable for me at least. I never knew what to do when Albert's mood grew this black.

I glanced around the room, trying to distract myself with its extravagant decor, its curlicued chairs and marble-topped tables. The hour was odd, somewhere in between lunch and dinner, and the café was largely empty. The white-coated waiters stood in an orderly but relaxed line against the back wall, looking relieved that the café wasn't bustling.

"Maybe if I was free to go where I like," Albert muttered, almost to himself. Almost.

I stared back at him, stunned. Too stunned to speak, in fact. Was he talking about me? Was he actually suggesting that I'd put some geographical limitation on his search that gave rise to his rejections? Or that I'd made some other sort of demand that was compromising him? How dare he? I had offered him unbridled support and the freedom to seek a job wherever he liked; I told him I would follow. I had even turned down an unsolicited job offer from a former instructor to teach at a high school in Zagreb, because Albert didn't want to live in eastern Europe. He deemed it too far away from the heart of scientific developments. I agreed because I knew he found the notion of following me for a job humiliating, especially when he couldn't find one himself. And throughout it all, I'd suffered the brunt of his frustration in silence.

I'd never yelled at Albert before, and now, when the words finally came, they emerged as a whisper. Not as the roar I felt inside. "I have never stood in the way of your career—"

"Albert? Miss Marić?" A voice interrupted me. I turned

away from an astonished Albert to see Mr. Grossman. Because he'd been the very first of our class to secure a job as a teaching assistant, he was possibly the last person Albert wanted to see. "I say, what are you two doing here? This is far from your usual stomping grounds at the Café Metropole."

Albert wasn't one for displaying his weaknesses to anyone but me, so he assumed a pleasing expression, stood up, and grasped Mr. Grossman's hand as if there was no one else in the world that he'd rather see. "Good to see you, Marcel. Miss Marić and I happened here after a stroll, but what brings you to this unlikely spot?"

Mr. Grossman smiled but said nothing about finding us here, alone, so far from the school grounds; I suspected that he'd long known about our relationship. He then explained that he had a bit of free time before a social call in the neighborhood and stopped in for an ale. We invited him to join us. Inevitably, as social convention required, the talk turned to his new role as the teaching assistant to Polytechnic professor Wilhelm Fiedler, a geometer. Even though Albert's inquiries seemed enthusiastic, I could see how forced they were and the toll they took upon him.

The conversation slackened, and out of politeness, Mr. Grossman asked, "Miss Marić, I know that you decided to sit for the exams next July and are undoubtedly busy studying, but what of you, Albert?"

"My dissertation, of course," Albert said hastily.

"Of course," Mr. Grossman answered just as hastily, sensing Albert's discomfort with the question. Something made him risk the topic again. Perhaps he knew of Albert's situation and how desperate it had become. "I only ask because my father just mentioned to me that his friend Friedrich Haller, who's the director of the Swiss Patent Office in Bern, might be looking for an examiner."

"Hmm," Albert said, feigning calm. Even disinterest.

"I don't know whether you've secured a permanent position yet—"

Albert interjected, "I have several posts for which I'm still being considered."

I wanted to scream at Albert. What was he doing, not leaping at this chance? He couldn't afford to play games. My future was at stake too. Damn his pride.

"I assumed as much," Mr. Grossman said, then gingerly continued, "The patent office job isn't a position in which you'd use theoretical physics, of course, but you would certainly have cause to utilize physics in a very practical way as you considered the inventions that sought patents. It would be an unconventional—even unorthodox—use of your degree."

With a single word—unorthodox—Mr. Grossman had offered Albert a way to preserve his honor. Brightening, Albert said, "You're right, Marcel. The position would certainly be unconventional. But then, I've sought out unconventionality. Perhaps it's just the thing."

"Wonderful," Mr. Grossman said. "It would be a great relief to my father's friend Mr. Haller to have a solid choice. I'm not certain exactly when this examiner position will become available, but I'm sure my father—whom you've met—would be willing to recommend you for the position."

Albert caught my eye and smiled. And in that moment of fresh hope and possibility, I forgave him.

CHAPTER 15

May 3, 1901
Zürich, Switzerland

THE PATENT OFFICE POSITION DIDN'T COME QUICKLY
enough. As the Swiss government proceeded through
their methodical, clocklike machinations of considering Albert,
necessity required he find a job. Any job really, as his parents
had cut off the support they promised only for his university
years. He submitted his name for tutoring positions, but nothing surfaced until a distant Polytechnic friend, Jakob Rebstein,
wrote, asking if Albert would substitute for him as a mathematics teacher at a high school in Winterthur while he went on
military duty. We were giddy.

Even though the job was only temporary, we celebrated
and ordered a bottle of wine at Café Schwarzenbach, a rarity
for us. Heady with the job and the wine, we giggled about
the future, truly lighthearted for the first time since early
fall. I allowed myself to forget about the months of mercurial behavior and harsh words, where I never knew whether
I'd see my loving Johnnie or the brooding Albert. After all,
with the tension of the job search behind him—for a few

months at least—I felt certain my Johnnie would return permanently.

There, in the warmth of the night air and the haze of the alcohol, the idea of a Lake Como getaway was born.

"Imagine it, Dollie. The famed waters of Lake Como lapping at our feet, and the snowcapped Alps wrapped around us." He wriggled a little closer to me but not close enough to raise the eyebrows of the proper Café Schwarzenbach patrons. "Just the two of us."

"Alone." I breathed in the idea, scandalized and magnetized all at once. I couldn't recall ever being alone with Albert, except in a public place or in the pension parlor. In neither venue were we ever truly alone.

"No Mrs. Engelbrecht."

I giggled. "I can't fathom kissing you without the worry of her unexpected appearances in the parlor. That woman creeps as silently as a cat."

The crinkles around Albert's eyes deepened; I loved this Albert. This was the man with whom I first fell in love, the one who had been missing most of this past school year. "Maybe she's so quiet because she's not quite human. A ghost or some sort of spirit perhaps. After all, Engelbrecht means bright angel."

I giggled again and ran my fingers through the long coil of hair that fell over my shoulder. In honor of the occasion, I tried a new, relaxed coiffure, one I'd seen other young women sport. Instead of my usual tight chignon, I wove my hair into a loose twist on the nape of my neck and very intentionally coaxed a single, thick curl out of the updo and arranged it over my shoulder.

"What do you think, Dollie?" Albert asked, lightly touching that same curl.

I stalled. "You mean whether Mrs. Engelbrecht is a cat or a ghost?"

"You know what I mean, Dollie," he said, sliding his hand around my waist under the starched whiteness of the tablecloth. "What do you think of Lake Como?"

I didn't know what to say. Part of me longed for a romantic escape with Albert, where we could flee from the restrictions of Zürich. But part of me was scared. I knew what the trip would entail. We had waited so long to take such a step. Perhaps it was best if we didn't dare to take it just yet.

By my silence, Albert sensed my conflict. "Just think about it, Dollie. It might ease our separation, however temporary. It might be the bridge to our new life together."

But Lake Como never came up again. Not in the harried days of packing before Albert left for Winterthur, when he'd left toothbrush, robe, and comb behind. Not in the abbreviated farewell in the train station, where an unexpected encounter with a family friend from Berlin dampened our ardor. He didn't mention the trip, and I let it drop, a little relieved.

Yet within days of his arrival in Winterthur, he wrote me about Lake Como. Begging me to meet him there, he professed his love, calling me by all my nicknames—Dollie, sweet little sorceress, and the like. Alone at the Engelbrecht Pension— Helene had moved to Reutlingen with her new husband, Mr. Savić, and Milana and Ružica had finished their studies and returned home—I was susceptible to his pleas. I knew that if Albert were standing before me and uttering those words in person, the choice would be so much simpler. One glance into his fox-brown eyes and I would have no choice but to say yes to the trip, no matter how mercurial he'd been in the months that he hadn't been able to find work.

If Albert were here, I wouldn't hesitate to ignore the damning note I received from Papa the day before, the one questioning my honor, and accusing me of casting *sramota*, or shame, upon my family that would last for generations if I went to Lake Como. Why had I even told him? Papa, worried that I would "give Albert my shirt"—my innocence—in Como, had informed me that he would no longer support my studies if I went away with Albert. How could my parents think I cared so little for my honor and for theirs? Yet how could I ignore Papa's threats?

But Albert was not here to embolden me to go to Como. With him went the external source of confidence he provided. The choice was mine alone.

What decision should I make?

I had penned two distinct letters—two very different responses—and I spread them before me. Each path was fraught with its own pleasures and perils. Which letter should I send?

I smoothed out the letters' wrinkled surfaces; they'd grown worn from my constant perusal over the past few hours. Did I really think that, by reading and rereading the letters, I could glean some sort of divine signal about which to send? Hours later, no sign from the heavens had arrived, of course, and I was still no closer to a decision about what to do.

I read the two letters for the hundredth time. In the first, I prettily refused Albert's invitation to Como, hinting at

objections from home. Should I send this letter and deny myself
the pleasure to which I'd been looking forward? What would
happen to our relationship if I did not go? He had referred to
the trip as a bridge to our new life, after all. Would Albert inter-
pret my refusal as a rejection of him? Our relationship had been
in such a transitional state lately, I was worried.

I read the other. Dutifully, I laid out my travel details and
sketched out a rough itinerary. I couldn't help but smile at the
professions of love that spilled out from its pages. These words
revealed my true self, not the person bound by fear and convention.

I tossed the letters down on my desk. How could it be that
I wrote both of these letters? It seemed incredible that I could
feel both of these emotions so strongly and simultaneously.
Longing and surrender. Duty and forsaking. But I did.

I rubbed my temples and paced my pension bedroom. What
was I going to do? Did I dare to pick up Papa's letter again to
help me decide? I didn't think I needed to see the actual letter
to remember his hateful words: *sramota*. Shame.

What would Helene advise? I wished she were still here
to talk it over with me. She would sit down across from me
on my bed and, with kindness and strength, help me make a
wise choice. A modern decision, not one dictated by Papa's old-
fashioned Serbian thinking, but still very protective. I could
almost hear her advice on my lamentations that an impending
separation from Albert would kill me or her guidance on my
impatience about whether he and I would ever reach the point
when we could profess our love before the whole world. She
would pat my hands and urge me to "bear it with courage."

I thought about our parting nearly six months ago, in early

November, when Helene finally left Zürich to marry Mr. Savić. I had awoken before dawn to say farewell before she took her train to Reutlingen, where she and Mr. Savić would be living. Her bags packed and stacked at the bottom of the steps, Helene looked small as she waited in the parlor for her carriage. When Mrs. Engelbrecht stomped off to find out why the carriage was delayed, I padded down the stairs in my nightgown and robe.

We embraced. "I will miss you terribly, Helene. I've never had a friend like you, and I never will again."

"I feel the same, Mitza." She broke from my arms to look into my eyes. "I've never stopped regretting that I broke our pact. Even in my happiness with Mr. Savić, it looms darkly."

"Helene, please don't let that old pact ruin even a second of your bliss. We have both broken from it now, haven't we?"

"Yes," Helene said wistfully, "but I was first. And I wonder what might have happened to both of us if I'd stayed the course. If I'd decided to pursue my career instead of marry."

"Helene, I'm pleased with both of our choices." I took her by the shoulders and, in mock seriousness, said, "Now, I'm going to give you the advice you've given me time and again. Remember to live in the moment. This is your moment with Mr. Savić. Please embrace it. And I will do the same with Mr. Einstein."

We embraced one last time, promising to always stay in close touch by letters and visits, and then she walked out the door.

Would she urge me to live in the moment and head to Como? Or would she suggest that I bear our separation with courage for a little while longer? At least until we were married. I could not guess, and I didn't have the luxury of time to inquire.

I felt utterly alone. My family was furious with me. My

friends had moved on. Even Albert's future was unsure once his teaching position ended in a few months' time, and I knew what path his mother wanted him to take. One without me. I shivered at the thought of the solitude I'd long assumed would be my fate.

Perhaps, having been part of a complete unit, I suffered the halving more deeply. I could almost hear Albert whisper words of love in my ear, that he felt half a person when we were apart. His words had lodged into my soul, spoiling forever the poetic vision of myself as the solitary intellect that I'd carried around for years. Because I felt the same.

I knew what path I would choose.

I grabbed one of the letters from my desk and quickly sealed it into an envelope. Without allowing myself another second to reconsider, I marched down the stairs of the pension. Ignoring the call from a parlor maid that breakfast was being served, I pushed open the front door and advanced toward the post and my future.

CHAPTER 16

May 5 through 8, 1901
Lake Como, Italy

A ROSE-INFUSED DAWN CREPT OVER THE MOUNTAINOUS Alpine backdrop as my train neared Como. In luminous stages, the landscape began to reveal itself. The deep blue waters of the legendary Lake Como were enveloped by emerald-green hillsides and villas and villages so picturesque they seemed to be painted by Renaissance master Titian himself.

The overnight journey from Zürich had taken hours, and I should have felt tired. But I didn't. To the contrary, I felt excited, as though I was stepping over the crumbling remains of my past life and crossing the threshold into my real existence.

The train slowed as we pulled into the station, and I peeked out the window. Would Albert actually be there? My letter noted the time of my arrival, but given his propensity for lateness, I didn't dare hope he would be waiting. I had already prepared myself for lingering over a cup of coffee in the station café until he arrived.

Chugging car by car into the vaulted, airy station, my suspicions proved true. An empty platform with an equally empty café greeted me. No one else seemed to be present at this early hour other than a lone ticket-taker in the barred ticket window.

But then, at the farthest end of the station, I saw a figure. Squinting through the haze of the steam-filled station, I recognized Albert's distinctive silhouette. Grabbing my bags, I hobbled down the long aisle toward the door nearest him. When the train finally halted, I stepped down into his waiting arms. He picked me up and swung me around.

Lowering me to the ground, he whispered into my ear, "My heart is pounding. I have waited so long for this."

Steadying my dizziness by staring into his eyes, I said, "I have as well."

Lifting the bags off my shoulders and hoisting them upon his own, he said, "Come, my little sorceress. I have much to show you."

We meandered through the wakening streets of Como. My hand nestled in the crook of his arm, he led me down the cobblestone streets and into the fifteenth-century duomo that loomed over the town. Treading down the black-and-white-tiled central nave, Albert guided me to two fading but intricate Flemish tapestries and to three beautiful paintings by Bernardino Luini and Gaudenzio Ferrari.

"These paintings of the Madonna and Child are exquisite." Eyebrows raised at his expert direction, I asked, "But how did you know they were here?"

"I arrived yesterday afternoon so I could map out our day. I wanted to ensure a perfect holiday for us." Eyes crinkling at the corners, he smiled at the success of his uncharacteristic planning. "I've also scouted out the best coffee in Como, which I'm sure you could use after your overnight train, Dollie."

I squeezed his arm. "You've thought of everything, Johnnie."

As we dunked our soft bread into steaming cups of coffee, Albert described our plans. We would wander the Como streets until noon, when we'd board the boat bound for Colico, a three-hour trip to the north end of the lake. But we would hop off midway through the journey at the small fisherman's port of Cadenabbia, where we'd visit the Villa Carlotta, famous for its fourteen acres of gardens.

He made no mention of where we would be spending the night, and I did not ask. I was both excited and scared about what the evening might bring. Its promise hovered between us like an anticipated but unfamiliar dessert.

After a morning spent staring at the luxurious goods displayed in the Como shop windows—the affluent people of Milan had begun flooding Lake Como's shores—we boarded the boat. The waves lapping its side seemed impossibly azure in the sparkling sunlight, and soon, it became so warm I removed my coat. With Albert's arm around me and the sun's rays on my face as we watched the ancient shoreline castles of Lake Como pass by, I almost felt like purring. Never before had we been so carefree or so able to display our feelings.

The gardens of Villa Carlotta did not disappoint. After crossing what seemed like endless marble staircases and walkways, we arrived at a kaleidoscopic landscape of verdant green, riotous red and pink, and shocks of yellow. Over five hundred species of shrubs and one hundred and fifty varieties of azaleas and rhododendrons alone competed for our attention. Even the plentiful sculptures by Antonio Canova could not compare with nature's full bloom.

I leaned close to one of the fuchsia flowers, wanting to breathe deeply of its scent, when a guard rushed to my side. "*Non toccare!*" he warned me. No touching.

Stepping back, I said to Albert, "They are all the more beautiful because we cannot pluck a single flower."

With a wry smile, he said, "That's how I've felt about you all these years. My unplucked flower."

I laughed. One of us had finally broached the unspoken topic.

"I hope you still feel that way after this holiday," I teased and then strolled off to examine a particularly bright red azalea.

I'd been somewhat saucy with Albert for years, but still, I surprised myself with the remark. Where had I learned to be so coquettish?

The patter of his footsteps increased behind me, and I felt his arms wrap around my waist. "I can hardly wait until tonight," he breathed into my ear.

My cheeks flushed, and a warmth spread over me. "Me too," I whispered back and leaned into his arms.

Colico was not our final destination. We escaped the dreary, seaside town at the end of the boat route by hopping on a train for a short ride to Chiavenna. Although the sky was darkening and I couldn't observe the village in detail, Albert described it to me as a quaint, ancient place, tucked into a beautiful valley at the foot of the Alps. He had visited once before, years ago, he said, and wanted to return with his love in hand.

His love.

Hungry and weary, we ambled out of the train station and into a small inn two blocks away that had a sturdy if a bit plain edifice. Albert pushed open the heavy oak door and introduced himself to the innkeeper, a haggard, older woman seated at a desk in the foyer. "My wife and I would like a room for tonight if one is available?" Albert asked.

I almost giggled at the sound of "my wife," but when I thought of the duties that came along with the role, I quieted. Nerves set in.

The innkeeper glared at him. Not the welcome I'd anticipated. "Where are you from?"

"Switzerland."

"You don't look Swiss. And you don't sound it," she croaked to him.

Albert gave me a quizzical glance; why was this woman so interested in our citizenship? This region was rife with tourists from all over Europe. "My apologies. You asked where we are from. We arrived from Switzerland. But I am originally from Berlin." Albert didn't offer his citizenship papers to her, because he was between countries. Despising the militaristic culture prevailing in his hometown of Berlin, Albert had renounced his citizenship and was awaiting Swiss papers in its place.

"You don't look German either. You look Jewish."

Albert's eyes narrowed in an angry expression I'd seen only once before, in an argument with Professor Weber. "I am Jewish. Is that a problem?"

"Yes. We have no rooms here for Jews."

Grabbing our bags and slamming the door behind us, we

walked out. "Albert, I'm so sorry—" I tried to soften the blow as we walked toward another establishment.

"Why are you apologizing, my sweet Dollie? Anti-Semitism is an ugly part of my world. I'm just sorry that you had to experience it firsthand."

"Johnnie, if it's part of your world, then it's part of mine. We will face it together."

Smiling at me, he said, "How lucky I am in you."

We arrived at another inn. White-washed with dark timber beams for support and ornamentation, it looked like a traditional inn for the region. Tentatively, Albert pulled open the front door. Warmth and a well-scrubbed reception prevailed on the inside. A few empty tables sat before a crackling fire, and before we could ask for assistance, a barmaid approached.

"*Würden Sie ein Bier?*" she asked.

An ale had never sounded more enticing. We accepted and settled into chairs. Without noticing, I downed several steins of ale before our dinner of *Wurst und Spätzle* arrived. We laughed over the day's adventures, and somehow, I found Albert's jokes funnier and his scientific musings more insightful than ever before. As he excused himself for a minute, I realized I was tipsy. And not at all nervous about what the night might hold. I took another swig of ale.

When he returned, he had an archaic-looking key in hand, and our bags were gone. "Are you finished, Dollie?" he asked and extended his hand.

Without a word, I placed my hand in his and stood up. Together, we walked up the creaky set of stairs to the guest rooms. When we reached a door inscribed with a number four, Albert inserted the key and jangled it in the lock. The door wouldn't budge. Looking down, I saw that his hands were trembling.

"Here, Johnnie, let me try," I said. Easily, I slid the key into the lock and opened the door to an immaculate bedroom, replete with a roaring fire, a small terrace, and a four-poster bed. A bed. All the ale had made me forget for a moment.

I froze. Sensing my nervousness, Albert turned me to face him. "We don't have to do this, Dollie. I can get another room for you."

In the pause, my father's accusations passed through my mind along with those of Albert's mother, and I almost asked for a separate room. Almost.

"No, Johnnie. I want to do this. We have waited too long."

A carafe of crimson wine sparkled on the small table before the fire. Albert hastened over to it and poured us each a glass. Even Albert, who rarely drank alcohol, except tonight, it seemed, quickly downed a glass of the sweet wine. A second glass in hand, he lifted it to mine. "My dearest Dollie, this night is the first of our unions. Soon, we will celebrate our marriage with the rest of the world. But tonight is our private, bohemian ceremony. For us alone."

I had made the right choice.

He kissed me. A full, deep kiss without worry of interruption. I relaxed into it, allowing it to envelop me. I felt his tongue on mine and his hand in my hair. He pulled the pin out of my chignon, and my heavy curls fell to my shoulders. Slowly, too slowly, he unbuttoned the tiny pearl buttons that ran the length of my navy dress. As it slipped to the floor, he gasped.

Standing in my undergarments, I felt horribly exposed.

Was he recoiling at my uneven hips? My deformed body? "Am I so ugly?" I whispered as I rushed to cover my chest with my long, heavy hair.

"No! Dollie, you are beautiful."

He ran his finger along the curves of my body, pushing aside my skein of hair and slowly unlacing my corset. I shivered at the deliciousness of his touch. "Your ivory shoulders, your tiny waist, your full bosom. I-I never expected—"

He wasn't disappointed. He was in awe. I reached for him, kissing him hard on the mouth. I fumbled over the buttons on his shirt and pants; I wanted to feel his chest and body against mine. For a long moment, we melded our bodies to one another, just breathing. And then he led me to the bed.

On our final day, Albert arranged a surprise. Holding his hands over my eyes, he walked me through the streets of Chiavenna. I'd grown accustomed to the scents of our little haven—the bitter roasting coffee beans at our local café, the spicy incense wafting out of a church mass, the rich floral perfumes of the one luxury store in the tiny town—and I had a fair idea of our path. But soon, we walked into a space whose smell I didn't recognize immediately. I sniffed again; it was the distinct aroma of horse.

Albert removed his hands from my eyes. We were in a barn. This was my surprise?

"We are off to the Splügen," he announced.

I clasped his hand in excitement. We'd often discussed the mad journey over the mountain pass that spanned Italy and Switzerland. But funds had never been available for this splurge.

"I have a job now, don't forget," he said proudly, answering the question I hadn't asked.

I embraced him tightly, then, with the coachman's hand at my elbow, settled into the snug sleigh. Albert squeezed in after me, and the coachman laid a thick layer of furs, blankets, and shawls upon us. It would grow cold as we ascended.

"It's delightfully close," I whispered.

"Perfectly close for us lovers," he whispered back, running his hands along my legs under the secrecy of the blankets. I shivered, and not from the chill.

The coachman assumed his position on a plank in the rear and cracked the whip. The horses were off, galloping gaily along the snow-laden paths leading to the Splügen. The coachman prattled on about the history of the pass and the natural wonders we encountered, but Albert and I paid attention only to each other. For hours, we wrapped ourselves together as we traveled through long, climbing galleries of open road, seeing nothing but snow and more snow.

"It's like a white eternity," I said. Eternity. Would I ever discover a scientific or mathematical truth that would have such an enduring impact as the theory of eternity?

"It is warm enough under these covers." Albert tightened his hold around me. "Last night was wondrous, Dollie. When you let me embrace you in that special way..."

I blushed at the thought of our intimacy and buried myself deep in his arms. Each night, we'd grown more comfortable—and more wanton—with each other. Chiavenna had indeed become the place of our bohemian honeymoon.

"I think I'll give this new Professor Weber our paper," Albert said distractedly. I was well used to his rapid shifts in conversation from our love to our work. Ironically, his new superior at the Winterthur school was also called Professor Weber.

"Which one?" I asked from deep within the curve of Albert's neck. There had been so many papers and theories over the past few years, and work wasn't exactly at the top of my mind.

"The one on molecular attraction between atoms," he answered. The faraway sound of his voice and the slackening of his arms told me his mind was elsewhere.

"'Conclusions Drawn from the Phenomena of Capillarity'?" I sat up. We had researched and written a paper theorizing that each atom related to a molecular attraction field that is separate from the temperature and the way in which the atom is chemically bound to other atoms; we left open the question of whether and how the fields are related to gravitational forces.

"Yes, that's the one."

We had finalized this paper last month with the intent of submitting it to an esteemed physics journal. Publication would increase both of our chances of securing positions. "Won't he ask who this other author is? This Miss Marić?"

Albert was quiet. "Would you mind if I listed only my name as the author? I'm hoping that if Professor Weber reads it and becomes as impressed as I think he will, he will offer me a permanent job."

I didn't answer. The thought of being expunged from the paper's authorship bothered me; we had worked on it as equals. But if he was only showing it to the new Professor Weber to impress him and if we'd later submit it to journals with both our names, I could agree. Anything to speed along Albert's ability to secure a permanent job.

"I suppose if you give it to him just to read…" I said, trailing off. I didn't think I needed to insist that the publication authorship remain the same. Albert always had my best interests in mind.

"Of course, Dollie," he said. "Just imagine how quickly we could be wed if I had this professorship in hand."

I leaned forward to kiss him when the coachman interrupted us. "Signor! We have reached the crest of the Splügen pass. Do you and the signora want to get out and cross the border on foot? Many of my passengers do."

"Yes," Albert called back. "My signora and I would love to cross the Splügen on foot."

The Splügen? I didn't care about the Splügen at that moment or how we'd cross it. I was Albert's signora.

CHAPTER 17

May 31, 1901
Zürich, Switzerland

M ISS MARIĆ, PLEASE ATTEND TO THESE NUMBERS MORE diligently. I had expected far better attention to detail from you." Professor Weber's nostrils flared in annoyance. We were reviewing the research underlying my proposed dissertation on heat conductivity, and I had never sat so near to him before. I could see the precision with which he combed his dark beard and the quick flush of his cheeks when he was irritated or disappointed. He was even more intimidating in close proximity.

"Yes, Professor Weber." As I uttered what seemed like my thousandth "Yes, Professor Weber" of the afternoon, I couldn't help but think that my return to Zürich from Como felt like the descent of the angels to earth. Even though Albert would laugh at such superstitious nonsense, a biblical passage from Jude, one Mama often quoted, replayed in my head: "The angels who did not keep to their own dominion but deserted their proper dwelling, God has kept in gloom…" Like them, I had fallen from the heights of pure bliss to the dark grind of my final days as a student in Zürich, with only Weber for company. How could I be satisfied with the drudgery of earthly things—and Weber's nastiness—once I'd had a taste of heaven?

"And don't think for a second that by quoting my theoretical work on the motion of heat in metal cylinders you can flatter me into an easy pass," he said, his voice even more thunderous.

"Of course not, sir." My relationship with Weber had degenerated once his suspicions of my relationship with Albert were confirmed when Albert and I, strolling hand in hand, unexpectedly encountered Weber in Universitätsspital park two months ago. Since my professional future depended almost entirely on him, I was trying anything at my disposal to please him. Obviously, my use of Weber's own data was a failure. It didn't help that I kept drifting off into daydreams about the trip to Como, and Weber had to call me to attention.

"Your dissertation research is otherwise sound, but if you cannot perform the calculations accurately, all will be for naught."

"Yes, Professor Weber," I answered meekly, almost welling up with tears. Why was I getting so emotional in his presence? I thought I'd been hardened to Weber after years in his company. For some reason, I was feeling more delicate than usual.

Was it attributable to Albert's inability to visit last Sunday? Required to tutor some struggling students in the hours he had free from actual classroom teaching, he had to stay in Winterthur unexpectedly. Perhaps without his bolstering company for a week, I felt more fragile when faced with Weber's tongue-lashing.

Still, my vulnerability surprised me. Could the cause

possibly be something else? Perhaps the separation from Albert—and the instability in our shared future—was hitting me harder than I'd anticipated.

Albert had been able to visit the past several Sundays, although I'd been all nerves before he arrived for the first Sunday after our tryst in Como. Even though his letters had brimmed with affection—"I love you, my Dollie, and I cannot wait to see you again on Sunday... The thought of you and our time together in Lake Como is the single thing that animates my days"—I worried that we'd be awkward with each other after our intimacy. Yet even with the constrictions on our behavior at the Engelbrecht Pension and the Swiss cafés and parks, we managed to fall back into our easy, familiar affections. And the following Sundays had been much the same.

But now I was back to dissertations and final exams. If preparing for my final exam was squeezing the natural joy out of physics for me, researching my dissertation with Weber was killing any hope of pleasure. Where had my natural exuberance for physics gone? I had once gravitated toward its patterns as the key to unlocking God's plan for his people and world, a sort of religiosity all my own. At the moment, it felt like godless drudgery. I saw no grand divine design.

"Now, let's turn our attention to page sixteen, where I noticed some sloppy calculations. Based on this work, I surmise that you are months away from completion, Miss Marić," Weber barked at me.

I suddenly felt violently ill. Without even excusing myself, I raced from the room to the sole ladies' lavatory in the building, two floors up. Unsure whether I'd make it in time, I swung open the door. I kneeled before the toilet bowl and began heaving. I had never been so sick in my life.

When the retching finally ended, I sat back on my haunches. Had I been served something spoiled at breakfast? I'd eaten only toast with jam and some tea with milk. I hadn't even touched the boiled eggs. What could be making me so ill? Surely not Weber's criticism alone.

Then something occurred to me, something I was unsure would ever be possible. I did some quick calculations, and I gasped.

It was very early days, but I was certain. After all, I was a mathematician and a physicist, even if Weber maligned my skills. I was pregnant.

CHAPTER 18

June 2, 1901
Zürich, Switzerland

I PACED THE FRONT PARLOR. THE THREADBARE RUSSET-and-navy Turkish rug no longer had a defined pattern, and I couldn't help but think that my nervous treading in the past week contributed greatly to its demise. Why must so many of my life events be played out in the Engelbrechts' parlor?

Unlike the last Sunday when Albert and I saw each other, the anxiety I was experiencing wasn't one of pleasant anticipation. It was the precursor to terror. What would Albert do when I told him my news?

When I finally heard his distinctive rap and saw his twinkling brown eyes in the doorway, my anxiety melted away for a moment. I wanted to leap into his arms. From the way his arms instinctively outstretched, I saw that he wanted the same. Only the judgmental sniffing of Mrs. Engelbrecht slowed us.

Instead, we exchanged a polite bow and curtsy, with Mrs. Engelbrecht lingering in the parlor, ensuring the propriety of our reunion. Under the shadow of Albert's mustache, I saw a mischievous grin at this contrivance, and I had to restrain a giggle.

Mrs. Engelbrecht normally hovered without a word, but I must have looked pitifully peaked, because she asked, "Are you quite all right, Miss Marić? Shall I have the parlor maid bring in some tea to restore the color to your face?"

"That would be most welcome, Mrs. Engelbrecht. Thank you for your kindness."

She left the room, and I heard Albert exhale. Not many people scared him, but something about Mrs. Engelbrecht's Teutonic firmness made him anxious.

He reached for my hand; he wouldn't dare embrace me until the parlor maid had delivered the tea and Mrs. Engelbrecht was safely gone. "Oh, Dollie. Two weeks is too long."

"I know, Johnnie. These have been terribly hard days."

"My poor little kitten. Preparing for your final exams and dealing with Weber are horrific tasks I remember well." He clucked sympathetically.

"It's been quite a bit more than that, Albert."

He reached for my fingers and said, "I know, Dollie. After Como, it's strange to be apart. Without you, I have no life." Craning his neck to make sure no one lingered in the hallways adjoining the parlor, we stole a kiss.

The uniformed parlor maid, whose name I never bothered to remember as there seemed to be a new one every week, entered with a rattling tea tray. Albert and I sat down on the settee and waited expectantly for her to finish setting up the cerulean-blue teapot, cups, and sugar, and strain the tea. My heart thunked louder as the moments passed, but the maid wouldn't leave. I wondered if Mrs. Engelbrecht had ordered her to keep watch over us.

Finally, Albert had enough of the maid's presence, and pulling me to standing, he whispered, "Come, let's leave this philistine prison. We need nature with all her freedom."

Arm in arm, we walked the distance to Universitätsspital Park. The air was clear and crisp, the sun agreeably bright, and for the first time in days, I felt light. We passed through the park gates, and I broke from Albert to admire a particularly bright bluish-purple alpine columbine.

As I leaned down for a whiff of its fragrance, I felt Albert's hands around my waist. He whispered in my ear, "Not unplucked anymore, my little ragamuffin."

I blushed.

We linked arms again as Albert talked about his week of teaching. After recounting the challenges of instructing high school boys, his focus returned to his private research—thought experiments, he called them—into thermoelectricity. Usually, we pursued projects together, but the demands of my dissertation and final exams made that impossible just now. "I'm not satisfied with my theory, Dollie."

"Why, Johnnie?"

"As you know all too well, parts of it rely on Drude. But I've found some mistakes in Drude's text. So how can I publish my paper if the research upon which it's based is riddled with errors?"

He described the problems he'd identified in Drude's work and asked for my advice. I thought for a moment, and said, "Well, perhaps if you wrote to Drude and pointed out his mistakes, you might feel more comfortable sharing your theories. You might even forge a useful alliance with him if you do it tactfully enough. One admirer of physics to the other, that sort of thing."

"That's a capital idea, Dollie. It's a bold move, but we are bold bohemians, are we not?"

I smiled; I adored making Albert happy. Particularly when I was about to share some very unsettling news. "We are indeed."

For a moment, we strolled in silence. Was this the right moment to bring up the pregnancy? Stuttering a bit, I lost my courage and instead asked him about something that had nagged me since Como. "Did you share our paper with the Winterthur Professor Weber?" I emphasized *our* paper; I wanted Albert to remember that I had given permission to remove my name from its authorship, but for this purpose only.

"Yes, yes," he said distractedly.

"What did he make of our theories on the phenomena of capillarity?"

"He was quite interested," he said, then returned to his musings on thermoelectricity. I didn't pursue the topic any further. Albert was like an unstoppable train once his mind had fastened onto a particular idea, and there was no shaking him from thermoelectricity. He often said that since his family's dwindling money supply was due solely to a short-lived electrical business his father had founded, it would be appropriate if he was the one who finally uncovered the scientific secrets about how electricity actually worked. It was soothing to see him happy and engaged after the long months of worry and moodiness.

I hated to spoil it. But I had no choice.

We stopped at the Café Metropole, securing a well-placed outdoor table with just enough seclusion. Albert was thrilled to be returning to our favorite spot now that he had a job, necessary armor for any acquaintances we might come across. Before I could say anything, Albert summoned a familiar waiter. "Two *Milchkaffee* please, Heinrich."

The very second the waiter placed the cups down, Albert proudly paid for us both. Heinrich's eyebrows raised in surprise—Albert never had the funds to pay for my coffee before—but he didn't remark. As we clinked our cups in a toast, he said, "I wish we could pursue a beautiful life together right away. But between my parents and the fact that I could only land a temporary job just now, fate seems to have something against us, my sweet Dollie."

"I know, Johnnie. It isn't fair."

Albert placed his cup down and stroked my cheek. "My love, this waiting will only make things better later on when the obstacles and worries have been overcome. Our luck will change soon."

"Our luck cannot change soon enough." Albert, of course, had no idea how very quickly I needed our luck to change.

He smiled. "I have some news for you. There is a secret I've been keeping from you."

His smug grin told me he wasn't serious, and I pretended at pouting. "We promised never to keep secrets from one another." Even though I'd kept my own for nearly a week.

"This is a secret you will like, my sweet sorceress." He paused before announcing, "In addition to the Bern prospect that Marcel suggested, Michele Besso has a possible job for me."

Proper etiquette be damned. I leaned over and kissed him on the cheek. The possibility of a position from a good friend like Michele Besso had more promise than any of the job applications Albert had submitted to universities across Europe. Perhaps our luck was indeed changing.

This was the moment.

"I have some news of my own. Although you may not like it quite as much as I like yours," I said, my voice quavering.

"Not another job offer, I hope? I confess that it was the teensiest bit humiliating that you got a job offer so easily when I was struggling. Not that I wasn't proud of my Dollie, of course." This reference to the job I'd declined in Zagreb reminded me again of my sacrifice. I hoped I wouldn't have to make more, but my current condition made things complicated. Sacrifice might well be the order of the day.

"No, it's not that." How should I say it? What words would soften the blow?

"What then, kitten?" he asked, nestling toward me.

I drew closer to him, so I could whisper in his ear. "I am with child."

Like a threatened snake, he recoiled from me, moving into the farthest recesses of his chair. "You are certain?"

"I am. A result of Como."

He ran his fingers through his hair. Then, instead of reaching for my hand as I'd hoped, he reached inside his jacket for his pipe.

"Whatever shall we do, my dearest little sweetheart?" he finally said.

We. While the mention of "we" wasn't an immediate offer

of marriage, this pregnancy was to be our problem, not mine alone. It was an enormous relief. "What do you think we should do, my love?" I asked back, wondering what he would say.

He puffed on his pipe for an interminable amount of time. After blowing a huge smoke ring into the air, he finally reached for my hand and looked at me. "Dollie, I'm not certain how we will manage this exactly, but I want you to be happy and not worry while I work out a solution. You will just have to wait."

Wait? I had been waiting for so long now, I could hardly remember a time when I had the luxury of impetuousness. I'd been waiting for nearly a year for Albert to secure a job so we could marry, and that was *before* I was pregnant. "I'm not certain I have an abundance of time, Johnnie," I said in as pleasant a tone as I could muster. I knew how poorly Albert reacted to pressure.

Running his free hand discretely across my flat abdomen, he asked, "When will the boy arrive?"

"The boy?" I laughed at his assumption.

"Yes." He smiled. "Our little Jonzerl." Little Johnnie indeed. "Or maybe a Hanzerl?" I laughed at his proffered diminutive of the name Hans.

"Not a little girl? A Lieserl?" I joked, suggesting a diminutive of Elizabeth. I'd been privately thinking of a girl. It felt good to be laughing with him.

"We shall see, I suppose."

"I estimate he or she will arrive in January."

"January." He smiled. "In January, I will be a papa. That's many months away, Dollie. By then, I promise that you'll have a wedding and a home of our own. Can you envision how wonderful it will be for us to be in our own home, completely uninterrupted in our work and with no Mrs. Engelbrecht to look in on us? We will be able to do whatever we like," he said with a slightly different smile. A naughty one.

Did he not understand that I couldn't wait until January? If there was any hope for me to work after I passed my exam in July, I needed to be wed *now*, before my exams and before my pregnancy became apparent. No illegitimate pregnancy could besmirch my name. My personal reputation wouldn't survive it, and I would have no hope of forging a professional one. All these years of hard work—and Papa's support—to create a life of science would dissipate in an instant. Even if we did marry immediately and a baby was born in seemingly proper course, I would still face intense criticism and resistance if I chose to pursue my profession while a mother. And what was this mention of working undisturbed in our "own home"? What peace did he think a baby would bring? I remember well the noise and work that followed the births of Zorka and Miloš. A baby would bring nothing but disturbance.

I wanted to scream. Couldn't Albert see that my world was shattering? I felt nauseated, and not from the baby.

But I said none of the things I thought. Albert valued me as a strong and independent partner. Now was not the time to dissolve into a nagging philistine like the women in his family. I could not risk alienating him in any way. What if he decided to walk away from me? All would be lost.

Instead, I said, "A home of our own? Where no one will disturb us? Johnnie, it nearly makes my worries about our parents' reactions and my fear about my profession evaporate."

"Dollie, all the things we want—jobs, a marriage, a home— we will have in the future. I promise."

Sipping his coffee, he said, "I need to tell you of a very exciting development I had this week."

"Yes?" Perhaps this was more job news.

"Yes, I had a free morning this week to read Wiedemann's *Annalen der Physik* in detail. Can you believe that, in his text, I found validation for the electron theory?" he said, his eyes shining.

How could he think that, at a moment like this, I wanted to hear about his ephemeral studies instead of his career prospects? Did he expect me to engage him in a spirited discourse on the matter of life right now?

I heard myself say, as if I were looking down on myself from above, "That is exciting." My tone must not have matched my words, because Albert stopped his monologue. He dragged himself out of the distracting inner workings of his mind and saw me. Really saw me. And for a second, himself.

"Oh, Dollie, I'm sorry. I want you to be free from pressure about this. I promise I'll continue hunting for any sort of permanent job, and I'll accept any role. No matter how inferior. As soon as I've secured this job, we will marry without even bothering to tell our parents until it's all done. When your parents and mine are presented with this certainty, they'll have to accept it."

"Really?" He was finally saying the words I was desperate to hear, although his focus was too locked upon parental reaction. At this point, I needed the armor of marriage far more than parental approval. I already knew how much his parents would dislike this news; his mother loathed me.

"Really. We'll live the bohemian life we've always dreamed of, working together in our own home on our research." His eyes crinkled deeply at the corners when he grinned widely. "Only with a little boy on our laps."

I closed my eyes and rested my head on his shoulder. And for an indulgent minute, I allowed Albert's beautiful dream to envelope me.

CHAPTER 19

August 20, 1901, and November 7 through 18, 1901
Kać, Serbia, and Stein am Rhein, Switzerland

T HERE HAD BEEN NO PRETTY PACKAGE OF A MARRIAGE
complete with a job for both of us to present to our parents. When Albert failed to secure a permanent position again
and again after his job in Winterthur concluded, we had no
choice but to inform our parents of our situation. After all, we
would be under their roofs for the coming months. I would
have to return to my parents at the Spire in Kać; I'd completed
the exams, and while I awaited results that I knew were terrible,
I couldn't remain in Zürich to work on my dissertation as my
pregnancy became more evident. Albert, who had no financial
net, had to retreat to his parents, who were taking their holiday in Mettmenstetten at the Hotel Paradise. The fact that he
would be in paradise while I would be facing hell at the Spire
in Kać rankled.

Papa's anguish over the baby was worse than any rage he
might have inflicted upon me. When I told him, his broad
shoulders slumped, and he cried for the third time in my life.
"Oh, Mitza, how could you?" He didn't need to speak aloud

what I knew he was thinking: that he'd carved a path for me through the all-male wilderness of science and math, and I had jettisoned it all for nothing. I let my entire family down.

Papa's disappointment when the exam results arrived in the mail had paled in comparison. Immediately after I shared my pregnancy news, I'd prepared Papa for the failing final exam grades I believed were inevitable. I told him how hard I'd studied but how horribly ill I'd been in the days and weeks leading up to and including the oral exams—the perpetual nausea, retching, and dizziness that plagued my days and nights, worsened by the ever more difficult lacing of my corset. I explained to him how I'd had to race midquestion from the examination room so that I did not heave in front of my examiners, Professor Weber among them. My descriptions to Papa almost didn't matter, and neither did the grades once they actually arrived as I'd predicted. He knew that all my professional dreams were lost the minute I became pregnant; failing the exams was a secondary defeat. Even the possible adoption for the baby that he kept hinting at could not restore my honor or my career.

Mama cared only for the redemption of my soul. Prayers to the Virgin, beseeching Mary to forgive my sin, were an hourly affair, although I detected a hint of vulnerability when Mama asked how I felt. She mentioned that it was rare enough for women with my hip condition to get pregnant and even rarer for them to deliver safely. New prayers were added for my health and the health of the baby, but her head hung low, heavy with her shame.

Only the letter from Albert's parents softened my parents'

treatment of me. "Whore," Mr. and Mrs. Einstein called me. Although both their signatures appeared on the letter, I knew that Mrs. Einstein was its author. Mr. Einstein was too soft for such invectives.

Hateful names. Hateful accusations. Words I wouldn't say aloud, let alone write to the mother of my grandchild.

"This letter is not only offensive, it's nonsensical," Papa said after his rare outburst of fury—punching sofas and kicking walls—subsided. A wry smile appeared on his rage-reddened face. "Who would want to trap an unemployed physics student?"

I had to laugh. He was right. On paper, Albert was no prize. It was the sole moment of merriment in weeks of misery.

"If Albert's mother thinks we would permit our beautiful Serbian daughter to marry her rapscallion son, she is sorely mistaken," Papa announced and sat down to write his response. Papa would rather I raise this illegitimate child on my own or have it adopted by another family, no matter the damage to my standing and our family's reputation, than entangle our family with Albert's evil parents any further.

I was better off without him, he believed.

To Helene, I confessed everything: the pregnancy, my concerns about Albert's commitment, our struggles with our parents. I wrote to Helene of Albert's mother: "How could the world contain such abominable people? It seems clear that her purpose is to ruin three lives: mine, that of her son, and that of her grandchild!" Helene alone displayed compassion for my situation rather than rage or worry or fear for my soul.

As the weeks passed and Albert still did not journey to Kać, pity set in. I overheard conversations between my parents about "poor Mitza" and clucks of sadness; I knew my parents had been bracing for this sort of rejection my whole life. Their pity wrapped around me like the tentacles of a giant squid until I could no longer breathe. I sometimes felt that I couldn't bear a minute longer.

After three months of alternating disappointment, worry, and pity, I needed to get out of Kać. In November, I manufactured a trip to Zürich, claiming that there was a chance I could salvage my dissertation with Weber. I doubted that Papa believed me—even tightly corseted, the bulge of my belly was hard to hide, and it was incredulous that I could get a doctorate having failed my undergraduate classwork—but he allowed me to go and even gave me money for the trip. I was, of course, headed to Albert. He was the solace I sought, the salve for my wounds.

⁓

The bold red sign announcing Schaffhausen flew past the train window so quickly, I nearly missed it. I craned my neck for a glimpse of the town's eleventh-century fortress that Albert had described so prettily in his letters. I saw nothing of the town with its cobbled streets and its astronomical clock tower, only the thick forest that encircled it. I wondered if those were the woodsy outskirts of Schaffhausen where Albert lived and worked tutoring a young Englishman for the Matura exams. It was a temporary job, the only one he could secure after his temporary teaching position in Winterthur ended in August.

I couldn't risk leaving the train to find out. Not in my condition. If anyone from his work saw us together, the mark on his reputation might affect his job. We couldn't afford that.

No, I would stay on the train until the next stop. I had decided to lodge in Stein am Rhein, the closest town to Schaffhausen to the north. I planned to write Albert of my surprise visit from there. He hadn't come to see me in Kać and explain our situation to my parents as I'd requested—his pay was only one hundred and fifty francs per month, and he claimed he couldn't go to his parents for the fare—so I traveled to him.

From my room in the Hotel Steinerhof in Stein am Rhein, I sent Albert some flowers and a note announcing my arrival. Then I settled into blissful quiet, my growing belly set free from the constraining corsets, and read without interruption or condemnation from my parents. And I waited.

For an entire day, Albert didn't write back. I became frenzied. What could possibly delay his reply? Could he be away? Or ill? Perhaps the mail system was to blame? I ventured another letter.

This time, a response came swiftly. Without mention of my other letter, Albert expressed his surprise and delight but maintained that he couldn't visit just yet. He proffered two excuses: one, that his cousin Robert Koch was visiting, and since Robert had lost his ticket home and was awaiting funds from his mother to purchase another, his departure date was unclear; and two, that Albert himself didn't have any money left from his one hundred and fifty francs a month to pay for a ticket to Stein am Rhein.

The letter ended with numerous "beloveds" and "sweet sorceresses," but no nicknames could appease me. Did he think I could be so cheaply bought? How dare he not come immediately? Had his mother finally gotten to him? I understood the issue of his cousin—I didn't want either one of our families to know about my visit—but the money? His pregnant sweetheart had traveled nearly two full days to visit him, and he couldn't muster thirty francs for a short train ride? One hundred and fifty francs a month wasn't much, but carefully managed, he should have already amassed a small sum to set up house in Zürich. A train ticket should not be an issue.

With the upsetting note came some books from Albert's collection, presumably to keep me well occupied until his visit. I tried to keep my focus on a psychology text from Auguste Forel, director of the famous Burghölzli Clinic in Zürich, but it was futile. Particularly when another letter arrived on the day designated for the visit, begging me to wait yet again. He blamed work, his cousin, his finances, everything but himself.

This time, I did not control my anger. If he could not even scrape together enough money and time to visit me one train stop away when I'd traversed countries to see him, what type of commitment could I really expect from him? I sent off another missive giving him three days to visit, the three days until my money ran out.

But Albert never came. I waited in vain until I could afford to stay at the Hotel Steinerhof no longer. Ten days after my arrival, I returned to Kać alone.

The trip had not helped heal my wounds but inflamed them. It seemed I would be facing this pregnancy alone, just as my parents feared.

CHAPTER 20

January 27, 1902
Kać, Serbia

I SCREAMED. AS MAMA MOPPED MY BROW, I HEARD guttural groaning in the room. Was there a creature in the birthing room with us? Surely, it couldn't be me making the noises. The screams yes, but not those desperate, animalistic sounds.

"What is that noise, Mama?" I asked, my voice hoarse from screaming.

Mama looked at me strangely. "Mitza, the only noise in here is coming from you."

How could that be my voice? How could this be my body?

Another wave of pain hit me. I clutched Mama's hand tightly as the midwife, Mrs. Konaček examined me again. I tried to breathe and calm myself as she had instructed, but my body convulsed as more stabbing sensations coursed through me. When would this end?

"It won't be long now," Mrs. Konaček announced.

Not long? I had already been in labor for two days. I couldn't endure this much longer. Mrs. Konaček had warned me that with a hip condition like mine, labor could be unusually protracted. I was so tired, yet the pain never let me sleep.

I looked up into the midwife's familiar eyes; she'd delivered all my brothers and sisters and me, dead and alive, as well. "Think on something pleasant while your mother and I go out to the well to get some fresh water," she said with a pat on my hand.

Something pleasant? Once, the pleasant distraction would have been Albert. After Schaffhausen, however, my distrust in him was too deep for innocent pleasure. How could I have faith in a man who couldn't even take a short train ride to meet me in Stein am Rhein when I'd traveled across countries to see him? It didn't matter that his letters since that time—letters I'd left unanswered for weeks—contained news of a near-certain job as a patent clerk in Bern, Switzerland, the position Mr. Grossman had mentioned in the Café Sprüngli, the very news for which I'd once longed. Understanding the condemnation in my silence, Albert strained to appease me, professing love in his letters and wondering whether the postman lost my replies in the mail, but his empty words no longer assured me. Once, Albert's words would have been enough; now, I needed action.

I would have insisted that my silence continue to wordlessly scream my disappointment and anger except for Mama. In the fall, when everyone else returned to Novi Sad, she and I stayed at the Spire for the birth of the baby. It was the safest choice given that we hadn't settled on the baby's future yet. We allowed only a single, well-trusted maid to attend us in an effort

to still Kać's wagging tongues, and consequently, Mama and I
were largely alone for the first time in my life.

To my surprise, I found her domestic routines calming,
and we soon established a quiet order to our days. I followed
her throughout the house as she changed the linens, mopped
the floors, hung the laundry, and prepared the meals. All the
housework that Papa had shielded me from as he urged me on
toward a professional life, a life of the mind and not the life
of a housewife, I learned for the first time as a twenty-four-
year-old woman. An unmarried and pregnant twenty-four-
year-old woman at that. Yet Mama never shamed me; instead,
with respect and caring, she initiated me into the traditional
province of women.

It was on one peaceful afternoon, when we were sitting
before the fire after preparing a fine stew for dinner, that she
noted the stack of letters from Albert and the fact that I had
not posted any in return. She asked, "Will you not answer
him, Mitza?"

I looked up at her in astonishment. Mama never brought
up Albert or the future. We existed in a bubble of the present,
creating a sanctuary in a house never meant as a winter retreat.
"No, Mama."

"I understand your anger, Mitza. Albert is the one who
led you toward sin, yet you must bear the burden of that sin
alone. But please don't saddle your child with that sin if you
have a chance at giving that child a proper family—a mother
and a father."

I looked up at Mama in astonishment. Her advice directly
contradicted Papa's counsel to break with Albert. "I don't know

if I can do that, Mama. Not after his failure to visit all these months." Papa had expressed his fury at Albert's absence, and I assumed that Mama shared his sentiments, though she never mentioned it. I didn't dare to explain to her the worse offense of his refusal to see me in Stein am Rhein; I might actually unleash Mama's carefully controlled wrath with the information.

"Forgive Albert as God forgives us and embrace any chance He offers you to give your child legitimacy."

Mama was right. Punishing Albert with my silence would only punish our child. In my anger, I had forgotten something so obvious. I began writing Albert back, and with Mama's help and encouragement, I even sent him a Christmas package, only days before the pains began.

Now, there were no pleasantries. It was just me and the pain and the sound of my screams.

"Mama!" I yelled. She and the midwife were taking forever to get buckets of fresh water. I could hear a storm rage outside; wind whipped against the window, and a thunderclap sounded in the distance. Had they gotten hurt fetching the water? I prayed to God for their safety. The contractions were coming faster and faster, and I didn't think I could manage alone. The pain seared through me, not just in the birth canal but through my back and hips. I felt like my body was being split wide-open.

They raced in and froze at the sight of me. Their expressions were worse than any of the pain I'd suffered. Something was horribly wrong. Mama muttered prayers as she set the buckets of water on the floor and kneeled next to me, and the midwife settled at my feet.

"Oh, Mrs. Konaček, the blood," Mama said with a cry.

"What's wrong?" I asked frantically.

"Pray to the Virgin Mother," I heard the midwife say to my mother. She then addressed me. "Miss Marić, your baby is not coming into the world headfirst as we would like. The baby is breech. I will have to reach inside and try to turn him."

Mama gasped. I had heard of such births. Injury and death to mother and child were commonplace. How could this be happening to me and my baby?

The pain was excruciating, worse than any I'd experienced so far. Just when I didn't think I could bear a second more, Mrs. Konaček said, "We have turned the baby, Miss Marić. The baby is now crowning. If you push one last time, I think the baby will be out."

"Are you sure she should push? What about the blood?" Mama implored.

"There is only one way through this, Mrs. Marić. Whatever the outcome." She placed her hands on my thighs. "Come now, Miss Marić, push."

Tunneling through the pain into a still place deep within myself, I took a breath and bore down. And then, suddenly, the pain and pressure stopped.

I did not hear the cry of a baby as I expected. I heard the sound of water dripping. More like pouring, actually. What water would be pouring in here? There was no well, no sink. Was there a leak from the storm? Looking down toward my feet, I saw the midwife holding a bowl, not a baby. Even in my pain-induced delirium, I could hear it fill with blood. My blood, not water, was the source of the sound.

What's wrong? I wanted to ask. *Where is my baby?* I longed to cry out. But I couldn't make the words form in my mouth. I clutched at the air, and then I went black.

I didn't remember when I first saw her beautiful face. My eyes may have fluttered open for a few seconds before I fell back into the void of blankness. It may have been hours after the birth or days; I lost so many days and hours in the weeks after she was born. I held her for a few minutes here and there, I thought. I even suckled her for a bit, I hazily remember, as I half listened to Papa read aloud a letter he'd written to Albert about the baby. But I vividly recalled the moment when she opened her bright-blue eyes and looked at me. Even though I knew it was impossible, that newborn babies are incapable of such a thing, I swore she smiled at me.

I had a daughter. Just like I secretly wanted. A little Lieserl. *Izgoobio sam sye.* I was lost to her.

CHAPTER 21

June 4, 1902
Kać, Serbia

LIESERL GRINNED UP AT ME FROM HER CRIB. I ADORED the way her toothless smile emphasized the pillowy softness of her cheeks. Stroking her impossibly silky skin, I thought how deserving she was of every and any sacrifice I could make for her. Physics was nothing compared to Lieserl. God's secrets were revealed in her face.

Her cornflower-blue eyes stayed open instead of fluttering shut for her nap as I'd hoped, and I almost reached into the carved oak crib for her, the same one Mama had used for me as an infant. Lieserl had fallen asleep in my arms in the rocker, and I had tried to place her as gently as possible onto her blanket-strewn bed. But the moment her sweet, blond head touched the heather-gray blanket I'd knitted for her, she woke up with that smile on her rosebud-shaped lips.

I heard Mama's footsteps thud down the hallway to Lieserl's bedroom, then the noise stopped. I didn't need to look at the doorway to know that Mama was leaning against the frame, watching us with a smile on her lips. Mama adored Lieserl nearly as much as I did, illegitimate or not.

"A letter has arrived for you, Mitza," Mama said. From her tone, I knew it must be from Albert.

"Will you stay with Lieserl until she falls asleep, Mama?" I asked, taking the letter from her hand.

"Of course, Mitza," Mama said with a squeeze on my arm.

Instead of heading downstairs to the comfortable front parlor with its open windows and early summer breeze, I walked upstairs to the Spire bell tower. I wanted solitude when I read the letter. There, in what had once been my childhood refuge, a time that seemed long ago, I slit the envelope open with a pair of sharp scissors.

Before I read Albert's words, I closed my eyes and whispered a small prayer to the Virgin Mary. Mama's habits had become contagious, and I needed help, especially since the religiosity I used to find in my work was outside my grasp these days. I wanted so desperately for Albert to come visit our baby girl; I'd begged him to come, and he'd continually demurred. He explained that he had to stay in Bern to await final governmental approval for the patent position and couldn't afford to do anything that might besmirch his reputation. While I understood that the Swiss were notoriously respectable and that Albert needed to be cautious, I couldn't see how a trip to Kać could possibly jeopardize the position. No one in Bern needed to know whom he was visiting.

I lowered my eyes to his familiar scrawl. He started the letter with his usual loving nicknames and musings on the baby, what she looked like, who she resembled, and of what she was capable at this stage. I looked up and smiled, thinking of Albert trying to envision Lieserl.

He then asked, "Couldn't you have a photograph made of her?" A photograph was an excellent idea. Kać didn't have a proper photographer, but I could take Lieserl to Beočin, a larger town nearby, for a formal portrait. Surely, if Albert saw his beautiful daughter, all curls and smiles and cherubic folds, he couldn't resist coming to see her in person.

I returned to the letter.

> *Dollie, I cannot come to Kać right now. Not because I don't want to meet our Lieserl but for a very good reason. One I hope you will see. The job as patent clerk in Bern has come through as Grossman promised, and I am to start in mere days. So travel is out of the question at the moment. But we have been apart for far too long. I beg you to come to Switzerland, but maybe not to Bern, where tongues may wag, perhaps to Zürich so we can visit each other more easily. And come alone. Come without the little one. At least for the next several months until we can arrange our marriage in Bern. I know this may sound strange, so let me explain. You know how notoriously prim the Swiss are. Well, on my application papers for the patent clerk position, a mere six months ago, I listed myself as not married. If I arrived in Bern with a wife and baby in tow, they would know immediately the baby was illegitimate, a fact that*

would undoubtedly jeopardize my new position.
You do understand this, don't you? Perhaps we
will find some other way to have Lieserl with us
at a future date. Maybe your knowledgeable papa
can find a way...

I threw the letter to the floor. How could he not come to Kać and see his daughter? More disturbingly, how could he dream of asking me to leave Lieserl just for the sake of convenient visits to him? Why had our marriage required a job, and why must the job require relinquishment of my child? Were his parents behind this? I knew that they were still adamantly opposed to our union, Lieserl or not. I had resigned myself to the surrender of my career and honor, but my consolation had been Lieserl. I couldn't stand the thought of not being by her side for an indeterminate period of time.

I lay down on the old sofa, and my body curled around itself as if I were an infant myself. I gave in to the tears building within me.

The stairs to the bell tower creaked with Mama's slow, heavy step. I felt her sit down next to me on the ancient sofa and wrap her arms around me. "What did he say, Mitza?"

Trying to talk between my heaving sobs, I told her. Saying the words aloud made them sound even more outrageous. How could Albert ask me to give up my beautiful child? For several months at least, but quite possibly for an unknown amount of time? Albert had never even seen her; he didn't know what it would be to miss her sweet smell, her clear blue eyes, her gurgles, and most of all, her smile. And he had speculated wrongly in a past letter that Lieserl must be incapable of laughter. Her laugh was like the ringing of the clearest bells.

"Albert mentions nothing of marriage and offers no plans for Lieserl. He just wants me to relocate—alone—to a convenient base from which he can summon me when it suits him." As I spoke the words, even though they were even more horrible spoken aloud than existing as mere thoughts in my head, my crying lessened, and my breathing slowed. An alternative path for my life illuminated before me—a life with Lieserl but without the physics I used to hold so dear and without Albert. I needed to become strong to face it. "We will just stay here in Kać, Mama. Me and Lieserl. This will become our home."

As Mama wiped the final tears away, she said, "Listen to me, Mitza. Do you remember our conversation about making a proper family for Lieserl?"

I nodded. That discussion had guided my actions toward Albert ever since. It had even resuscitated some feelings for him as well. But I wasn't so sure I wanted to continue down that path, not now.

"You must go to Zürich; this is the only way to keep your marriage plans in motion. I know you don't like what you are learning about Albert—his reluctance to see Lieserl, his selfishness in wanting you near but not setting a firm date for your wedding, his lack of courage with his family—but you aren't doing this for you. You are going to Zürich for Lieserl."

I knew she was right, even though I didn't want to listen to her or accept her words. But I also knew how mercurial Albert was.

"But, Mama, what if I make that sacrifice and go to Zürich

as Albert wants, and he still refuses to allow Lieserl to live with us? You know that he has agreed with Papa's position on adoption in several of his earlier letters. Marriage isn't worth that to me. I will never give up Lieserl."

Mama's eyes narrowed, and her nostrils flared. She looked like a bull in a matador's ring. "I will not let that happen, Mitza. Have I not defied your father's wishes to send her away to some remote family member for a secret adoption? Have I not insisted that we keep her here with us in Kać?"

Mama had indeed risen up with a ferocity I didn't think she possessed. I'd been wrong about her my whole life. Her quietude was not weakness; it was an ardent watchfulness that would be replaced by a roar when required. Single-handedly, she fought Papa for my right to keep Lieserl with me in seclusion at the Spire, with only Mama and a maid for company.

"Yes, Mama."

"So can you believe me when I tell you that I will love and protect your daughter here until you return for her as a married woman? And that I promise we will find a way for Lieserl to live with you then?"

"Yes, Mama."

"Good. Then you will go to Zürich as Albert requested. The rest will fall into place. I will make sure of it."

CHAPTER 22

January 6, 1903
Bern, Switzerland

M Y RIGHT HAND INTERLACED WITH ALBERT'S LEFT, WE
stood before the officious Civil Registrar Gauchat.
In my left hand, I clutched a bouquet of dried alpine flowers
thoughtfully selected for the occasion by Albert as a nod to our
holiday in Lake Como. Some of the buds even matched the
vivid blue dress I'd selected. Today was the day for which I'd
prayed and waited for years, the day of our wedding. What I
once wanted for myself, however, I now needed desperately for
another. For Lieserl.

The registrar was so heavily bespectacled and mustachioed
that Albert and I nearly laughed when he entered the room. He
shot us a look of such stiff Swiss respectability that we quickly
collected ourselves and assumed our place before him. Registrar
Gauchat took a long minute to center himself on the dais. After
making certain he stood framed by the imposing backdrop of
the Alps, he began a speech carefully crafted to convey the
solemnity of the occasion.

Our witnesses—Maurice Solovine, a Bern University student who came to Albert for tutoring but became a friend instead, and Conrad Habicht, a friend of Albert's from Schaffhausen who had recently moved to Bern—marched into their positions on the registrar's signal. We hadn't dared include our families; Albert's mother's objections were still too vociferous, and my parents had Lieserl in their charge.

"It seems all your paperwork is in order, Mr. Einstein and Miss Marić," the registrar said.

"Thank you, sir," Albert responded.

"Are you ready for your vows?"

"Yes, sir," we answered together, and I felt Mr. Solovine and Mr. Habicht draw nearer to us.

"Then let us begin." The registrar cleared his throat and then bellowed, "Will you, Albert Einstein, take this woman, Mileva Marić, to be your wife?"

"I will," Albert answered as he fumbled for the simple silver band in his pocket. Hands shaking, he slid the band onto my ring finger.

The registrar turned to me and asked, "Will you, Mileva Marić, take this man, Albert Einstein, to be your husband?"

Time slowed, and I stared into Albert's deep brown eyes. Eyes that I once trusted implicitly and now had no choice but to rely on entirely. I had once longed for this moment with an almost painful urgency, and indeed, Mama and Helene assured me that this was the right thing to do—the only thing, for Lieserl's sake—but I wondered what the future as Mrs. Einstein held for me. Since our student days had ended, trouble had reigned over our relationship, and Albert had disappointed me mightily with his mercurial treatment, with the endless waiting, and with his recalcitrance over Lieserl.

"Mileva?" Albert asked as I hesitated. "Are you all right?"

"I'm perfectly fine, just overwhelmed with the momentousness of this day." The registrar nodded approvingly at my serious reaction to the vows. "Of course I will marry you, Albert Einstein."

He grinned at me, the corners of his eyes crinkling in that way I once adored. Part of me still loved him, despite all I'd suffered. With steady hands, I slid a silver band, identical to mine, on his finger.

The registrar handed us our certificate. It listed us as Mr. and Mrs. Albert Einstein. No children. My heart lurched at the absence of Lieserl's name. I painted a smile on my conflicted face and clutched Albert's hand tightly, and we turned to our witnesses for their congratulations.

Directed by the registrar to sign the certificate, we paused our merriment to finalize the ceremony. As I watched, Albert received good-natured chuffs on the shoulder from Mr. Solovine and Mr. Habicht. I knew that I should have been happy, but a sadness gnawed at me. At what cost had I secured this marriage?

As we left the civil registrar's office and walked down the stairs of the imposing governmental building, our wedding bands glistened in the weak winter sun. Bern was picturesque even in winter; encircled by the Aare River and surrounded by cliffs, the city perched on a dramatic promontory. The city itself was prettily decorated with red tile roofs, medieval buildings, cobblestone streets, and gurgling fountains. While it might have been more charming than Zürich, it lacked the capital's cerebral energy and, to use a favorite word of Albert's, bohemian spirit. Respectability ruled the day.

Albert grabbed my hand as we strolled down Bern's uneven cobblestone streets, and I tried not to think of the moment I handed Lieserl to Mama and left her behind for Zürich. I attempted to banish from my mind the four months after that I spent alone in Zürich at the Engelbrecht Pension, wandering aimlessly during the day and crying myself to sleep every night while I waited in vain for Albert to visit or summon me because he was too busy on hikes and sails with his new friends in the hours he had free from the patent office. I squirreled away the painful memories of my move to Bern one month ago into the Herbst Pension on Thunstrasse, then the Suter Pension on Falkenplatz, and finally Schneider Pension on Bubenbergstrasse, where my empty arms ached to be filled by my warm plump Lieserl. I tried to bury my anger that it took the October deathbed permission of Albert's father to finally make Albert move forward with our marriage plans. Instead, I forced myself to think about the union Albert and I had just formed and the promise it held of reuniting us as a whole family with Lieserl. My mood lightened.

"Let's toast the newlyweds at Café im Kornhauskeller!" Mr. Habicht cried out.

Albert and I hadn't planned any particular celebration to follow the ceremony; we had no family to laud the occasion with us, and I didn't know Mr. Solovine and Mr. Habicht well. Both dark-haired, mustachioed, and dark-complected, on first glance, they looked alike, with the primary distinction between the two men consisting of Mr. Habicht's glasses. They were

Albert's friends, the ones who had kept him well entertained in Bern while I languished in Zürich. Still, I was determined to make this day a fresh and happy beginning for us, so I called out, "Excellent idea, Mr. Habicht!"

Mr. Solovine held the door open for me as I entered the famous old Bern café. The establishment was surprisingly noisy and crowded given the midafternoon hour, but Albert and Mr. Habicht were able to secure a table from some older gentlemen about to depart. As Messrs. Habicht and Solovine excused themselves to purchase a bottle of wine for our foursome, Albert and I settled into two of the chairs. He leaned over to me and whispered in my ear, "Congratulations, Mrs. Einstein. We are now *Ein Stein*, one stone. I am looking forward to carrying you over the threshold."

Blushing, I smiled at his sweet use of my new marital name, although in truth, it still reminded me of his mother, Pauline, the original Mrs. Einstein. I shivered at the thought of her. She had continued her strident opposition to our marriage, despite Albert's father's deathbed approval, and even sent a damning missive as recently as this morning.

But when Messrs. Solovine and Habicht returned to the table with bottle and glasses in hand, I banished the image of Albert's mother from my mind and reached for a glass. Holding it out for Mr. Habicht to fill, I smiled and said, "Thank you for keeping Albert such good company for me."

As Mr. Habicht poured the glimmering, rich red wine into my glass, a few drops spilled on the white tablecloth in the process. I stopped short for a moment; the droplets reminded me of blood.

Mr. Habicht set the bottle down, and he said, "Thank you for loaning him to us. We wouldn't have the Olympia Academy without him."

"Hear! Hear!" The three men clinked glasses at the mention of the Olympia Academy. Together with Albert, they shared a restless quest to understand the world, and they had formed their "academy" to pursue this mission. Parsing through books by mathematicians, scientists, philosophers, and even Charles Dickens, they held lively debates; most recently, the men read Karl Pearson's *The Grammar of Science*.

Mr. Solovine raised a glass in the direction of Albert and me and said, "To the newlyweds."

As we sipped our wine and kissed lightly at their insistence, Mr. Habicht then stood and raised his glass. This time, he toasted me alone. "To Mrs. Einstein, a beautiful and brilliant lady. We can't imagine what Albert did to deserve you, but we would like to make you an honorary member of the Olympia Academy."

I laughed out loud. I'd been convinced that lively discussions about science and the nature of our world of the sort I'd grown used to at Café Metropole would be out of my reach, and I was delighted at the inclusion. For a fleeting minute, I felt like a Polytechnic student again, brimming with hope and wonder at the universe's mysteries. Not at all like the grown woman who'd failed her physics exams and spilled her blood in the birth of her child.

"I would be honored," I said with a nod of my head. "I welcome a vigorous discussion with Academy members on your latest reading, Pearson's *The Grammar of Science*. I wonder if you all agree with his statement that it's impossible to separate science from philosophy."

Messrs. Solovine and Habicht looked over at me, surprised and impressed. What a relief. I'd been quiet around them until now, having grown rusty in thought and speech after months spent solely with Lieserl and her simple routines and then mostly alone in Bern and Zürich while I awaited Albert's summoning.

"Brilliant idea," Albert concurred. "Wish I'd thought of it myself."

So do I, I thought ruefully. I buried this sentiment deep within myself and instead said brightly, "I insist that the Olympia Academy meet at our apartment from now on. Dinner, drinks, discussion."

Albert beamed at my invitation, proud of the bright, bohemian wife who sat next to him. The woman he'd always wanted me to be. I smiled back and continued in this lighthearted way for the rest of the day. I kept my step light even when we said farewell to Messrs. Solovine and Habicht, and Albert led me by the hand down the cobblestone streets of Bern to the red-tiled roof of our new apartment on Tillierstrasse, high over the winding Aare River. Because every step brought us closer to Lieserl.

CHAPTER 23

August 26, 1903
Bern, Switzerland

T HE BELL DOWNSTAIRS RANG. GLANCING UP AT THE CLOCK
from the floor I was scrubbing, I saw that it was nearly
four o'clock. The postman must have rung. Individual delivery
notification wasn't his normal practice, but I'd begged him to
signal me whenever he had a delivery for us, and he'd begrudgingly agreed. I didn't want to wait a single moment to read
Mama's letters about Lieserl.

Placing my scrub brush in the bucket, I wiped my hands
on the apron I wore over my flowered housedress and raced
down the stairs as quickly as I could. My mobility and speed
had diminished since Lieserl's birth. The damage that labor did
to my hips would probably not heal, the midwife admitted, but
I learned to adjust. I'd never been quick, after all. I felt dizzy as
I descended; maybe I stood up too quickly in this August heat.

In the eight months since our wedding, I put to use all the skills
I'd learned from Mama in our time alone at the Spire. Cooking,
cleaning, shopping, and mending filled my days, the work Papa
had barricaded me from as he urged me toward a life of the mind.
I'd become the embodiment of an old Serbian phrase, *Kuća ne*

leži na zemlji nego na ženi; the house doesn't rest on the earth but on the woman. I tried to tell myself that I enjoyed taking care of Albert in the way Mama took care of Papa. I even wrote to Helene that Albert and I were more blissful as a married couple than as university students. Was I trying to convince myself with those words? Because in my honest moments, I found the work of caring for Albert and our home mind-numbing.

Fortunately, the nights kept my brain engaged. After dinner or sometimes during, Conrad and Maurice arrived, and with them, the self-dubbed Olympia Academy was convened. Honorary member that I was, I sat in the background, knitting, listening, and occasionally chiming in when my natural reticence allowed. But once the Olympia Academy left, I really came alive. Returning to our original shared passion and my secret quest— discovering where God's secrets are hidden in the language of math and science—Albert and I researched the nature of light, the existence of atoms, and most of all, the notion of relativity. In those moments, late at night huddled together over our kitchen table with cups of coffee in our hands, despite my doubts and my suffering, I allowed myself to fall in love with Albert all over again. He had promised that he wouldn't allow me to fall away from science, and he had delivered. Together, he said, "we would unlock the secrets of the universe," and I believed him.

Since she was never far from my thoughts, sometimes I mentioned Lieserl. Albert never initiated conversations about her. He would quietly listen while I recounted Mama's letters. But he always changed the subject when I raised the specific question of bringing Lieserl to Bern, muttering "later" if I dared ask him when we might fetch her. And he would shake his head at any construct I fashioned—a cousin's daughter, an adopted child—to explain Lieserl's existence.

Still, I hadn't entirely given up hope. In my last letter, I'd asked Mama to have a formal portrait done of Lieserl and send it to us. I was certain that if Albert saw his beautiful daughter, he couldn't resist my pleas to have Lieserl live with us. Surely, we could come up with some excuse that would appease the Swiss authorities and any inquisitive friends. I prayed this postal delivery would contain the photograph.

A single envelope sat in the mailbox, and I examined it. From the handwriting, I knew it was from Mama, but the slim package couldn't fit the photograph for which I'd hoped. I trudged upstairs to our tiny living room. Dust flew out of the cushions as I settled onto the ocher settee. No matter how hard I scrubbed, I couldn't clean away the must of the previous tenants.

Dear Mitza,

I am sorry to write you with terrible news. Scarlet fever has been running rampant throughout the countryside again. Although we have taken every precaution to protect Lieserl against it, she has contracted the disease. The red rash has already appeared on her face and neck and has begun spreading to her trunk. Her fever is very high, and cold baths will not abate it. This, of course, presents the biggest concern. The doctor has examined her and informed us that there is nothing to do but let nature take its course. And pray.

We are giving her the best possible care, but
she is quite uncomfortable and longing for you. You
may wish to come.

Much love,
Mama

Scarlet fever? No, no, no, not my Lieserl.

Children died from scarlet fever all the time. Even if they didn't die, they suffered terribly during the illness. Scars, deafness, kidney and heart failure, encephalitis, and blindness were just a few of the long-term ramifications for survivors.

I had to go.

Wiping my tears away, I raced to our bedroom to pack my things. As I pulled down my trunk from the top of the armoire, I heard the front door slam. Albert was home early. I kept packing. There was a train—the Arlberg train—that evening that would start the long journey to Novi Sad and from there to Kać, where Lieserl was staying with my parents now that Papa had gone to the Spire for the summer months. I didn't have a spare moment to fuss over Albert's return home.

"Dollie?" he called out, sounding perplexed. He was used to me greeting him at the door.

"In the bedroom."

The smoke from his pipe preceded him into the bedroom. "Dollie, what are you doing?"

I handed him the letter from Mama and continued packing.

"So will you go to Kać?"

I looked up, startled at his question. How could I stay away? "Of course."

"For how long?"

"Until Lieserl recovers."

"Can't your mother handle this? You could be away for an awfully long time. A proper wife shouldn't leave her husband alone for too long. How will I manage?"

I stared at him. Had he really just asked me those questions? For all his selfish inquiries, he hadn't asked a single question about the scarlet fever or Lieserl's condition. Where was his compassion and concern for his daughter? All that seemed to matter was his inconvenience at my absence. I wanted to scream at him. Shake him senseless, even.

Instead, I said, "No, Albert. I'm her mother. I will handle her illness."

"But I'm your husband."

I could not believe what I was hearing. "Are you telling me I cannot go?" I said loudly with my hands on my hips. Albert looked shocked. He had never heard me raise my voice.

He didn't answer. By his silence, was I to surmise his objection? I didn't have time for his selfishness or whatever ridiculous thoughts were passing through his head.

I snapped the lid of my trunk closed, grabbed my citizenship papers, and put on my gray traveling coat and hat. Lugging my battered tin and leather trunk off the bed, I began to drag it out the front door of our apartment and down our steep stairs, no small feat with my limp. As I pulled the trunk out onto the street to hail a passing hansom cab to take me to the train station, I looked back up the steps.

Albert stood at the top of the staircase, watching me walk away.

CHAPTER 24

August 27, 1903, and September 19, 1903
Salzburg, Austria, and Kać, Serbia

A TERRIBLE THOUGHT PLAGUED THE INITIAL LEG OF MY long journey to Kać. Had I gone too far with Albert?

Part of me hated that this thought even occurred to me, but storming off and defying his wishes, no matter how outrageous and unjust they were, could undo all the groundwork I'd laid for his acceptance of Lieserl into our life in Bern. If she survived the scarlet fever, that was. Should I appease him in some way? The thought of it rankled terribly, but I needed him on my side. Especially since I suspected I was pregnant with another child.

At 3:20 p.m., the train pulled into the Salzburg, Austria, station. I had exactly ten minutes while the train boarded more passengers before it continued on to the next stop. Was it enough time to write and send Albert a note? I decided to take the chance.

Weaving through the throngs of new passengers boarding my train, I hobbled down the aisle and steps and over to the nearest kiosk. I grabbed a sepia postcard of Schloss Leopoldskron, a castle near Salzburg, and two five-heller stamps. Four minutes until the train departed. What should I write? I contemplated several approaches but couldn't decide.

I finally settled on a greeting—a familiar nickname to signal that I was no longer fuming, but I wouldn't lead with an actual apology—when the whistle sounded. Glancing up, I realized that I had only one minute to board the train before it left the station. I'd spent too long on the postcard. With my limp, the distance stretched out long before me, and I panicked. Could I make it? I tried to race toward my train car—toward my daughter—but a surge of passengers disembarking from another train blocked my way. As I tried to dodge through them, my lame foot caught on the hem of my skirts, and I fell to the ground. A kindly older couple reached down to help me up, but it was too late. My train had left the station.

Hysterically crying, I shrugged off the couples' hands and rushed over to the ticket master's office. When would the next train for Novi Sad, Serbia—where Papa would pick me up and take me by carriage to Kać—depart? The first one left in fifteen minutes, and it would require that I take two additional connections to make it back anywhere close to my original arrival time. I bought the ticket.

I raced to send a telegram to Papa about my change in arrival and the whereabouts of my luggage and then hastened to board the train. Even though it had factored into my delay, I decided to take the postcard with me back on board and send it from our next stop, Budapest. But this time, I wouldn't deliver it to the post for mailing myself; I would enlist a train agent to do it for me. I wouldn't take the chance of leaving the train again.

As the train bumped along—my stomach along with it—I

scrawled a note to "Johnnie," inquiring after him and updating him on my journey. I needed to know that Albert and I were settled as I went to go fight for Lieserl's life.

The train arrived in Novi Sad the next afternoon, a whole half day later than I'd planned. Papa, who'd already secured my trunk from the earlier train, was waiting with a carriage to take me the twenty kilometers to Kać. He greeted me with a grave smile and warm embrace, and he confirmed that, as far as he knew, since he'd been at the train station for nearly a day awaiting me, Lieserl's condition was unchanged. Then we slipped into an uncomfortable silence. The controversial topics of my marriage and my failure to visit the baby since the wedding loomed large between us, preventing any of our historical intimacy.

When the carriage pulled into Kać, red crosses outlined in black were painted on nearly every door in town. The symbol of scarlet fever was everywhere. I had never seen so many red crosses, not in any of the scarlet fever epidemics I'd experienced before. No wonder Lieserl was ill. I felt sick at the thought and instinctively clutched my stomach. How would I protect this new baby from infection should I catch it?

"Is it so bad?" I asked Papa.

"It's the worst outbreak I've ever seen," Papa answered. "With the worst symptoms."

The Spire's towers grew closer, and instead of being elated at reuniting with my daughter, I grew more afraid. What would be the state of my poor Lieserl? What if I'd arrived too late?

Before Papa could even stop the horses entirely, I jumped from the carriage and ran into the house. I passed the local doctor's carriage parked out front. Had Lieserl taken a turn for the worse?

"Mama!" I called out, dropping my traveling bag at the foot of the steps.

Climbing the curved stairs as quickly as I could, I heard her call back, "In the nursery, Mitza."

I pushed open the door to the nursery and gasped at the state of my daughter. Her face and throat were a deep crimson, as, undoubtedly, was her trunk. Her eyes were rolled halfway back in her head, an undeniable sign of high fever. Mama was dipping a cloth into a bowl of ice water and rubbing it on Lieserl's body, while the doctor sat at her side. I smelled rose water and wintergreen in the air and spotted a row of jars along the dresser. Mama was using her arsenal of home remedies: quinine; dressings of rose water and glycerin mixed with oil for the skin; wintergreen for fever; mint for the itching; monkshood, belladonna, and woodbine combined with jasmine to calm the system. Would any of them help my poor baby?

Mama and the doctor looked up at me, their eyes full of worry. "She took a turn for the worse this morning, Mitza," Mama said. "The fever took her in its grasp."

I kneeled beside Lieserl's bed. I had arrived too late. Stroking her blond hair, damp from sweat or Mama's ministrations, I whispered in her ear, "Mama is here, Lieserl. Mama loves you." And I wept.

The days passed in a haze as I kept vigil by Lieserl's side. The doctor was right; there was little we could do for her besides make her comfortable and pray, which Mama and I did constantly. I gave up worrying about my own health and scarlet fever's potential effect on my unborn baby and focused instead on the very sick but still living child who lay before me. Lieserl hadn't opened her eyes fully since I returned home—the fever never lifted—so I had no idea if she realized I was there. Or indeed, if she even remembered who I was. She had grown so much in the year since I had last seen her; I'd left behind a six-month-old infant, and I now stared down at a year-and-a-half-old child.

What sort of mother was I? How could I have left this beautiful being behind for so long?

After nearly three weeks in which Albert sent three concil-iatory letters, I wrote him about her state. I didn't stint on the description or the possible outcome, and there was no longer any need to beg for her admission into our family. Her survival was my focus now.

On September 19, he responded, asking about Lieserl and her scarlet fever symptoms. After inquiring about how she was registered in the governmental records—an odd question under the circumstances, I thought—he begged me to return to Bern. Three weeks was too long for a proper wife to be separated from her husband, he claimed, and I needed to join him again.

How dare Albert admonish me about my duties as a wife? Was he even concerned about Lieserl's condition? He seemed more focused on his own well-being and asked more questions about her birth registration than her health. Why was he asking about that? If he was finally considering having her with us—when, and if, she recovered—he knew that a child born out of wedlock automatically becomes legitimate after its parents' marriage under Swiss law. He would simply need to list Lieserl's name on his passport and be present at the border to escort her into Switzerland. His question didn't make any sense—unless he was thinking about adoption again. Surely, he could not consider such a thing at this grave juncture.

I wouldn't be going back to Bern any time soon to minister to Albert's needs and tidy our home. Not without a healthy Lieserl, in any event. She was my priority and my life. Albert could not think I would leave her again.

CHAPTER 25

October 12, 1903
Novi Sad, Serbia

I CLUTCHED MY STOMACH AND TRIED TO KEEP FROM CRYING. The last time I was in this train station, almost two months ago, I promised myself I wouldn't pass through on my return to Bern without my Lieserl. Yet here I stood, empty-handed.

Scarlet fever broke my promise. The disease ravaged my poor baby—peeling her skin from her blistering body, taking her sight, singeing her with relentless fever, and damaging her sweet heart—until she could no longer hold on. After the life slowly drained from her, I clutched her limp body, rocking her back and forth, until Mama gently pried her from me. I didn't stop sobbing from the moment she died until we lowered her tiny coffin into the hallowed ground of a churchyard near Kać. On that terrible evening, Mama and Papa, our shared grief linking us together once again, had to carry me back to the Spire once night fell.

I did not leave Lieserl. She left me.

How would I go on without her?

While I waited for the boarding announcement for Bern, I

sat down on the station bench, giving in to the grief I'd penned up since I hugged Mama and Papa good-bye at the station entrance. If I wasn't pregnant again, I would insist on a very different future. I would stay in Kać, never leaving Lieserl's resting place behind. I would become like Mama, perpetually dressed in funereal black and making daily visits to the grave of my beloved departed. Albert and physics would become a distant memory, a hazy piece of a past I'd foresworn. They would be penance for my sin in abandoning Lieserl in the first place.

Questions and regrets plagued me. Could I have staved off the scarlet fever if I'd never left her behind for Albert? Could I have stopped the fever from sinking its final talons into her if I had arrived just a little earlier? If I hadn't gotten off that damned train in Salzburg to write to Albert?

But I *did* have another baby coming. I rubbed my growing belly, this time unencumbered by restraining corsets, and willed myself to stop the tears, if only for a little while. No matter my grief, I would have to mother this new baby and create a family for him or her, regardless of how I felt about his or her father. Albert's response to my pregnancy still angered me. "I'm happy about your news. I've thought for some time that you needed a new little girl…"

A new little girl? I wanted to scream. How could he think a new baby would replace Lieserl, the unique soul I had just lost? A child he had never bothered to see.

A child I wanted God to give back to me.

If only God would let me go back in time, I wouldn't make the same mistakes again. I would stay in Kać and never leave Lieserl; surely a mother's savage love could ward off the scourge of scarlet fever. If only God's rules permitted me to freeze time or change it. Instead, I was stuck with Newton's rigid laws of the universe.

Or was I?

An idea crept into my mind. I'd spent the better part of my life trying to uncover God's hidden rules for the universe through the language of physics. Who was to say there wasn't a rule of physics as yet undiscovered? One that would help me with my pain and suffering over the loss of Lieserl.

Perhaps God had a rule He wanted me to find. Perhaps there was a purpose for my devastation. After all, Romans 8:18 said, "For I consider that the sufferings of this present time are not worth comparing with the glory that is to be revealed to us."

Where was the glory amid my grieving?

I stared at the station clock and the train waiting patiently beneath it. I sensed—no, I knew somehow, some way—that the answer lay before me. What was it?

The clock.

The train.

Lieserl.

In a rush, it came to me. What would happen if the train left the station not at sixty kilometers an hour but at close to the speed of light? What would happen to time? I ran through the calculations in my mind, roughing out a solution.

If the train left the station at rapid speeds approaching the speed of light, the clock's hands would still move, but the train would be moving so quickly that light could not catch up with it. The faster the train accelerated, the slower the hands would move, ultimately freezing once the train reached the speed of light. Time would effectively freeze. And if the train could go faster than the speed of light—an impossibility, but for argument's sake, assumed—then time might roll backward.

There it was. The new rule was so simple and natural. Newton's laws about the physical universe only applied to inert objects. No one needed to be bound by the old rules anymore. Time was relative to space. Time was not absolute. Not when there is motion.

This new law was so simple and natural. Elegant, even as it challenged Newton's physical laws that had held fast for hundreds of years and the new laws about light waves proposed by Maxwell. It was the sort of divine law for which I'd been searching my whole life. Why did God only allow me to see his handiwork after so much suffering?

But I did not have a train that traveled the speed of light or faster. I had no way to halt or roll back time. My newly uncovered law wouldn't bring Lieserl back.

CHAPTER 26

October 13, 1903
Bern, Switzerland

O N THIS OCCASION, ALBERT CAME TO THE BERN STATION. "Dollie," he cried out merrily as he lifted me down the final step from the train. "How your belly has grown in only two months!"

In truth, my belly was a little larger than when I'd left, although hardly big enough for the usually dreamy Albert to notice in normal circumstances.

I tried to smile as we left the station and hopped in a hansom cab to our apartment. I attempted to leave the sadness of Kać behind as I breathed in the familiar antiseptic smells of Bern—the crisp Swiss air with hints of evergreen, the freshly scrubbed laundry drying in the wind, the woodsy smell of freshly lit fireplaces. I struggled to focus on our new little girl, as Albert kept calling the baby in my belly, and his warm welcome home. I even endeavored to listen to his chatter about his boss, the director of the Swiss Patent Office, Friedrich Haller. I even nodded encouragingly when he said, "You'll see. I'll get ahead so we don't have to starve."

Very obviously, Albert was trying to divert the mood from

the melancholy loss of Lieserl to the more hopeful future. But I couldn't pretend for long. How could I act as if our beautiful daughter hadn't lived? How could I forget her horrible, pain-filled death?

My tears began falling as soon as we entered our apartment. When I left for Serbia, I'd hoped that when I next crossed the apartment's threshold, Lieserl would be in my arms. Instead, my arms hung unfilled at my sides—superfluous limbs.

"Oh, Dollie, it's not so bad as that!" Albert said, gesturing around the dusty, paper-strewn living room. "I tried to keep up on the cleaning, but your Johnnie doesn't have the knack. Anyway, I think a cluttered, busy house signals a cluttered, busy mind…and, well, I'll let you guess what I think a clean, empty house signals."

He smiled at me, those familiar crinkles appearing around his eyes. I reached up and stroked his cheek gently, wishing desperately that affection without sadness or anger would return to my bereft interior. Instead, the tears flowed again.

I let my hand drop down and ignored his beseeching eyes. Walking into the bedroom, I lay down on our bed, curling into a ball. I didn't even have the strength to remove my traveling coat or boots. I was so very tired and soul-sick. Albert stared at me for a long minute and then sunk down into the mattress at my side.

"What is it, Dollie?" He sounded genuinely perplexed, as if he'd expected me to bustle in from the train station and whip up a four-course dinner with a radiant smile.

"How can you not know?" I asked, not hiding my anger at his ignorance. When he didn't respond, I muttered, "You are a genius at everything but the human heart."

The loquacious Albert was rendered momentarily speech-less. Finally, incredibly, he guessed, "It's Lieserl, isn't it?"

I didn't answer. There was no need. My silence, broken only by sobs, answered for me. Albert looked over at me helplessly.

"I imagined her here with us, Albert," I tried to explain. "Every single day I was in this apartment with you, I was wait-ing for her to join us. Each time I passed a park or strolled to the market, I thought, 'I will bring my Lieserl here soon.' But that will never happen now."

Our bedroom was absolutely still for a long time but for the ticking of our bedside clock. Finally, Albert spoke. "I'm very sorry about what happened to Lieserl."

His mouth uttered the correct words of solace and consola-tion, but I couldn't hear any emotion in his voice. He sounded hollow and false, like an automaton.

It seemed I had a choice. I could cling to my fury at the unfairness of Lieserl's death and my anger at Albert for his incomprehension and selfishness. Or I could surrender my wrath and instead embrace hope for a new family life with this baby. The sort of life I'd wished for Lieserl.

Which path would I choose?

Inhaling deeply, I stilled my breathing and wiped my tears. I chose life. For a successful life with Albert, that meant choos-ing science. It was the language in which we first communi-cated and the only one Albert comprehended perfectly.

"I had a scientific epiphany, Johnnie," I said as I sat up.

"You did?" His flat eyes began to glimmer in the glow of the streetlights streaming in the window.

"Yes, in the Novi Sad train station. You know how we

have been struggling to reconcile Newton's physical laws with Maxwell's new theories on electromagnetism and light waves? How we've been trying to bridge the divide between Newton with his matter and Maxwell with his light waves?"

"Yes, yes," he exclaimed. "It's been confounding. Not just to us but physicists everywhere. What did you discover, Dollie?"

"I think that the notion of relativity—the one we've read about in Mach and Poincaré—might hold the answer. Relativity might bridge the gap between the theories of Newton and Maxwell, the new and the old. But only if we shift our understanding of space and time."

I explained to him the thought experiment I'd had in the Novi Sad train station. "The logical outcome is that the measurements of certain quantities—such as time—are *relative* to the velocity or speed of the observer, particularly if we assume that the speed of light is fixed for all observers. Space and time should be considered together and in relation to each other. In this way, Newton's classic laws of mechanical physics remain accurate but only in situations of uniform motion."

He gasped. "That's brilliant, Dollie. Brilliant."

Had he really just called me brilliant? It was a word Albert reserved for the great masters of physics—Galileo, Newton, and periodically a couple of the modern thinkers. And now me?

Rising from the bed, he started pacing around the bedroom. "It seems you've grieved for Lieserl thoughtfully, such that something extremely important has come out of it." Pride shone in his eyes, and I couldn't help but be pleased with myself, despite all my self-loathing over Lieserl.

"Shall we write a paper on your theory?" he asked, his eyes

sparkling. "Together, we could change the world, Dollie. Will you do this with me?"

A spark of excitement ignited within me, but guilt immediately dampened it. How dare I be pleased with Albert's reaction? How dare I long to research and write this theory? It was my daughter's death that inspired the insight and allowed me to see God's patterns in science. Yet, another voice argued, couldn't I write this theory in her memory so that her death was not in vain? Maybe this was the "glory" I was meant to uncover.

What was the right course?

I allowed my lips to form the words that my heart yearned to say. "Yes, Albert. I will."

CHAPTER 27

May 26, 1905
Bern, Switzerland

THE PAPERS AND BOOKS WERE HEAPED HIGH ON THE large rectangular table in our living room. This table, once burnished and scrubbed and ready for meals, had become the battered hub of our research, the place from which the spark of our creativity emanated, not unlike the spark of life between Adam and God depicted in Michelangelo's Sistine Chapel, we joked to ourselves. These papers were to be our own miracles.

Peering between the stacks, I made eye contact with Albert. Whispering to ensure that one-year-old Hans Albert stayed asleep, I said, "Johnnie, tell me what you think of this." Holding my paper close to the oil lamp, I read aloud to him from my paper on relativity: "Two events that appear concurrent when observed from one spot can no longer be considered concurrent when observed from another spot that is moving relative to it."

Albert puffed on his pipe, squinting at me through the haze of its smoke. A long pause ensued before he answered. "It's very good, Dollie."

I glanced down at my paper, pleased with Albert's reaction

and the sound of the words read aloud. "It captures well the notion of relativity, doesn't it? I wanted at least one sound sentence in the paper, separate from the thought experiment and the bolstering calculations, that would be understandable and quotable to a larger audience."

"That's wise, Dollie. This notion will reach wide, I think."

"You do? You're certain the wording isn't a mistake, Johnnie?" I asked. Although my theories on relativity were indeed simple at their core, the notion itself was hard to grasp—it completely contradicted prior learning—and the math was beyond the average person. I needed to be certain I'd boiled it down to its essence.

"We may need to play with the verbiage a bit, but when we're trying something new, there will be some mistakes along the way," he muttered distractedly. These days, Albert repeated this phrase fairly often. With my paper and the other two we were working on together, we were generating *many* new theories. Between us, we jested that not only were the papers a miracle, but it would take a miracle for people to accept their revolutionary notions.

"True enough." I slid two papers between a stack toward him. "Please take a final look at my calculations on the velocity of light and empty space."

"Dollie, we've gone over and over your calculations. They're magnificent. Anyway, you're the mathematician in the family, not me. It's you who I rely upon to correct my own numbers!" he cried out in mock exasperation.

"Shh," I said with a giggle. "You'll wake the baby." Albert was right. For the past eighteen months, we'd been working on three papers, although the relativity paper was largely my own. The others—an article on the quantum of light and the photoelectric effect, and another article on Brownian motion and atomic theory—were coauthored by both of us. On those two, Albert primarily drafted the theory while I handled the mathematics, although I was intimately familiar with every word and idea.

"We are just days away from submitting this paper to the *Annalen der Physik*. I want to make certain every detail is perfect."

"I know, my little sorceress," Albert said, and I smiled. It had been a long while since he'd called me his sorceress. The past two years of our marriage had been content enough, but the childish passions and frivolities had faded in the reality of daily living. "Anyway, we've run it by Besso too. I know he's not a certified physicist, but he's as smart as any of the jokers we went to school with. And he thinks it's sound."

I nodded. Albert reviewed our papers with Michele Besso, who had indeed served as an excellent sounding board. Given that Michele now worked at the Swiss Patent Office too, as a technical expert a grade above Albert, and that they walked home from work together every evening, Michele had ample time to consider our theories. I knew Albert was right, but my nature tended toward worry and exactitude.

He yawned. "Shall we call it a night, Dollie? I'm exhausted."

Funny that I didn't feel tired at all. I should have. I rose before Albert to make sure breakfast was ready when he and Hans Albert awoke. I spent the day cleaning and cooking and caring for our one-year-old, a cherubic but fatiguing little fellow. Once Albert arrived home, I hastened to serve dinner while he spent a precious few minutes tossing the baby about. After I cleared the dinner dishes and put Hans Albert down, more often than not, the Olympia Academy arrived, picking up the debate from where we had left it the night before, whether on Sophocles's play *Antigone*, David Hume's *A Treatise of Human Nature*, or Henri Poincaré's *Science and Hypothesis*. Only then, when the academy left, the baby was down, and the house was clean, did Albert and I sit down to our real work.

It was the time of day when I came alive.

Not that the rest of my day didn't hold pleasure. No, the birth of my sweet, brown-eyed Hans Albert had brought me great joy. Caring for him and undertaking with him all the activities I'd imagined with Lieserl—strolls to the market, walks through the park, even his nightly bathing ritual—had been a great balm for the scars left by Lieserl's death. As my feelings for Hans Albert, or Hanzerl, as we sometimes called him, grew, so my anger at Albert diminished. My contentment with our family and our little apartment at 49 Kramgasse, one of the most beautiful streets in Bern, ran deep. I adored strolling with Hans Albert down the lengthy Kramgasse, once part of the medieval city center, and pointing out to him the Zytglogge, Bern's famous clock tower, as well as the obelisk-adorned Kreuzgassbrunnen fountain, the Simsonbrunnen fountain with its sculpture of Samson and the lion, and the Zähringerbrunnen fountain that showed an armored bear. I had written of my joy to Helene, who, having read much of my sadness in recent years, replied with a confession of relief.

"You go to bed, Johnnie. I'll just read through this paper one last time, and then I'll join you." Bringing the oil lamp closer to me, I began to reread the familiar words for perhaps the hundredth time.

I felt Albert's hand on my shoulder, and I glanced up at

him. His eyes gleamed in the low light, and I sensed his pride at watching me toil away. I hadn't seen that expression from him in a long while. For a brief, blissful second, we beamed at each other.

"Our life is just as we promised each other in our student days, isn't it?" I asked him. "You used to say that we would work as students of science forever, so we don't turn into philistines. That prediction has finally come true."

He paused for an eternity of a moment and then said, "Quite right, my little ragamuffin." It was another name he hadn't used for some time. After gently stroking my hair for a moment, he whispered, "This is indeed our miracle year."

As I watched him amble down the hall to our bedroom, I smiled to myself. I had been right to return our relationship to the language of science; love followed in science's footsteps with Albert.

My eyes blurry from staring at the minuscule calculations, I smoothed down the cover of the paper: "On the Electrodynamics of Moving Bodies." Our names—Albert Einstein and Mileva Marić Einstein—shone beneath the title. The work was largely mine, but I understood that without my degree or doctorate, it must come with Albert's name as well.

My new theory on relativity had revealed that time may not have the same fixed qualities that Newton, along with nearly every other physicist and mathematician since him, once believed. But an even more ancient philosopher, Seneca, had certainly understood one aspect of time perfectly: "Time heals what reason cannot." Time and my work with Albert, in honor of Lieserl, had healed much.

CHAPTER 28

August 22, 1905
Novi Sad, Serbia

HELENE SQUEEZED MY ARM IN DELIGHT. OUR CHILDREN ran around the square in front of the Queen Elizabeth Café, where we sat sipping watery coffee. Thrilled by the little chase, Julka led the merriment, followed by Zora and finally, unsteadily toddling in their wake, Hans Albert. As they dodged in and out of passersby, it was all I could do to quell my protective instincts to jump up and prevent his fall, even though I knew Albert wasn't far behind them.

I glanced over at my friend, who was squinting into the bright summer sun. Deep vertical lines creased between her heavy, dark eyebrows, making her appear older than her years. Despite the worry evident on her brow, her blue-gray eyes were as soft and kindly as they'd always been.

I squeezed her arm back and said, "This time with you has been a gift, Helene."

"I agree, my old friend," Helene said with a satisfied sigh. "I'm so happy that you convinced us to come with you to Novi Sad."

Just two days ago, we'd stood crying on the banks of Lake Plitvice in the tiny resort village of Kijevo. Our husbands and children stood by, confused since we'd spent a blissful week in each other's company on holiday. "Why were you crying?" little Julka asked. Helene and I explained that we found the idea of parting hard to bear. What we didn't say was that the languid days at Lake Plitvice with water lapping at our feet, surrounded by low red hills and fields of green dotted with blue periwinkles and reveling in each other's easy company, had been almost too perfect. Our lives back on Kramgasse in Bern and Katanićeva Street in Belgrade, respectively, seemed bleak by comparison. A life of housework and the blank eyes of other housewives, women who found us odd and too academic for their household cares.

I made the case to Helene for an extension of our visit, but I didn't need to beg her. The invitation to join us in Novi Sad was accepted readily, for which I was now grateful. Having Helene, Milivoje, and their children with us made easier the awkward introduction of Albert to my parents in their Novi Sad home base. Mama and Papa had grown to accept Albert from afar, but shaking hands with the man who'd impregnated their daughter—and never visited their poor, late granddaughter— was quite another thing. The presence of Helene and her family and my parents' delight in meeting Hans Albert softened an otherwise challenging occasion.

"I think how we used to walk together every day along Plattenstrasse in Zürich completely carefree. At the time, I didn't know how wonderful that was," Helene said with a faraway expression on her face.

"I know. I often imagine that I'm studying in my little bedroom at the Engelbrecht Pension. Is it strange that I like to think of that time so often?"

"No," Helene answered with a wistful smile. "Do you ever wish we'd kept that pact?"

"Which pact?" As soon as I asked the question, I remembered. There had only ever been one pact between us; I simply hadn't considered it for some time.

"The one about dedicating ourselves to our studies and never marrying," she said.

The pact seemed so long ago, struck by an entirely different person. One who hadn't had her body riven in two—from the pain of childbirth and the inexorable suffering of child loss. That girl seemed so innocent, standing on the brink of limitless possibility, mercifully unaware that she would have to morph herself and sacrifice her ambitions to persevere in the world.

I stared at Helene. "I would be lying if I said there haven't been moments when I wished we'd stuck to the pact. Certainly, there were dark days when I was pregnant with Lieserl and terrified." My eyes welled up with tears. Helene was the only person in the world to whom I could speak openly about Lieserl. "But I would never have wished that my beautiful Lieserl did not exist, no matter the fear and pain. No matter the shortness of her life."

We held hands in silent understanding. Then, gesturing to our giggling children, I said, "And anyway, if we'd kept our pact, we would never have had this."

"True enough," Helene answered with a broad smile.

Just then, Hans Albert, finding his sea legs at fourteen

months and resembling nothing more than a young sailor on a swaying ship, fell to the ground with a cry. On instinct, I jumped up, but I wasn't fast enough. Albert raced from the nearby table where he was holding court on physics with a group of local students, swooped down, and hoisted Hans Albert on his shoulders.

"Albert should have two children on his shoulders, Helene. Lieserl would be three and a half now." I watched Albert march around the square with our son cackling away.

She squeezed my hand tightly. "How you bear it, I don't know."

"I don't. Just when I'm having a moment of joy with Hans Albert, Lieserl's absence fills the room like a black chasm. I try to channel that energy into work." I had told Helene about the work I was doing with Albert, the papers we were writing and the theory that Lieserl's death had spawned. I'd described the scientific partnership we'd formed and how it filled the void left by my own professional failures. I was on the verge of expressing my excitement over the publication of my paper in the esteemed journal *Annalen der Physik*—in just a few short weeks, I could hardly believe—when I stopped. I had no wish to make Helene, who had no such outlet for her history degree, feel badly.

Reaching for my coffee, I took a sip and changed the conversation's course. "How about you, Helene? Do you wish we'd kept to the pact?"

So complete was Helene's pleasure in her children, I expected an emphatic no. Instead, she said, "Lately, yes, although I wouldn't wish away my girls for anything in the world. You see, Milivoje and I are having troubles."

"No, Helene!" I exclaimed, accidentally putting my cup down too hard and spilling black coffee all over the marble tabletop. "You haven't mentioned anything in all these days together."

"Milivoje has always been within earshot, Mitza. Or the girls. I had to be careful."

"What has happened?"

Voice quavering, she whispered, "A certain distance has grown between us."

Before their engagement in Zürich, Milana, Ružica, and I had speculated about their match, wondering whether the brusque Milivoje could satisfy our gentle, intellectual Helene in the long term. But we'd kept our concerns to ourselves and decided not to mention it to her. Perhaps we'd been wrong to keep quiet.

"Oh no, Helene. What will you do?"

"What can I do?" She gazed at me with tears in her eyes and shrugged.

I didn't answer. What could I say? I knew, as did Helene, that she and the girls were dependent on Milivoje and that she would never do anything to jeopardize her children's welfare. Not only would it be hard for Helene to support herself and the girls on her own, but the stigma attached to divorced women was immense. Surely, some other sort of escape must be possible.

My mind raced with all sorts of arrangements, and I started to suggest that she and the girls come to Bern and live with us for a while when Papa approached our table. Helene and I had been so engrossed in our conversation that I hadn't noticed him crossing the square. He wasn't alone. He had Mrs. Desana Tapavica Bala in tow, the wife of the Novi Sad mayor.

Pushing back our black metal chairs with a swift scrape, Helene and I exchanged curtsies and greetings with Mrs. Bala. She looked me up and down, sizing me up as dispassionately as Mama would assess a side of beef at the market, and said, "Your father is proud of you, Mrs. Einstein. A physics degree, a successful husband, and a nice life in Switzerland. What father wouldn't be proud?"

I smiled over at Papa, whose chest had swelled at Mrs. Bala's compliment. Obviously, he was overstating my Swiss education, but I was relieved that after all the shame my parents suffered over Lieserl and my scholastic failures, they still felt a modicum of pride in me. Their strangely intelligent, "deformed" daughter had exceeded everyone's expectations, including their own. This was due in no small part to the fact that our secret from the Spire—the existence of Lieserl—had been kept.

"Do you ever get a chance to use your fancy education now that you have a son and husband to care for?" Mrs. Bala's tone and choice of words was strangely confrontational. Was she suggesting that my unusual education was useless in the face of the actual women's work I now did daily?

Mindful of Papa's eyes upon me, I squared my shoulders and said, "Actually, I do, Mrs. Bala. I work with my husband on all sorts of articles and studies. In fact, just before we left for Novi Sad, we finished some important work that will make my husband world famous."

Did I sound too boastful? Defensive? Mrs. Bala's scrutiny and her odd, challenging questions had made me prickly, but really, I wanted Papa to still see me as a *mudra glava*. Our busy visit home had left little opportunity for me to share my ongoing work with him.

"My, my. No wonder I overheard your husband saying, 'My wife is indispensable for many things, including my work. She is the mathematician in our family.'"

"He said that?" I blurted out and then immediately chastised myself. This wasn't the image I wanted to convey to Mrs. Bala or Papa.

"Oh yes." She gloated at my reaction. "In fact, he said that he bases his assessment of Serbia as a brilliant nation on what he knows about his wife."

I didn't make the mistake of showing surprise at Albert's comment again, but I couldn't stop myself from blushing. Thank God I'd returned our relationship back to the language of science. Albert and I had forged our early relationship upon its embers, and it continued to stoke our fires.

CHAPTER 29

September 26, 1905
Bern, Switzerland

O N OUR RETURN TO BERN, MY WORLD GREW SMALL
again. Housework, child care, science. Me, Hans Albert,
Albert. As if in a fixed gravitational loop, we circled each other
in a constant cycle.

I missed Helene terribly. The camaraderie, the keen understanding we shared, the empathy and total acceptance was
found nowhere else in my life. Not with the other hausfraus.
Not with my own family. Not even with Albert. I longed for the
return to my purest, truest self—the self of my youth—when I
was with her.

Instead, I spent the days in an anxious impersonation of
my life. Even while I was cleaning the apartment, caring for
Hans Albert, cooking meals, and mending Albert's clothes, I
was thinking about the fall publication of the relativity article
in the *Annalen der Physik* and waiting to see my name in print.
My mind could settle on little else but my tribute to Lieserl.

I returned to stalking the postman, a practice I'd abandoned
with Lieserl's death. Day after day, I trudged up the four flights

of stairs empty-handed but for the hefty Hans Albert. I had nearly given up when the bell rang. Wondering who would be calling—visitors almost never appeared until Albert's Olympia Academy friends arrived after dinner, as I'd never made friends with the Bern hausfraus—I hoisted the stocky Hans Albert onto my chest and hobbled down the stairs. Swinging the front door open, I stared into the wide eyes of the postman.

"Good afternoon, Mrs. Einstein. I'm guessing this is the package you have been waiting for?" He handed over a brown-paper-wrapped parcel, about the correct size and weight and bearing a German return address.

"It is," I cried out excitedly, hugging him. "I cannot thank you enough."

Bobbing respectfully, the postman scurried away. Used to Swiss stoicism, my unusual show of affection had unsettled him. It had astonished me too; I didn't even know the postman's formal name.

I could barely restrain myself from ripping open the packaging immediately. The very second Hans Albert and I entered the apartment and I settled him with his wooden stacking blocks, I tore into the package. The cover of the *Annalen der Physik* peeked out, and I pulled it from the tangle of twine. Flipping through the table of contents, I saw the listing for "On the Electrodynamics of Moving Bodies," with the author Albert Einstein listed next to it. The omission of my name left me unfazed; there was probably only enough room for one author in the table of contents, and Albert's name *was* listed first in the manuscript. As the only one of us with a formal degree, it was necessary.

Thumbing through the volume, I finally reached page 891.

There was the title I'd labored over so diligently—"On the Electrodynamics of Moving Bodies." It looked marvelous in print, even better than I'd hoped. My eyes scanned the rest of the page. Where was my name? I carefully processed each word of the article, but my name was nowhere to be seen. Mileva Marić Einstein didn't even appear in a footnote. Underneath the title was one author only: Albert Einstein.

How had this happened? Why would the editor have removed my name without consulting us? Was it because I was a woman? This went against every ethical code of scientific publication.

I sank to my knees. What had happened to my tribute to Lieserl? The article had been my way of making sense of her poor, short life and the many months I'd left her behind. I sobbed at the thought of my lost memorial to my secret daughter.

Hans Albert toddled over to me from his block stacking. Laying his warm, chubby body over me, he patted me softly on the back. "Mama," he said sadly, making me cry all the harder.

Hours later, Hans Albert sat up in the porcelain tub, merrily splashing water all over the kitchen. I rubbed the soapy washcloth over the soft folds of his arms and the chunky rolls of his legs. Delighted with his bath, he kicked his legs harder, spreading water all over the towels I'd set aside for him. For the first time in my life, I did not relish the gentle washing of my young son, usually one of my favorite activities of the day.

I couldn't get the betrayal by the editors of *Annalen der Physik* out of my mind.

Laying Hans Albert down to sleep, I finished preparing dinner and began waiting for Albert. Seven o'clock passed, then eight. Where was he? The Olympia Academy could be arriving any minute. Albert could be forgetful and easily distracted, but I'd never known him to arrive so late without giving me advance notice. Had something happened to him?

I paced the entryway of our little apartment. When I finally heard his key in the lock and I knew Albert was fine, I grabbed the copy of *Annalen der Physik* and met him at the threshold. I didn't bother with my usual polite greetings, or the normal pleasantries, or even questions about his tardiness. I spit out the words that had been building inside me all day.

"Albert, the article on relativity was published today, but you'll never believe what happened. It lists only you as the author. Can you believe that the editors would do that? We must write them and demand a correction."

Putting his fingers to his lips, Albert said, "Be quiet, Mileva. You'll wake Hans Albert."

His admonition shocked me. Albert never worried about Hans Albert's sleep. Only one explanation was possible.

"You knew," I whispered, backing away from him.

He walked toward me. "Listen, Dollie. It's not what you think. It's not as it seems."

"Is that why you were so late tonight? You were reluctant to come home. You knew that I'd be upset with what the journal has done."

He didn't answer, but the expression on his face told me I was correct.

I withdrew from him and backed away until I hit a wall in the living room. If I could have wormed my way into the plaster, I would have. Anything to get away from him. "How could you have let this happen? And not tell me? You know where that idea came from. You know how important it was to me to memorialize Lieserl by publicly authoring that article."

Flinching at the mention of Lieserl, he grabbed me by the forearms. "Listen, Dollie. Please. One of the editors of *Annalen der Physik* wrote me, asking questions about you and your credentials. I explained that you were my wife and fully trained as a physicist, even though you didn't have your degree. In his reply, I sensed hesitation."

"Did he ask you to remove my name?"

"No," he said slowly.

"*You* asked him to remove my name?" I was incredulous. But only in part. I suddenly remembered another time he'd removed my name from an article we'd coauthored. The one on capillaries, for the other Professor Weber.

Never loosing his grip of my arms, he nodded.

"How could you do that, Albert? For the other articles, I wouldn't have been happy, but I would have understood. But not for the relativity article. That was for Lieserl. You should have insisted."

"What does it matter, Dollie? Aren't we *Ein Stein*? One stone?"

In the past, Albert had often used this clever play on his last name to describe our "oneness." In my innocence, I'd allowed this fanciful image to color my decisions. How could I let this plea—that we are as one, that what benefits one benefits the other—sway me in the matter of Lieserl? Hadn't I already sacrificed enough for the "oneness" of our relationship? Didn't I deserve this one lasting tribute to my dead daughter?

Wrenching my arms out of his hands, I said, "Albert, we may be *Ein Stein*, but it has become clear that we are of two hearts."

CHAPTER 30

August 4, 1907, and March 20, 1908
Lenk, Switzerland, and Bern, Switzerland

WITH THIS MACHINE, WE WOULD BE ABLE TO MEASURE very small amounts of energy," Albert announced to the brothers Messrs. Paul and Conrad Habicht over a strong pot of coffee at the inn restaurant. The brothers had traveled from Bern to the inn near Lenk where Albert, Hans Albert, and I were holidaying for ten days in August. Albert and I had an idea for an invention, and he hoped to refashion the Olympia Academy without Maurice, who had moved to Paris, to help us create it.

"Why would we want to do that?" Paul asked. The brother of an original Olympia Academy member, Paul, as a talented machinist, was more practical than his theoretical sibling Conrad. His practicality made for lively discussions during the Olympia Academy meetings that he had occasionally attended over the years.

"To record tiny electrical charges, of course," Albert answered dismissively.

Paul still looked confused, so I tried to clarify. "The *Maschinchen* would permit us to amplify minuscule amounts of energy and measure them, which would help scientists everywhere assess various molecular theories." Conrad was used to my comments during our frequent Olympia Academy meetings—including my translations for the often terse Albert—but I wasn't certain that Paul would be as receptive. I never knew how a particular man would react to a woman speaking the language of science.

"Ah," Paul said, finally comprehending the link between the machine and one of the great debates among physicists: what was the precise "stuff" of our world. He seemed comfortable with my involvement; perhaps his brother had prepared him, or maybe my brief remarks at Olympia Academy meetings had readied him.

Conrad chimed in, understanding the lucrative nature of the undertaking. "Every lab would want one."

"Exactly," I said with a smile.

I passed Hans Albert to Albert and unrolled the rough sketches I had made of the *Maschinchen*, primarily electrical formulas and circuitry diagrams. I reviewed the plans with the brothers and proposed a schedule for the work. Albert had somehow secured a spare room in a local Bern gymnasium where we could cobble the machine together.

"You will work on this with us?" I offered a silent prayer to the Virgin Mary as the brothers glanced at one another. I didn't invoke Mary often—without Mama around, I'd become unaccustomed to the ritual—but when I really wanted something, she came to mind. Albert and I were all theory and little practicality; we needed the Habicht brothers to make the *Maschinchen* a reality.

"We will share the profits?" Paul asked.

"Of course. Twenty-five percent each," I said. "If you agree, I will consult a lawyer to draw up an agreement. Once we finalize the device, Albert will take charge of getting the patent filed. He has some expertise in that field, of course," I said with a smile at Albert.

Albert grinned back, visibly pleased at my finesse with the brothers. While he had apologized for the painful omission of my name in our four 1905 papers in the *Annalen der Physik*— the relativity article in particular—my forgiveness didn't come from his mere proffered words. An invitation to work was the key to unlocking my absolution, Albert finally learned after months of silence from me. This *Maschinchen* project, conceived by us both over the past year, with wide berth given for my leadership, was the only form of amends I would accept. In this way, Albert's words of remorse were finally accepted. And, in theory, I forgave him.

⌘

Months after our meeting in Lenk, I stood before Albert and the Habicht brothers, waiting to see the fruits of that conversation. Albert rubbed the stubble that had grown on his chin over the long March weekend which he'd spent holed up with Conrad and Paul working on the machine. His face had thinned recently, hollowing out his pudgy cheeks. He suddenly looked older, not at all the student I'd once known.

The back room we'd seconded from the local Bern gymnasium was littered with wires, batteries, sheet metal, and a host of unidentifiable parts, not to mention the detritus of used coffee cups and tobacco that had accumulated over the months since the summer. Setting Hans Albert down in a seemingly safe corner, I examined the machine.

The cylinder finally resembled my sketches. After seven months of evening labor, once their day jobs came to an end, Albert, Paul, and Conrad had finally tinkered the *Maschinchen* into being. The men had summoned me for the momentous occasion of testing the device.

"Shall we try it?" I asked them.

Albert nodded, and Paul and Conrad began hooking up wires and setting switches. Then Albert started the machine. Sputtering at first, with a steady stream of smoke emanating from one of the electrical leads, the machine began to work.

"The two conducting plates made the charge, and the strips actually measured them. It works!" I cried out.

The men clapped each other on the back and bowed in my direction. Just as Conrad reached for a dusty bottle of wine hidden behind a pile of wires, the *Maschinchen* made a horrible screeching sound. And suddenly stopped.

The men hastened to the device and played with wires for what seemed like an hour. As I bounced Hans Albert on my lap to keep him entertained for just a little longer—it was well past the little fellow's bedtime—I said, "I suppose we were premature on the congratulations."

Paul looked up at me. "Why do you say that?"

I gestured to the still smoking *Maschinchen*.

"This is nothing. Just some faulty insulation. We'll fix it in no time."

"Truly?" I asked, relieved.

"Truly," Conrad answered for his brother. "Once we get it running consistently, we will file the patent application right away. Albert already has most of the application finished, including the blueprints. Right, Albert?"

Albert hadn't mentioned this to me. I was surprised at his speed, but then, this must be what he'd been working on in the gymnasium workroom while the Habicht brothers assembled the machine. I knew Albert wasn't as skilled on the practical side as Paul and Conrad.

"Can we take a look at the patent filing, Albert?" Conrad asked.

Albert, his hair a wild, dusty mess around his face, glanced up as if he'd forgotten I was there. "Surely," he said and stood up. Sorting through a table covered with electrical parts, he pulled out a disorganized pile of papers.

"Here it is. It's still rough, but this is the general idea," he said, spreading out the sheets before me and the Habichts.

The sketches were an exact replica of the machine as it had evolved, and the descriptive verbiage necessary for the filing was precise. Paul and Conrad suggested a few minute changes, but otherwise, they expressed pleasure at the draft. I made no remarks, as the patent particulars were outside my expertise. All seemed in order. Now we just had to ensure the proper working of the *Maschinchen* before we actually submitted the filing.

"Why isn't Mileva's name on the patent filing?" Paul asked Albert, a quizzical expression on his face.

I stared at the papers again. Surely, Paul was wrong; Albert would not commit such a grievous sin twice. Not after the months of silence he had endured. My name must be on the filing somewhere. Scanning the page containing the applicants' information, I saw that Paul was right. Nowhere was the name "Mileva Einstein" listed.

How dare Albert?

The room grew still. Albert, Paul, and Conrad understood the offense and waited uncomfortably for my response. Even the typically frenetic Hans Albert didn't move, as if he felt the unusual tension in the room.

I wanted to rage at Albert for his thoughtlessness and cowardice. Surely, he could have predicted my reaction, if he had even given me a second thought. Had he been too scared to talk to me directly about the applicants he'd listed? Did he really prefer this public vetting? If Albert would have raised the issue with me in private, explained that the patent would fare better without an uncredentialed woman on the applicant list, I wouldn't have been happy, but I would have appreciated that he cared enough about me and my feelings to spare me embarrassment in front of Paul and Conrad.

I wasn't going to let Albert humiliate me, privately or publicly. Not again. I forced a smile upon my face, and as if I'd known about the omission of my name all along, I calmly said, "Why should my name be listed, Paul? Albert and I are *Ein Stein*—one stone."

"Of course," Paul said too quickly.

Albert said nothing.

Very pointedly, I stared at Albert. As my mouth moved to form the words, I felt something pure and trusting harden within me. "Are we not of one stone, Albert?"

CHAPTER 31

June 4, 1909
Bern, Switzerland

Albert and I slowly began to ignite the world of physics in the months after we received our patent on the *Maschinchen*, the invention I'd hoped would bring us a steady income. Letters from physicists around Europe began to pour into our Bern apartment on Kramgasse. But none of the letters contained requests for the *Maschinchen*, which was struggling for acceptance in labs. Instead, once Europe's most esteemed physics professor Max Planck began teaching relativity to his students, other physicists began inquiring about the four articles we'd published in the *Annalen der Physik* in 1905, my article on relativity in particular. Not that any of the letters came for me, since my contribution had been erased. No, the letters all came for Albert.

Like a spider, Albert became busy building a name for himself in the center of the intricate web of European physicists. Offers to write more articles and comment on others' theories for various journals began to appear. Invitations to physics conferences and convocations formed piles around the apartment.

Strangers started stopping him in the Bern streets when they learned who he was. But Albert's new web lacked a sticky foothold for me and Hans Albert. We became merely the tree branches to which the web was attached.

Day after day, I tended to the house, cared for Albert and Hans Albert, and even took in student boarders to live in our two spare rooms, cooking and cleaning for them too. The extra work exacerbated my already aching legs and hips, which had never really recovered from Lieserl's birth, but I did it without complaint, because I was waiting for Albert to invite me back into the secret world of physics we'd once wrapped around ourselves. Since the Olympia Academy had unofficially disbanded when Maurice relocated to Strasbourg, France, and Conrad returned to Schaffhausen, only Albert could invite me into that world again. I conjectured that if I freed him from financial worry through the student boarders, he could begin theorizing again, and an invitation would ensue. It angered me that I had to take such measures, but there was no other avenue for me to return to science.

But no true invitation came in the months after we completed our work on the *Maschinchen*. Albert was no longer available for collaboration, no matter how well I freed his time to focus. Occasionally, as he responded to letters from physicists on the four *Annalen der Physik* articles or drafted reviews of others' articles for scientific journals, he requested emergency consultation in the nuances of the relativism theory or mathematical calculations. I kept myself ready for his invitation by reading the latest journals and studying the textbooks Albert left at home, but we slowly lost the language of science that we once spoke to one another. Childish chatter to Hans Albert and worried mutterings over our finances took the place of those sacred conversations.

The trusting part of me that had hardened during the *Maschinchen* patent omission solidified further, and the spark of hope that Albert and I might rekindle our scientific projects transformed into a flame of anger instead. Only to Helene could I confess my feelings, that fame had left Albert with little interest in his wife, that I worried his desire for notoriety would overtake any humanity remaining within him.

I had become the philistine hausfrau I never wanted to be. The sort Albert had always mocked. This wasn't the bohemian life I wanted, but what choice had he left me?

Hope for our relationship—marital and scientific—came in the form of a job offer. On the heels of his growing acclaim in the physics world, Albert received the professorial position he'd sought since our school days. He was asked to be a junior physics professor at the University of Zürich after a protracted debate among the professors over his Jewish heritage and a rocky conclusion that he didn't exhibit the more "troubling" Jewish traits. We planned to settle there some months before the winter term began in October. I began praying again to the Virgin Mary, this time for a fresh start in the city of our school days. The city of a very different Mileva.

The packing for Zürich was left to me, of course, while Albert finished up his days at the patent office. One day, after I busied the studious five-year-old Hans Albert with the piano, I turned to the heaping mass of papers Albert had strewn about the dining room table, kitchen counters, and bedroom floor, including piles of documents he had begun to bring home from his patent job. It was like a trail from "Hansel and Gretel." I began to organize the articles, notes, and other assorted papers into categorical piles.

It was then that I saw it. A postcard stuck out from between two pages of an article Albert had been sent for review.

> *Dear Professor Einstein,*
>
> *I hope you will indulge a congratulatory note from an old girlfriend that you may well have forgotten in the ensuing years. If you will recall, I am the sister-in-law of the owner of the Hotel Paradise in Mettmenstetten, and we spent several weeks in each other's company one summer ten years ago. I noticed an article in our local Basel newspaper about your appointment as extraordinary professor of theoretical physics at the University of Zürich, and I wanted to wish you well in your new role. I often think of you, and I treasure the weeks we spent together in our youth at the Paradise hotel.*
>
> *Best wishes with all my heart,*
> *Anna Meyer-Schmid*

I almost laughed at the cloying, sentimental note. I'd grown accustomed to Albert receiving adulatory notes from scientists and lay people alike; I was always cleaning them up around the apartment. A note from an old girlfriend was a first, but perhaps I'd raise it as a little joke over dinner.

I continued with the sorting when I came across another postcard in the same handwriting.

Dear Professor Einstein:

How wonderful to receive such a rapid reply! I never expected that a man of your reputation and busy schedule would have the time to respond so quickly to a simple Basel housewife. I am surprised and delighted that you recall fondly the weeks in Paradise. What a wonderful invitation you've extended to meet you at your offices in Zürich once you are settled. I would be very honored to see the professor in his new offices. I will send dates for our rendezvous.

With all my heart,
Anna Meyer-Schmid

My heart began racing. Albert had written back to this woman. In his reply, he must have invited her to visit him in Zürich. This was no joke I'd be raising over dinner. This was the beginning of an affair.

Outrage simmered within me. I had suppressed my own ambitions, even sacrificed some of the little time I had with my daughter, for Albert. To tend to his wishes and desires. He had become my life, my pathway to love and work, even if he was blocking that route at the moment. The blood of bandits, as Papa would say, began to boil within me. If Albert thought that I would hand him over to some Basel hausfrau without a battle, he was wrong.

I picked up a pen and a sheet of paper. Addressing a letter to Mr. Georg Meyer, the woman's husband, at the address she helpfully provided, I described to him what his wife had begun: "Your wife has written a suggestive letter to my husband—"

The door slammed. I hadn't expected Albert back so early. I started to hide the postcards and letter I was drafting, then thought the better of it. Why should I hide? I wasn't the one who'd done something wrong.

When Albert called for me, I responded, "I'm in the bedroom," and continued writing my letter.

I heard the clop of his footsteps, and then his voice. "What are you doing, Dollie?"

I answered without looking at him. "Writing a letter to Anna Meyer-Schmid's husband about the exchange between you two."

After a long pause, in a quivering voice, he said, "What are you talking about?" As if he did not know.

"In my packing, I came across two postcards from Mrs. Meyer-Schmid in which it seems you two have arranged a rendezvous in Zürich. I thought Mr. Meyer had a right to know."

"It's not what it seems," he stammered.

"I believe I've heard that excuse before." I continued writing, my eyes locked on the page. I feared that if I saw his face, I would soften.

"Really, Dollie. Her note seemed innocent to me—the congratulations of an old friend—and I don't know what led her to write another letter."

"You didn't invite her to visit you in Zürich in your reply?"

"Only in the most general way, as I would to any friend."

"Good, I'm glad to hear that." I did not believe him. I recognized the bluster in his voice too well for that. "Then you won't mind if I explain that to Mr. Meyer."

He launched into me. "How dare you make this so public, Mileva?"

"How dare I? How dare *you* arrange an assignation with an old girlfriend! And how *dare* you express frustration at me!"

He grew quiet. "It's not what it seems."

"You've already said that. So you should have no objection to me sending this letter."

Silence filled the room as fully as a scream. I knew why Albert was desperate for me to *not* send the letter—because he was lying to me. I had to call his bluff and end this relationship before it began. This time, I looked directly at him and held his gaze. But I said nothing. I simply waited.

"Go ahead, Mileva, send the letter. You create problems at the most important times in my life. First, by having a baby when I was about to get the patent office job, and now, just as I'm finally about to start my university professorship. You only ever think of yourself."

CHAPTER 32

August 14, 1909
Engadine Valley, Switzerland

L ET ME TAKE HIM FROM YOU, DOLLIE," ALBERT SAID AS
he lifted the sleepy Hans Albert from my arms.

I almost said no, just like I'd almost said no to this entire
trip. I'd resisted Albert's thoughtful show of niceties—his
manner of apology for Anna Meyer-Schmid—since we arrived
in the Engadine Valley for our summer holiday. But my leg and
hip ached with the grade of the climb and the weight of Hans
Albert in my arms, so I relented.

The hill grew steeper as we neared the flat apex. The final
crest was almost unbearably precipitous, and I nearly stopped.
I pushed myself along on the waves of my ongoing anger
over Anna Meyer-Schmid and Albert's hateful words. No
more weakness.

I could no longer accept Albert's grand shows of affection—
this holiday as compensation for his flirtations with Anna
Meyer-Schmid, the *Maschinchen* project as atonement for his
omission of my name on the 1905 paper on relativity—instead
of what he knew I wanted in the way of amends. Work. I

withdrew into the shell of my exterior, like the mollusk I'd once stopped myself from becoming. That hard, protective layer was necessary to survive the turbulent waters that were my relationship with Albert.

The beautiful Engadine Valley spread out before me, giving me momentary relief from my inner turmoil. The azure River En cut through the verdant valley, turning the high mountainous peaks into a dramatic snowcapped backdrop. Picturesque spire-laden towns dotted the valley, and trails cut through the hills like swooping paint strokes. I knew why Albert brought me here: to reawaken old memories and loving affection. Feelings that seemed like faraway memories. Feelings that would make me forget about his failings.

Albert laid the sleeping Hans Albert down on a soft, mossy patch of green, pulling off his jacket and tucking it around our son. Turning away before he caught me staring, I gazed back out at the vista. Albert walked over to my side and placed an arm around me. I stiffened at his touch.

"The headwaters of the Rhine River are over that ridge, Dollie." Albert pointed into the distance.

I made no movement. Did he think he could sway me with a simple "Dollie"? I wasn't the guileless girl I'd once been.

"The Maloja Pass is just there." Albert pointed to a cleft in between two mountains. "It links Switzerland and Italy."

I did not answer.

"It is only a few miles from the Splügen Pass. Do you remember our day there?" He wrapped his other arm around me and bored his eyes into mine. I met his gaze, but still I wouldn't speak.

"Remember how we called it our bohemian honeymoon?" Albert said.

The reference to our "bohemian honeymoon" was a misfire. The mere mention of our time in Como conjured up images of Lieserl, the two-year wait until our actual wedding and honeymoon, and the destruction of my career. It hardly enticed.

"What *is* this quiet all about, Dollie?"

I heard the first pangs of frustration in his voice. How dare he be frustrated with me? I'd clung to silence, but how could I let such a stupid question go unanswered? "I think you know, Albert."

"Listen, Dollie. I made a mistake. Mrs. Meyer-Schmid's card stirred up old feelings from my youthful holidays in Mettmenstetten, and I overreacted in my response to her. I don't know what more I can say but that I regret it."

My anger stemmed from more than his attempted dalliance with Anna Meyer-Schmid, although that had inflicted a deep enough wound. "Do you regret your harsh words to me too?"

"Harsh words?"

How could he have forgotten?

"You don't really believe that the pregnancy with Lieserl was some sort of hysteria I manufactured as you were starting your patent job, do you?" I asked.

His arms dropped to his side, and he grew quiet. "No, I don't, Mileva. If I said that, I didn't mean it."

"You do realize how difficult that pregnancy was for me? Unmarried and alone, no prospects for a future career, bearing a child? Having Lieserl changed my life. For better and worse."

I had never spoken to Albert of Lieserl so bluntly. At the time, I'd been too afraid of losing him. Or of losing Lieserl.

"Yes, yes, of course." He answered too quickly. I sensed that he didn't truly understand the impact the pregnancy had on my life, that he just wanted peace from me and would say whatever he thought I wanted to get it.

He must have sensed the dissonance between us, because he wrapped his arms around me again and said, "Dollie, can we please make this move to Zürich a fresh start? A new beginning of love and work and collaboration?"

Collaboration? Albert knew my susceptibilities. I allowed myself to stare into his coffee-brown eyes. Within their liquid depths, I swear I saw a different future. Or perhaps I saw what I wanted to see.

I longed to say yes, to believe in Albert, but I couldn't be so foolhardy. "Do you promise that we will work together again? That in Zürich, you will make time for the sort of physics projects we created for the *Annalen der Physik*? The articles that have made you so famous and secured you this new Zürich job?" I needed to remind him on whose back he climbed for the heights he now inhabited.

He blinked but didn't waver. "I promise."

Did I believe him? Did it matter? I had my vow and couldn't hope for more. So I said, "Yes, Zürich can become our fresh start."

CHAPTER 33

October 20, 1910, and November 5, 1911
Zürich, Switzerland, and Prague, Czechoslovakia

T HE FAMILIAR CHARMS OF ZÜRICH WORKED THEIR MAGIC
on me from the very beginning. The aroma of coffee and
evergreens in the air, the animated chatter of students in cafés
batting about the latest notions of the day, and the allure of
strolls through the ancient streets and along the banks of the
Limmat River transformed me back into a younger, livelier version of myself. I became the hopeful Mitza of my youth, even
when Albert failed to keep his promise of undertaking a project
with me.

In lieu of a project with Albert, I found a surprising outlet
for my scientific longings. By happy coincidence, we discovered that a Polytechnic graduate who started the mathematics
and physics program after our departure and was now assistant to the head of the University of Zürich's physics program, Friedrich Adler, and his wife; Katya Germanischkaya,
a Lithuanian-born Russian who studied physics at the
Polytechnic after we left, had an apartment in our building
on Moussonstrasse. We became fast friends with the couple,

sharing meals with them and their young children, music, and scientific and philosophical discussions. My satisfaction became even more complete when I learned I was pregnant, a state for which I'd prayed for years. For a time, we inhabited the blissful bohemian world of which Albert and I once dreamed—as long as I didn't allow myself to reflect on his broken promises of work.

But then, a mere six months after our arrival, just as I'd gotten fully settled back into Zürich life, Prague began calling. The prestigious German University of Prague dangled before Albert a full physics professorship and the accompanying position of director of the Institute of Theoretical Physics. I knew this to be an irresistible carrot for him. Double the money, a full professorship instead of his junior professor status, and the head of a theoretical physics institute—how could he resist? Still, I begged him not to take us away from our happy life in Zürich, particularly when our second son Eduard was born on July 28, 1910. Tete, as we called him, emerged into the world very sickly, suffering from one childhood infection after another and sleeping very little. I worried how he would fare in Prague, notorious for pollution as industrialization increased in the ancient city. For nearly a year, Albert acquiesced to my wishes and declined the job, although his displeasure grew.

I sought to alleviate his discontent by expanding our world beyond the Adlers and arranging regular Sunday evenings of music with Polytechnic professor Adolf Hurwitz and his family. I wanted to remind him of the lure of Zürich and reconnect us through our shared love of music. But nothing helped his darkening mood.

His desire for the Prague job soured him on Zürich. And because of my resistance to Prague, his feelings toward me soured further.

One crisp autumn afternoon, the fall sun reflecting off the Limmat River in the distance, a large envelope arrived in the mail. It was addressed to Albert in formal script and bore a Swedish return address. Who could be writing Albert from Sweden? I didn't think his notoriety had spread that far.

Climbing up the stairs, I placed baby Tete in his bassinet and settled Hans Albert with a book. Because I handled the family finances and, consequently, all correspondence fell to me, I sliced open the letter, even though it was addressed to Albert. To my astonishment, the letter came from the Nobel Prize Committee. It informed Albert that Nobel Prize chemistry laureate Wilhelm Ostwald had nominated him for the Nobel Prize based on the 1905 paper on special relativity.

I lowered myself to the couch, my hand trembling. My paper was being nominated for the Nobel Prize? No matter how many accolades the paper had already garnered, this tribute was beyond my wildest speculation. Even if no one ever learned of my role in the creation of the relativity theory, I felt a certain sense of peace that Lieserl's death yielded this magnanimous laurel.

Admittedly, a tiny part of myself smarted that no recognition would fall to me. But when I realized that this award might be exactly what I needed, I tucked away my disappointment. Perhaps the Nobel Prize nomination would soften the loss of the Prague position and make staying in Zürich more palatable for Albert. Maybe he would realize that to climb to scientific heights, he didn't need to leave Zürich.

That evening, I waited for Albert by the door with the letter and two congratulatory glasses of red wine, one for each of us. And I waited.

Nearly two hours after his usual arrival time home, he finally arrived. Instead of chiding him for his lateness, I smiled and handed him the wine and the letter.

"What's this?" he asked gruffly.

"I think you'll be pleased."

As his eyes scanned the pages, I stretched out my glass, ready to toast him when he finished reading. Without clinking his glass to mine, he tossed back the proffered wine and muttered, "So the old boys are finally recognizing me."

Recognizing "me"? Had he really just said that? As if he'd forgotten my authorship of the paper now in contention for the Nobel Prize. As if he'd rewritten history in his own mind such that he'd actually created the article himself. I didn't know what to say; his statement stunned me. It was one thing to present the special relativity theory to the world as his own, but it was quite another thing to pretend to be its creator to me.

"You are happy that the committee is recognizing *your* paper?"

"Yes, Mileva, I am." His eyes dared me to say more.

If I was stunned before, I was dumbfounded now.

Abruptly, he asked, "Is dinner ready?"

I realized then I had become only a hausfrau to Albert. Mother of his children. Cleaner of his home. Launderer of his clothes. Preparer of his meals. There would never be anything more.

These were the only crumbs Albert had left for me. Yet he seemed to loathe me for accepting his scraps.

I had a choice. I could leave Albert and take the children

with me, destroying forever their chance of a normal family life and exposing them to the reputational stigma emanating from divorce, all because their father abandoned his promise to me. Or I could stay and try to fashion the best home life for them, walking away from the dream of a scientific partnership with Albert. A partnership, if I was truthful with myself, whose time had passed long ago. Either way, there was no hope of another collaboration. Only the happiness of my children. Certainly not myself. And all of that was dependent on Albert and his satisfaction.

As Albert walked to the dining room and sat at the table, ready for me to serve him dinner, I said, "Albert?"

"Yes?" he asked without bothering to turn back to me.

"I think we should go to Prague."

⊂⊗⊃

Black industrial soot clogged the Prague air, and it settled on me like a deep depression. I felt as if I were swimming through sludge when I made my way through the dense warren of Prague streets with the boys. The unpleasantness of the city's atmosphere was mirrored by the attitudes of its ethnically Germanic rulers and elite, whose rumored dislike of Slavic people and Jews was confirmed from the start. The mounting political instability in Austro-Hungary of which Prague was a part, as relations between the Ottoman Empire and Austro-Hungary continued to break down and the Serbs tried to create a nation for Southern Slavs within the Austro-Hungarian borders, only reinforced their adherence to their Germanic roots. They wanted to distance themselves from Slavs at all costs. How could I create the home life I'd decided upon in this setting?

Still, I tried. When brown water began running from the taps in our apartment in the Smíchov district on Třebízského Street, I traipsed to a fountain up the street and hauled cooking water into our apartment, boiling it before use. When bedbugs and fleas infested our bedding, I made a grand show of heaping the beset items in a bonfire and exchanging the mattresses and dour blankets with brightly colored replacements. I turned the boys' attention away from the lack of fresh milk, fruit, and vegetables and refocused them on the plentiful music available in concert halls and churches and the city's exquisite architecture, particularly the famous town clock that sat above the Old Town Hall.

I stopped clamoring for work from Albert and tried to mold myself into the hausfrau role that he'd left for me. Yet Albert wasn't present very often to witness my efforts. Theoretical work, teaching, and conferences filled his days, and nights out became his mainstay, leaving the boys and I alone for weeks. The only evidence of his continued presence was trails of clothes on the floor or the sound of his voice lecturing to colleagues in the living room late at night, after the Café Louvre had finally kicked them out or the weekly salon at Mrs. Berta Fanta's home on Old Town Square closed down.

It wasn't constant marginalization. Albert would sense that I'd reached the limits of his neglect and show up for a few family dinners. He'd toss the boys in the air and tickle them, and once, he even hinted at collaboration. "Should we return to relativity, Dollie? Should we explore the connection that gravity might have to relativity?" The next day, it was as if he'd never spoken the words. I tried not to let it bother me.

Sometimes, I wanted to give up, but I needed to stay stalwart for Hans Albert and Tete. I shared the toll on my self-esteem only with Helene, telling her how starved I was for kindness and affection, how alone I felt, and how thankful I was to have her in my life. Only with her could I be my true self.

I thought I was bearing it with a certain outward grace when I caught sight of myself in the mirror one afternoon. "Who is that woman?" I asked myself as I stared at my own reflection.

Broad hips from bearing children, the still trim waist hidden under the voluminous folds of an ugly housedress. Thickened nose and lips, coarsened brow. Once-lustrous skin and hair now dull. I was only thirty-six, but I looked fifty. What had happened to me? Was my neglected appearance one of the reasons Albert had turned away from me?

Just as my eyes began to well with tears, a loud, barking cough came from Tete's bedroom. Creaking open his door quietly so as not to wake him from his nap, I stared down at my youngest son. With his dark hair and soulful brown eyes, he resembled his older brother, but his constitution was quite different. Where Hans Albert had always been a sturdy lad, Tete was delicate, always catching the latest illness. Unclean Prague had been hard on him.

His cheeks looked flushed, so I placed my hand on his forehead. He was burning up. Fear bubbled up within me. I ran out to the desk, wrote a note to the doctor, and then, asking a neighbor to watch Tete for a moment, I raced out to the street to summon a messenger. Within the hour, a doctor knocked on our door.

"Thank you so much for coming, Doctor. You were quicker

than I imagined." I had waited eight hours for a doctor the last time Tete came down with a fever, so I had expected a long, anxious wait.

"I was just in the building next door. There's been an outbreak of typhoid, you see," he explained.

My heart beat wildly. Typhoid? Tete had managed to survive countless colds, ear infections, and even a bout of pneumonia, but typhoid? His constitution was far too weak.

The doctor saw the terror in my eyes. He took my hands and said, "Please let me examine him, Mrs. Einstein. He may simply have one of the many flus I've seen around Prague. It may not be typhoid at all."

I led him into Tete's room, thankful that Hans Albert was still at school, and watched as the doctor examined my listless son. Whispering the Hail Mary to myself over and over, I prayed for a common cold or one of the recurrent ear infections to which Tete was so prone.

"I don't think it's typhoid, Mrs. Einstein. I believe that your little boy has some other sort of infection, however. He's going to need ice baths to bring his fever down and close watching. Can you manage that?"

I nodded gratefully, made the sign of the cross, and leaned down to smooth Tete's hair. For a moment, I saw Lieserl's flushed, feverish face burrowed into the sheets, and my heart stopped. *This isn't Lieserl*, I reminded myself. *This is Tete, and he will survive. And this is not scarlet fever or typhoid but a typical flu.* Yet I also knew that I couldn't continue to expose the children to Prague's contaminated water, air, and food. We needed to get out of Prague.

Three days after Tete's scare, Albert returned home from the Solvay conference in Brussels, a prestigious gathering of twenty-four of the brightest scientific minds in Europe. I took special care with my appearance that evening. Then, without mentioning Tete's illness or exerting pressure upon him of any kind, I gave him dinner and let him relax with his pipe to tell Hans Albert and me stories about the event. Albert had been so distant since we arrived in Prague, it was a relief to watch his animated face and hear about the conference. All the physics luminaries were there, the ones we'd been reading and discussing for decades—Walther Nernst, Max Planck, Ernest Rutherford, Henri Poincaré, and the like. But it wasn't these old-school scientists who impressed him; he was drawn to the new band of Parisian physicists, Paul Langevin, Jean Perrin, and the famous Madame Marie Curie, who had won the Nobel Prize herself while they were in Brussels.

I had questions about Madame Curie; she'd long been a hero of mine, and I admired the scientific partnership she and her late husband had formed, the sort of relationship I once thought I'd have with Albert. Yet as his stories continued and the hours ticked by—hours in which Tete's disturbing coughing must have become apparent even to the often oblivious Albert—my impatience grew. At the two-hour mark, after I put Hans Albert to bed and checked on Tete, I plunged in and asked him the dreaded question. "Albert, do you think that there's any way we could leave Prague? Return to Zürich or move to any other healthier European city?"

He paused, a deep furrow appearing between his brows. "That sounds awfully bourgeois of you. I know Prague doesn't have the comforts or sophistication of Zürich or even Bern, but it's been quite the opportunity for me. It's quite a selfish ask, Mileva."

Mileva? I didn't think he had called me Mileva since we had first eschewed the formal "Miss Marić and Mr. Einstein" all those years ago in Zürich. Putting aside my concern at the use of "Mileva" and his unkind labels of "bourgeois" and "selfish," I said, "I'm not asking for me, Albert. It's for the children. I am worried about the effect of Prague on their health, Tete's in particular. We had quite a scare while you were in Brussels."

"What do you mean?"

"Tete became very sick last week. We suspected typhoid from the contaminated Prague water."

"I thought you'd been getting water from the fountain and boiling it."

"It wasn't enough, unfortunately."

He didn't speak. He didn't even ask how Tete was faring.

I got down on my knees before him. "Please, Albert. For the children."

As he stared at me with his dark brown eyes, I wondered how he saw me. Did he see only my haggard face and thick hips? Or did he remember the quick intellect and deep affection as well? The Dollie he'd once loved.

His face expressed no sympathy or concern, only disgust. "I've been prolific in Prague, Mileva. You are asking me to give that up." Albert stood up suddenly, causing my balance to waver, and I fell back on my heels. Without offering a hand of help, he stepped over me, and as he walked toward the kitchen, he said, "You only ever think of yourself."

CHAPTER 34

August 8, 1912
Zürich, Switzerland

FORTUNATELY, A RETURN TO ZÜRICH DIDN'T REST SOLELY on my unheeded supplications. As if answering *my* prayers, prayers that had become increasingly commonplace, Zürich began wooing Albert. Our alma mater, the Polytechnic, had summoned Albert with a job offer he couldn't refuse—senior professor of theoretical physics and the head of the department. I told myself that I wasn't delusional, but still, I hoped that a return to Zürich would lead to a return of civility between us.

The time in Prague had been hard. Hard on the bodies and minds of me and the children. Hard on our relationships as husband and wife and father and sons. The accusation I'd once made against Albert—that he and I were "one stone" but "two hearts"—proved an uncanny prediction, particularly in Prague's inhospitable clime. But surely, the bohemian atmosphere of Zürich would soften him, and his very separate, mercurial heart would cease its constant fluctuation. We could return to steady decorum at least. I'd stopped hoping for more.

Arms full of produce from the market, I pushed open the

door to our new apartment in Zürich. Outside, I had paused for a moment to admire the five-story stucco building, mustard-colored with bay windows, a red-tiled roof, an iron gate, and a view of the lake, city, and Alps. How far we'd come from our student days.

"Hello? Is anyone home?" I called out once I'd walked up the stairs and headed into the kitchen. I'd left the boys with Albert for a half hour while I shopped for dinner, and it was strangely quiet. The boys didn't get a lot of time alone with Albert, so I expected them to be loudly clamoring for his attention.

I rubbed my joints as I began to unpack the produce; my legs and hips had worsened considerably in recent months, and the steep climb to our apartment would be challenging. But Albert would never hear me complain a word about my health; I was too happy to be back in Zürich.

As I placed the final canister into the cupboard, I heard male voices boom from the living room. Not the youthful male voices of our boys but adult male voices. It was Albert and someone else. But who? We'd just arrived at 116 Hofstrasse, halfway up the steep Zürcherhof from the Polytechnic, and while we had acquaintances aplenty in Zürich, we'd shared our address with no one. Or so I thought.

A laugh reverberated through the foyer. It sounded oddly familiar. Could our old family friends the Hurwitzes or the Adlers be here? I knew we'd assume our routine of musical evenings with them soon, but I hadn't sent them our details yet. I placed the peppers and onions down on the kitchen counter and stepped into the living room to identify our guest.

It was Marcel Grossman, our old Polytechnic physics

classmate. He appeared much the same but for some graying at his temples and wrinkles around his eyes. I wondered how aged I seemed to him; my own hair was shot through with gray now, and my skin was lined. Still, my heart surged with joy. Wouldn't Mr. Grossman be a wonderful addition to our lives? A friend who knew me from my student days. A fellow mathematician and scientist who had consulted *me* on tricky problems in the past. Someone who knew of my intellect and not just my skills as a mother and housekeeper.

"Mr. Grossman!" I cried out and embraced him. "How wonderful to see you!"

"You too, Mrs. Einstein!" he replied with a tight squeeze. "We have been so excited that the Einsteins have returned to their old stomping ground."

"Please, after all these years of knowing one another, don't you think it's time you called me Mileva?"

He smiled. "And don't you think it's time you called me Marcel?"

"So, Marcel, Albert tells me that you are the chairman of the Polytechnic math department now."

"Yes, it's hard to believe sometimes."

"Congratulations. You are young for the job but up to the task."

"Thank you," he said with a smile. "How about you, Mileva? Do the boys occupy all your time?"

I glanced over at Albert. An idea occurred to me. Wouldn't Marcel be the perfect person with whom to hint about my earlier work with Albert? Marcel had the power to start me on a path of my own if he knew that I'd continued to work on my math and physics in the years since the Polytechnic. Nothing formal of course, as I had no degree, but maybe some tutoring or research. Then I wouldn't have to depend on Albert at all to feed my scientific cravings. Perhaps some of the tension between us could lift.

"Albert and I have been known to collaborate on some papers from time to time," I said.

"I knew it!" he said with a slap on his leg. "I reviewed some of his articles and knew Albert couldn't manage all those mathematical calculations on his own. You were always better at math than him. Than most of us, actually."

I blushed. "Coming from the head of the Polytechnic math department, that's quite a compliment. And here I am, just a housewife."

"The department chair could have been yours if this old man hadn't stole you away from science," Marcel said, nudging Albert.

I laughed. It had been so long since someone thought of me as anything but Albert's wife. His shy and strange and gimpy wife, as I'd been declared by the gossips in every place we'd landed. Someone always let this appraisal of me slip in the guise of "helping" me reshape myself into a better semblance of a professor's wife. They wanted me to be Albert's match, outgoing and charismatic. This was the only Albert they knew, of course, the public Albert.

"Speaking of math, you are one of the main reasons I've come to Zürich." Albert interrupted our banter with a furious glare at me.

What had I done wrong to warrant that look? Maybe he

was angry simply because I was talking with Marcel. Lately, any sign of my youthful exuberance irritated him. He had no concrete reason for his temper; it wasn't as if I'd identified which part of his articles I'd authored. I had only hinted at collaboration on the 1905 papers to Marcel, something that anyone who knew us from our student days would assume.

Was it so wrong that I wanted scientific work for myself? That work was the core of my being, the link to my long-neglected spirituality and intellect. Without it for so long, I felt hollow. Perhaps if I had work of my own, science could become less of a battlefield between Albert and me, a symbol of my sacrifice and neglect, and science could again return to its original sacred place in my world.

"Me?" Marcel asked now, clearly surprised. "What could I possibly offer that would lure you to Zürich? I assumed that taking over the physics chair of your alma mater was enticement enough."

"I am searching for the connection between my theory of relativity and gravity—the impact they have on one another—to further the special relativity article that was nominated for the Nobel Prize in 1910 and again this past year as well. And your math genius will lead the way."

Had I heard Albert correctly? Was he proposing that Marcel collaborate with him on the math for an expansion of *my* theory?

"Would I have to do any of the physics?"

"No. I will handle the physics, if you manage the math."

Marcel looked at Albert skeptically for a moment, as if he was trying to reconcile the irresponsible college student he'd once known with the successful physicist in front of him.

"Please, I need you, Grossman," Albert begged. Then, very pointedly, he stared at me. "Compared with this problem, the original theory of relativity is childish."

When Marcel still didn't answer, Albert asked, "Will you work with me?"

The successful physicist standing before him must have won out, because Marcel finally said, "Yes."

So this was to be Albert's new collaborator. He gave the work long earmarked for me away—to Marcel. I'd told myself that the hope of collaboration was long past, but to actually witness the passing of the baton was unbearable. How could Albert make me stand by and watch as he utterly robbed me of the bohemian partnership he'd promised? On the theory I created. He knew how much this must hurt me. Since an Easter trip to Berlin to see his extended family four months ago, he had become noticeably more callous. But I never thought he could be this cruel.

CHAPTER 35

March 14, 1913
Zürich, Switzerland

Happy birthday, Papa!" Hans Albert and Tete yelled out as they marched into the living room. My little men carried a cake to Albert, who put his pipe on the stand to collect it from them. The boys and I had prepared a surprise birthday celebration for Albert before we headed out for our usual Sunday evening of music at the Hurwitzes.

"Mmm, boys, this looks delicious. Shall I eat it all myself? It's my birthday after all," Albert teased with a twinkle in his eye. In these brief moments of familial contentment, with a rare, lighthearted Albert, I remembered why I stayed. Despite the betrayal with Marcel. And so many other deceptions.

"No, Papa!" Hans Albert protested. "It's for sharing."

"Yes, Papa. For sharing," Tete piped in, a high-pitched echo of his serious older brother.

After slicing the chocolate cake into generous pieces and passing them around for everyone to enjoy, I cleared the plates and headed to the kitchen. I could hear Albert toss Tete into the air and Tete's squeals of delight. The exchange pleased me. Tete had been a delicate child until recently—he suffered from chronic headaches and ear infections—and Albert had avoided playing with him as a result. Albert's relationship with the sturdier, serious Hans Albert had always been more solid. No matter my disappointment, even anger at Albert, I wanted the boys to have strong relationships with their father. Like I'd had with Papa.

"Careful," Hans Albert cautioned his father on his tossing Tete about. Ever old beyond his years, he took seriously the paternal role that fell to him so often in Albert's absence.

The past seven months in Zürich hadn't brought the new life for which I'd hoped, although the familiar surroundings and network of old friends helped keep things civil between Albert and me, particularly our Sunday evenings of music at the home of our old friends the Hurwitzes. Otherwise, any spare time Albert had available from his new professorship was spent with Marcel. As I washed dishes, reviewed homework, read books to the boys, and readied them for bed, I quietly listened to Albert and Marcel work into the night. The beginning of their partnership had been giddy as they hammered out the notion that gravity creates a distortion in space-time geometry and, in fact, bends it. But as the days grew longer and the math became more elusive, their despondency grew. As did their desperation. They delved into a version of space-time geometry invented by Georg Friedrich Riemann and played with various vectors and tensors. They struggled with the goal I'd set out for myself since the death of Lieserl, a generalized theory of relativity that extended the principle of relativity to all observers, no matter how they were moving with respect to one another, and posited the relative nature of time.

At this juncture, they couldn't make it work. They couldn't achieve the holy grail that Albert had convinced himself that he, and not I, had created. In fact, the men were preparing a paper called "Outline of a Generalized Theory of Relativity and of a Theory of Gravitation," or "*Entwurf*," in which they laid out the beginnings of their theory but acknowledged a failure, that they hadn't yet found a mathematical method to prove their theory.

I could've led them toward the answer. Even though Albert hadn't invited me into his theoretical world for years, not with any regularity since the *Maschinchen*, I hadn't exactly slept through that entire time in a haze of dishes and diapers. I'd been reading and thinking and quietly writing about the broader reaches of my relativity theory. I knew that they needed to jettison the goal of finding a law of physics applicable to all observers in the universe and focus instead on gravity and relativity as it applied to rotating observers and those in steady motion—by using a different tensor. But I had been waiting to be asked to the dance before I shared my knowledge. If Albert wasn't going to invite me, I wasn't going to dance for him.

I let him struggle. It was my only actual rebellion against his ever-mounting annoyance with me.

As Albert grew gloomier, I retreated into myself and grew darker still. Only to Helene did I confess the black fog that had descended upon me, explaining that, as Albert had become a renowned physicist and an important member of the scientific community, the boys and I had faded into the background of his life.

Birthday dishes done, kitchen clean, instruments and sheets of music assembled, I had an hour or so to tackle the piles of paper in the dining room before we left for the Hurwitzes. Ever messy, Albert had left the detritus of his work with Marcel all over the dining room table. Inwardly, no matter how willingly I seemed to assume the hausfrau role, I snarled at having to be his maid. How had my life devolved entirely into this?

Heaped on top of some notes left behind by Marcel was an array of letters conveying birthday wishes. Work colleagues like Otto Stern, old friends like Michele Besso, Albert's sister Maja, his mother Pauline, even his cousin Elsa, all remembered the famous professor's birthday. Never mine. Not even Albert recalled mine.

I was curious about this cousin Elsa, the one he'd stayed with in Berlin to see over the Easter holidays last year instead of returning home to celebrate with us.

Dearest Albert,

Please don't be upset with me for breaking our agreed-upon silence by sending you birthday wishes. Daily, I think of our trip to Wannsee last Easter and recall your words of love. Since I cannot have you, since you are a married man, can I at least share your science? Can you recommend a book

of relativity suitable for a layperson? Can you send
a photograph of yourself for my private reflection?

I remain your devoted,
Elsa

Swaying a little, I sat down on a dining room chair. The submerged sensation I'd experienced when I read the suggestive letters from Anna Meyer-Schmid returned. But this time, they reappeared laced with terror. This was no affair contemplated. This was an affair consummated. I had no ability to stop it before it began.

I read the sickening words again, praying I'd misinterpreted them. That I was overreacting. But there could be no mistake. Albert and Elsa had professed their love for one another.

I started crying. My last thread of hope—that even if Albert wasn't my scientific partner, he was still my husband—disappeared before me. He loved someone else.

Albert walked into the room. "What is it, Mileva?" Mileva is what he always called me now. Never Dollie. Never even Mitza.

Not trusting myself to talk, I stood up. I wanted desperately to leave the apartment. I didn't care that the streets were icy and dangerous, especially with my limp. I didn't care that I wasn't wearing a coat on a frigid day. I needed to flee.

But I had to pass by Albert to leave the room. As my arm brushed his sleeve, he grabbed my hand. "I asked you a question, Mileva. What is wrong?"

Handing him the letter, I started to walk away from him. To

the streets, to a café, anywhere but the apartment. He grabbed me. "Where do you think you're going?"

"I have to get out of here. Away from you."

"Why?"

I glanced at the letter in his hand. A silent invitation for him to read it.

Keeping one hand on me, he skimmed it quickly. "So you know?" He let out a sigh that almost sounded like relief.

How dare this be a relief.

Something sprung loose in me. "How could you! After Anna, after all your promises in the Engadine Valley, how could you betray me again! And with your cousin."

"You drove me to it, Mileva. With all your disappointed looks and dark moods. When I was back in Berlin over the Easter holidays last year, how could I not be attracted to Elsa's lightness?"

Berlin. Easter. Elsa. The worsening in his heartlessness. It all made sense.

I started to screech and wrenched free from his hold. Drawing closer to me, he gripped my shoulders and muttered, "Don't make a scene in front of the boys."

Squirming away from him, I lunged for the door, but he held me down firmly. I wriggled my hands out of his grasp and shoved him off of me. He grabbed me again, and I slapped his hands away.

Hands and arms flew until I felt the force of his hand fully upon my face. Like a slap. Whether accidental or intentional, I didn't know. All I could think about was the pain.

I sunk to my knees, hands on my face. The pain was nearly

as intense as the childbirth that had wrecked my body. It seared so badly I could barely breathe, let alone sob. Warmth trickled down my cheeks. I looked at my palms. They were crimson with my blood.

Two sets of little feet pattered down the hall.

"What's wrong, Mama?" Hans Albert cried out, fear and concern bubbling up in his voice.

"It's all right, boys. Mama will be okay," I answered, quickly placing my hands over my face again. The boys would likely become hysterical if they saw the blood streaming down my face.

Tete whimpered, "Mama's hurt," and started to creep toward me.

I didn't want the boys to see what Albert had done, so I stood up and said, "No, no. Mama is just fine, just…just…a bad toothache. I'm going to lie down in my bedroom until it passes, all right?"

I was halfway down the hallway when I heard Albert say to the boys, "Let's just write a little note to the Hurwitzes to explain that we cannot come for the recital tonight because Mama has a toothache. Then we will have some more cake, okay?"

As I took refuge in my room, one of Newton's basic laws of motion crept into my mind unbidden: the law told us that an object will continue on a particular path until a force acts upon it. I had continued on the fixed path as Albert's wife for years, but now three forces acted upon it that I couldn't ignore— Marcel, Elsa, and Albert's hand on my face. Surely, the path must alter.

Izgoobio sam sye. I was lost. But I could no longer afford to be.

PART III

To every action there is always opposed an equal reaction: or the mutual actions of two bodies upon each other are always equal, and directed to contrary parts.

Sir Isaac Newton

CHAPTER 36

March 15, 1913
Zürich, Switzerland

T HE KNOCK ECHOED THROUGHOUT THE APARTMENT. My hand froze in midair, and I stopped scrubbing the pots. My stomach churned. Who could it be? I wasn't expecting anyone. I considered not answering, but the boys were playing loudly, and the person outside the door could certainly hear them.

Cracking open the door, I peeked through the slit. It was Mrs. Hurwitz and her daughter, Lisbeth, the closest things to friends I had in Zürich. By God, what was I going to do?

"Hello, Mrs. Einstein. We missed you last night and wanted to see how you were feeling. You know, with your toothache." Mrs. Hurwitz spoke through the crack.

"Thank you so much for coming," I answered without opening the door any wider. "I'm still in pain, but I'm able to manage the children."

"Can we come in and help?"

"No, we are doing fine, but many thanks for your offer."

"Please, Mrs. Einstein?"

How could I decline to open the door? Which would be

worse to circulate around the Zürich academic circles: the peculiar tale of Mileva Einstein—already considered recalcitrant and strange—refusing to open her home to social callers, or the story about my bruised and swollen face? The blame for one would fall on me; the blame for the other would fall on Albert.

I chose Albert.

"Of course, please forgive my rudeness," I said as I unlatched the door and opened it for the Hurwitzes to enter. "I wasn't expecting visitors, so I'm still in my housedress. My apologies."

The women gasped when they entered the foyer. "Oh, Mrs. Einstein, your face!" Mrs. Hurwitz exclaimed, her hand covering her mouth in horror.

Instinctively, I shielded it from view. "Not pretty, I know. Toothaches can be grueling. You understand why I couldn't come to your gathering last night."

The women were quiet and staring at me. They knew perfectly well that my face didn't look like this because of a toothache. No toothache in the world would batter its owner in this manner. Papa would strangle Albert if he saw me right now.

"Can I get you ladies some tea and cake? I just pulled a strudel from the oven," I stammered into the silence.

Mrs. Hurwitz recovered herself and said, "No thank you, Mrs. Einstein. We wouldn't want to trouble you. Particularly in your state. We simply wanted to make certain you were all right."

"Well"—I gestured to my face—"I am as well as can be expected. I appreciate the visit," I said with a curtsy. The women returned the gesture, and we said our farewells.

The pot roast simmered in the oven, sending a warm, comforting smell throughout the apartment. The boys were playing on the floor of the living room, building a fortress together, Hans Albert in the lead and Tete as his assistant. Books I'd just read aloud to them were piled up on the floor next to the sofa. The scene in our apartment conveyed contentment to the observer, yet anything but serenity brewed beneath the surface.

Albert arrived home with a slam of the door. He greeted the boys first, tickling them and asking about their day. I heard him whisper, "How's Mama today?" but I didn't want to eavesdrop, so I turned my attention to setting the dining room table.

Once I finished, I reentered the kitchen and nearly bumped into a waiting Albert. Dark circles under his eyes cast shadows on his face, and he held a bouquet of alpenrose and bird's-eye primrose—alpine flowers carted in from the valleys—in his hands. He'd never given me flowers before, except on our wedding day.

"I'm sorry, Dollie." He gestured to my face and handed me the bouquet.

Without a word, I took them from him and began searching for a vase. My action wasn't an acceptance of his apology but a nod to the beautiful fragility of the flowers themselves.

He followed me. "I feel terrible about your face. And about Elsa."

Silently, I busied myself with cutting the bottoms off the flowers' stems and arranging them in the blue-and-white porcelain vase. The vase had been a gift from a scientific admirer, Albert once told me. Now I wondered who really had given it to him. How many other lies had he told me? How many other women were there? Was there any scrap of my life that remained true?

"I broke it off with Elsa only a few weeks after it began last Easter, Mileva. I swear to you. Even Elsa's letter refers to our separation."

I nodded but didn't answer as I continued preparing our evening meal. Slicing bread, spooning out the pot roast onto plates, quartering beets to accompany the meal. Wasn't this the last remaining service Albert wanted from me? I might as well be any housekeeper for hire. There wasn't anything else left of value in me, he'd have me believe. He had hollowed me out.

"Mileva, please say something."

What did he expect me to say? That I forgave him? I didn't. Not for hitting me, intentional or not. Not for Elsa. Not for Marcel. Not for Lieserl, most of all. And certainly not for promising me a marriage full of scientific partnership and breaking that promise right in front of my now-battered face.

"Mileva, I want to make things right between us. I've been invited to lecture on photochemistry and thermodynamics at the French Physics Society, and Marie Curie has invited us to stay in her home in Paris while we are there. I know you've wanted to meet her, and we've never been to Paris. Will you come with me?"

I stared at Albert's face, but I wasn't looking at him. Images of Paris and photographs of Marie Curie floated in my mind. I had long admired the famous scientist, the winner of the 1903 and 1911 Nobel Prizes, in physics and chemistry, respectively.

I didn't know what to do, but I would agree to this trip. Only for my own purposes, however. Not for those of Albert.

CHAPTER 37

April 1, 1913
Paris, France

I'D ALWAYS BELIEVED ZÜRICH TO BE THE EPICENTER OF ALL things academic and sophisticated. Certainly compared to Novi Sad, Kać, Prague, and even Bern, it was. Yet as I strolled through the glittering streets of Paris on Albert's arm and at Madame Curie's side on our way to dinner, along with her daughters and several male family members serving as chaperones, I understood that Zürich was provincial in comparison to the exquisite French capital.

After a languorous walk through the Bois de Vincennes, an enormous, fastidiously maintained park bordering the Seine, Albert asked why the park was largely empty. Madame Curie explained, "I'm told that the only fashionable time to promenade through the park is between three and five o'clock. It is past that hour. My apologies if you were hoping for a glimpse of the latest Paris fashions."

"We have never cared about being fashionable, have we, Mileva? How about you, Madame Curie?"

A chortle escaped unexpectedly from the somber Madame

Curie's mouth. "Fashionable? Oh my, Albert, no one has ever accused me of being fashionable. Quite the opposite. And how many times have I asked you to call me Marie?"

While her laughter surprised me, her response did not. Fashion was, quite obviously, the last thing on her mind. The frizzy, almost unkempt, grayness of Madame Curie's hair and the textured black of her simple dress made her appear dour, a darkness that made me feel oddly comfortable. She looked familiarly Slavic, particularly in comparison to the Parisian trends.

We stepped onto one of the wide, elegant boulevards for which Paris was justifiably famous. As we strolled down a sidewalk bordered by tall, manicured trees, I felt the ground rumble under my feet. I looked over at Albert in alarm, but before I could ask the source of the vibrations, Madame Curie said, "That is the movement of our underground electric railway, called the Metropolitan Underground Railway or 'Metro.' It takes travelers from one end of the city to the other—and back again if they choose—in an eight-mile loop."

With the mention of electricity, Albert and Madame Curie launched into a discussion about the elusive power, and Albert shared his own family's struggles to set up an electrical business. She laughed at Albert's garrulous account of his family's failings, and I saw that she enjoyed Albert not just for his intellect but his casual manner. I imagined that his relaxed, charming demeanor must be a welcome respite from the usual serious formality with which the Nobel Prize winner was treated. Watching him like this—exuding a charismatic disposition he could turn on and off at will—reminded me of the Albert of my youth. Now lost to me when we were alone.

Madame Curie's face lit up when she and Albert engaged in this spirited scientific exchange. In that moment, I could see the youthful Marya Sklodowska she had once been, the young Polish student eager to excel at the disciplines reserved for boys. The sort of young girl I'd once been.

At they chatted, I assumed that, as had become typical, Albert wouldn't invite my participation in their conversation about electricity. I stayed respectfully quiet and allowed myself to marvel at the omnibuses and tramcars whizzing past us on the boulevard. How antiquated and slow the horses and buggies that still roamed the Zürich streets seemed in comparison to all this motion. I felt the same way about the many cafés we passed en route to the restaurant; Zürich's establishments appeared stuffy and few compared to these plentiful bistros, brimming with patrons engaged in animated chatter.

Madame Curie turned to me and asked, "What are your thoughts on the interior makeup of atoms that Mr. Ernest Rutherford raised during the Solvay Conference, Mrs. Einstein?"

Was Madame Curie actually asking for my opinion? I panicked; I hadn't been closely following their conversation. "Pardon me?"

"Mr. Rutherford's hypothesis is that, based on his experiments with a sort of radioactivity called alpha rays, atoms are almost entirely empty with only tiny nuclei orbited by electrons at their centers. Do you have any thoughts on this?"

Once, Albert and I would have hashed out Rutherford's idea and arrived at conclusions of our own. Not now. Now, I was utterly unprepared for her question. I stammered, "I didn't have the honor of hearing his presentation firsthand at the conference."

"I understand. I am sure, however, that your husband spoke of Mr. Rutherford's theories to you. In addition, Mr. Rutherford has fleshed out this theory in papers since the conference, which I'm guessing you've read. Many have dismissed him, but I'm withholding judgment. Do you have an opinion on them?"

I racked my brain for the nuggets of information about Rutherford's ideas that I gleaned from Albert and the cursory reading I'd done on his work and said, "I have wondered whether the idea that light is composed of quanta, as Albert has advanced, might be applied equally to the structure of matter as light and could bolster Mr. Rutherford's notions about the construction of atoms."

Madame Curie was quiet at first, and Albert looked over at me in horror. Had I said something idiotic? Should I not have responded? I didn't care what he thought, but I cared very much what Madame Curie thought.

Finally, she spoke. "Well said, Mrs. Einstein. That's a perspective I hadn't considered. It's revolutionary, but I quite agree. Do you, Albert? It would certainly be an interesting link to and expansion on your own theories."

Albert's expression morphed from embarrassment into pride. But it was too late for me to care about his feelings toward my intellect. I had conversed with Madame Curie and held my own. That was my treasure.

The next morning, Madame Curie and I sat under the leafy green branches of a horse chestnut tree in the garden outside her family apartment on rue de la Glacière, cups of tea balanced on our laps. Albert had left for his lecture, and she and I were alone for the first time. Even though I'd made a solid contribution to the conversation the night before, my palms were so sweaty at the thought of a private discourse with a scientific legend that I could barely keep a grip on my cup. What topic should I initiate with this amazing woman? I'd read her most recent article on polonium, but my science was so outdated, I feared raising it. And chemistry, for which she was more recently noted, had never been my field. Aside from the favorable exchange we'd had about Mr. Rutherford's views on the way to our dinner at Tour d'Argent, the oldest restaurant in Paris and one of the finest, she and I hadn't spoken much.

I glanced at Madame Curie, who had asked me to call her Marie last evening, but I struggled to think of her as anything but Madame. In the silence, I blurted out the first thing that came to mind. "I studied physics at university as well."

She nodded but didn't respond. Had I said something utterly stupid?

"Not that I'm comparing us, of course." I hastened to explain myself. I never wanted to appear presumptuous.

After staring down into the depths of her teacup, she said, "Mrs. Einstein, I'm familiar with your extensive education and your intellect. And I know you completed your coursework in mathematics and physics at the Zürich Polytechnic. But I wonder why you never returned to work. Your mind must be so active, so full of science. How can you squander it on the home?"

I was speechless. Was I receiving compliments from Madame Curie? What excuse could I offer for my failure to return to science? Did I dare hint at my involvement in the authorship of the now-famous 1905 papers? I couldn't. Albert would kill me.

I offered the only explanation I could cobble together without inciting Albert. "The children have made it challenging. And please call me Mileva."

Madame Curie sipped her tea and thoughtfully responded. "Mileva, I'm frequently questioned, especially by women, on how I reconcile family life with a scientific career. Well, it hasn't been easy. But nothing is easy for people like you and me. We are eastern Europeans living in countries that look down upon people from our lands. We are women, who are expected to stay in the home, not run labs or teach at universities. Our expertise is in physics and math, exclusively male fields until now. And on top of it, you and I are shy in a scientific realm that requires us to speak publicly. In some ways, managing a family has been the easiest part."

How could I respond? Thank God, she didn't make me.

"You and I are not so different except in the choices we've made." She chortled. "And the husbands we chose, of course."

Nearly spitting out a mouthful of tea, I guffawed at the unexpected, almost inappropriate, remark. Madame Curie's late husband Pierre was well known for his unstinting support of her career. Was she insinuating that Albert was not Pierre in this regard? I'd often considered the scientific marriage of the Curies and coveted their union. Once, I had thought that would be the path that Albert and I would travel.

"I didn't have the honor of knowing Monsieur, but his encouragement of you and your work is well known. He must have been an extraordinary man." I said the only diplomatic thing that came to mind, the only statement that wouldn't directly compare Albert to Monsieur Curie. A comparison in which Albert would suffer greatly.

"I have no idea how the division of labor works between you and Albert, but my husband fostered my career from the start. When the Nobel Prize committee was being petitioned to remove me from consideration in 1903, Pierre publicly lobbied for me. He insisted to influential people on the committee that I had originated our research, conceived the experiments, and generated the theories about the nature of radioactivity, which was, indeed, the fact. But many a lesser man wouldn't have made that effort." She didn't ask, but implicit in her statement was the question of whether Albert would have gone to those lengths.

I tried to answer her question as vaguely as possible while still being respectful. "From the beginning of our marriage, our situation didn't allow for my work outside the home. Though I certainly longed for it."

Madame Curie was quiet for a full minute. "Science certainly needs practical men, but science also needs dreamers. It seems to me that your husband is one of those dreamers. And dreamers often need caretakers, don't they?"

I laughed. Was I really having this frank and insightful conversation about the state of my marriage and career with Marie Curie? "They do indeed."

"Whether Albert has championed your scientific efforts or not, he certainly supported mine. Did you know that he came to my defense last year when all that unpleasant business with my Nobel Prize arose?" Madame Curie paused, aware that further elaboration on her "unpleasant business" was unnecessary. Scientists worldwide had called her unfit for the Nobel Prize when her affair with married fellow scientist Paul Langevin became public.

I shook my head. Albert hadn't told me. Interesting that Albert was more willing to champion a known adulterer—brilliant and worthy though she was—than his own hardworking and deserving wife. What did this say about his moralistic worldview and allegiances these days?

She continued. "Perhaps, when your circumstances allow, Albert will encourage your scientific efforts again."

"Perhaps," I answered quietly, knowing full well of Albert's lack of interest in my work.

"Remember my words, Mileva, when you withdraw into the deadening cycle of home. You and I are not so different except in the choices we've made. And remind yourself that a new choice is always possible."

CHAPTER 38

July 14 through September 23, 1913
Zürich, Switzerland, Kać, Serbia, and Vienna, Austria

J UST AS I'D BEGUN TO DEVELOP A TENUOUS CONFIDENCE on the strength of Madame Curie's words, Berlin came calling for Albert.

The directorship of the soon-to-be formed Kaiser Wilhelm Institute for Physics. A professorship at the University of Berlin with no teaching duties. Membership in the Prussian Academy of Sciences, the greatest scientific honor aside from the Nobel Prize. The package, the prestige, and the money—all with no requirement that he do anything but *think*—were so over-whelming that they made Albert forget how much he'd hated the Berlin of his youth. His loathing of the city and its people had been so strident that he renounced his German citizenship to become Swiss in his early twenties.

Or perhaps it was something else entirely that washed away all those awful memories.

Berlin, for me, held only fear. Berlin was Albert's family, who despised me. Berlin was notoriously hostile toward Slavic eastern Europeans, and I plainly was anything but Aryan. More than anything, however, Berlin was Elsa, who I suspected engineered this position somehow. With Elsa in the wings—no matter Albert's assurances that he had broken off their affair—I feared that Berlin would be the death knell of my marriage.

But it wasn't a choice, according to Albert. In the past, we'd always deliberated new opportunities and new locations together, but not this time. After Max Planck and Walther Nernst made a trip to Zürich to persuade Albert to take the package—a job, they dramatically informed him, that was critical for the future of science—Albert announced that we were moving to Berlin. At first, I begged him not to, but after his emphatic insistence, I said little else in the passing weeks, even when he baited me about it. It was as if he was hoping I'd refuse to go so he could leave me behind.

Onward to his fame. And to Elsa, I didn't doubt.

Still, I clung. Why, sometimes I didn't know. Was it because I'd sacrificed so much for him that the idea of losing him felt like losing everything? Was I so fearful for the boys' future with divorced parents? Had I started to believe the awful things Albert said to me? The more passive I acted about the move, the more hateful he became, as if he wanted a fight so he could internally justify abandonment. One night, in front of the boys, he yelled, "You suck the joy out of every occasion." Another time, in front of the Hurwitzes, he called me "the darkest of sulkers." But when I looked into my sweet boys' doleful eyes, I wondered how they'd survive the nasty stain of divorce, and I stayed.

Surprisingly, Albert agreed to a summer reprieve in August before we began planning for the move in the fall. I never thought he'd agree to visit my parents in Kać at the Spire—he'd resisted since Hans Albert was quite young, so my parents hadn't seen the three-year-old Tete since he was a newborn—but he proved more than willing. Almost suspiciously so, to my mind. As soon as we arrived in Kać, he began inciting arguments with me about Berlin, and the reason for his complaisance dawned on me. He had hoped to anger me enough that I'd insist on staying in Kać with my parents. That way, he could abandon me with a clear conscience. After watching his mistreatment of me during our visit, Mama and Papa would have supported the boys and me in staying behind.

But nothing he could say or do would shake me. For after Kać, on September 23, he had agreed that I could accompany him to a conference in Vienna. There, Helene awaited.

Helene and I clung to each other like life rafts in turbulent seas.

"Girls, girls, your reunion is beautiful, but we do have places to be," Albert said with a puff of his pipe and a humorous tone. Astonishing how quickly he could revert to his charming public personality after just yelling at me to walk behind him, not at his side. He found me embarrassing these days.

But Helene and I didn't listen. "I've missed you so much, Mitza," she said.

"I've missed you too, Helene," I said into her hair. Her once chestnut locks were shot through with streaks of gray, and the furrows between her brows had deepened even further. No wonder. Helene and her family had contended with the Balkan Wars for the past two years, a conflict that made obtaining even basic necessities hard and travel impossible.

How grateful I was that we were together. We would have three glorious days while Albert spoke, conducted meetings, and hobnobbed with his peers. Helene and I would be left to our own devices for most of the time, apart from Albert's lectures, which Helene asked to attend out of politeness, I supposed. And we would be utterly alone since I'd left the boys in Kać with my parents.

"We haven't seen each other for years, but I talk with you daily. I'm always conversing with you in my mind."

Helene giggled, making her sound like the schoolgirl she'd once been. "Me too, Mitza."

Albert interrupted us again. "Ladies, we really must depart. The 85th Congress of Natural Sciences awaits, and my lecture begins in less than an hour."

We left the train station where we'd met Helene and hopped into a hansom cab to the hall. Chatting about her girls and my boys, with Albert piping in constant comments about the boys' intellectual promise and musical talents, the time passed in a blur. Before I realized it, we were ensconced in our seats, awaiting Albert's lecture.

Helene glanced around the packed lecture hall, her eyes wide. She hadn't experienced the breadth of Albert's fame before; my letters had been her primary source about his growing popularity. I scanned the room for familiar faces, but none of the kind professors from Zürich, Prague, or Bern who I'd gotten to know over the years were visible. It was simply an anonymous bobbing sea of sober mustaches and beards. No other women.

"All this is for Albert?" Helene asked.

"Yes," I answered with an attempt at a smile. "He has become quite a star."

As soon as Albert walked up the steps to the stage, the hall thundered with the audience's raucous applause. He beamed at the adulation, his eyes sparkling, a wide grin forming on his lips, the spotlight catching the gray streaks in his wild, dark hair. It was an impersonation of his somewhat impish, eccentric student self, a persona he'd begun to cultivate. Understanding the dichotomy of his transformation immediately, Helene squeezed my hand.

We didn't need to speak to communicate. Even after all these years.

He cleared his throat and spoke loudly to his fans. "Greetings, esteemed colleagues. I appreciate your invitation to speak at this 85th Congress of Natural Sciences. As you have requested, my lecture today will focus on my new gravitation theory, as it expands on my special theory of relativity as set forth in 1905."

"Isn't that your paper?" Helene whispered.

I nodded.

She glanced over at me with a distressed expression. As the only person in the world besides Albert who knew the full extent of my authorship of the 1905 papers—including what it meant as a tribute to Lieserl—she understood how hard it was for me to have my name erased from the project. Tears welled up in my eyes at her sympathy; I was unused to compassion these days. I stared up at the ceiling, not wanting anyone in the crowd to see me cry.

Albert began explaining the work that he and Marcel completed to date. He wrote out their equations and compared the development of his gravitation theory with the history of electromagnetism. When he launched into the two relativity-based theories he was considering and then set forth his own theory, grumblings built in the crowd. When Albert opened up the floor for questions, countless hands rose like a wave, and Professor Gustav Mie from Greifswald stood up without waiting to be called upon. Visibly impatient, the professor contended that Albert's theory didn't meet the principle of equivalence, a serious criticism.

Even after the question period ended and Albert stepped down from the stage, he was swarmed with scientists. Some sought answers to esoteric inquiries, and others sought his autograph on various papers and articles he'd drafted. When the throng thinned out, he walked toward us.

"What did you think, Helene?" he asked. Incredibly, even after all the flattery, he sought more. From everyone but me.

"Most impressive, Albert." Helene spoke to the number of attendees and their fawning reaction, the exact response Albert sought. What else could she say? I knew she didn't understand the math or the physics; she was a history student.

Walking down the long aisles toward the hall exit and then out onto the sidewalk, Helene and Albert nattered on. I overheard her ask about Berlin, and he responded enthusiastically above the move.

As Albert had requested, I walked a few steps behind them. When peers stopped Albert with questions or comments on his talk, they addressed Helene as "Mrs. Einstein," no matter her attempts at correcting them. Me, a dark shadow cast behind Albert's light, they utterly ignored.

On one street corner, Albert became engrossed in a debate with the persistent Professor Mie, and Helene and I took our leave. Albert had other meetings to attend anyway. Spotting a cozy café on a nearby street corner, we ordered coffee and two Linzer tortes, the city's specialty.

Biting into the intoxicating blend of cinnamon, almond, and raspberry, Helene sat back and sighed as she chewed. "It's been so long since I tasted anything this decadent."

"You have suffered so much hardship, Helene." I had taken note of her frayed blue gown—almost a patchwork quilt with its mending and stitchery—which was undoubtedly her best.

"Things haven't been easy for you either, Mitza."

"Oh, not nearly as bad as for you. I haven't had trouble finding healthy food or basic necessities. I haven't had the specter of war looming over me. I'm fine; it's just the same sort of marital distress that you've suffered too." Although she hadn't mentioned marital troubles for some time, I was ever mindful of it.

"Mitza, you may not have been dealing with the harsh reality of war on a regular basis, but your situation is terrible. Why do you think I'm here? Your letters had me so worried I found a way to travel to Vienna to check on you. But now that I see you and Albert in person—and I stare my beautiful friend in the eyes—I think you are far worse than you described. Worse even than when you lost Lieserl."

Conflicting feelings coursed through me. I wanted to protest that all was well enough, the mantra I'd been uttering to myself for years, the rationale I'd offered over and over to Mama and Papa, but my true feelings bubbled to the surface. I started crying.

"Mitza, you walk behind Albert like a servant. His colleagues were calling *me* Mrs. Einstein, for God's sake, and neither you nor Albert corrected them. No matter the private troubles I've endured with my husband, I always have his public respect. How has it come to this?"

"I don't know, Helene," I said through my tears. "I don't know."

"I no longer care for Albert," Helene said. "I do not like the person he has become."

It was as if a great weight had been lifted from me. No one else saw the man behind the public mask. "Truly, Helene? I could hug you for saying that. Other friends still admire him for his scientific achievement, even when they've witnessed his treatment of me. It's as if they've transformed their professional admiration into unshakable personal affection, no matter how contemptibly he has acted."

Helene grabbed me by the shoulder, forcing me to look her in the face. "Where are you, Mitza? Where is the brilliant girl I knew from the Engelbrecht Pension? You seemed so quiet back then, but you were always ready to lance anyone with your sharp wit when necessary. Where has that girl gone? We need her back."

Terrible heaving sobs wracked my body. The prim café's patrons stared at me, but I didn't care. "I don't know where she's gone, Helene," I cried.

"Mitza, you must wake up that latent part of yourself, that strong girl you've allowed to fall asleep for so many years. Because the future has become clear to me, even though I'm no soothsayer. You are going to have to do battle."

CHAPTER 39

July 18, 1914
Berlin, Germany

A LBERT HAD BEEN GONE FOR SIX DAYS, HIS LONGEST unexplained absence since we arrived in Berlin. Six days of Hans Albert and Tete asking about their father's whereabouts. Six days of running into Albert's colleagues, who shared tales of wondrous lunches and dinners they'd just experienced with the lauded professor. Six days of pretending that all would be well when he *chose* to return to our apartment at 33 Ehrenbergstraße after storming off when I simply asked if he would be home for dinner that evening.

But all wouldn't be well when—or if—he returned. At Helene's urging and Madame Curie's example, I had awoken my strength. I would not endure humiliation at Albert's hands again, whether personal or professional. If Albert didn't appreciate the meek helpmate I had become in our latter years together—the failed physicist from whom he could pilfer ideas at will and the wife bendable at his beckoning—he positively loathed the return of the old Mileva in Berlin. And that was precisely who would greet him at the door when he returned from his cowardly flight to his lover, Elsa.

The very thought of Elsa—all perfumed and dyed blond hair, exactly the sort of idle, pampered, bourgeois woman about which Albert used to complain—sickened me. Less because she had "stolen" Albert from me and more because of her perfidy.

"Please, Mrs. Einstein, allow me to help you," Elsa had said with an obsequious smile when the boys and I went to Berlin alone in the days after Christmas to find an apartment. Albert had sent her over to the hotel to "assist" us without my foreknowledge.

Staring at the ruby-red smile painted upon her lips, I couldn't speak. Her audacity coming here, seeking out the woman she'd betrayed, silenced me.

Elsa, as she insisted we call her, continued regardless. "I know all the best real estate brokers in Berlin. It would be my pleasure to help you find just the right apartment," she cooed. As if her angelic offer of assistance were for the benefit of me and my boys—not for the true purpose of securing an apartment convenient for Albert to visit her.

With Tete tugging on my arm and Hans Albert eyeing her suspiciously, I refused. My boys could see what their father could not. What sort of human being gazed into the eyes of one she's betrayed and pretended to offer salvation?

The door slammed. The boys flew to my side. Even though I never told them what was transpiring between Albert and myself, they sensed it. Their protective instincts were on high alert. Looking into their chocolate-brown eyes, so like Albert's, and whispering in their ears that everything would be fine, I sent the boys off to their bedrooms. No matter how I felt about Albert, I didn't want them to witness this exchange.

I followed Albert into his study, where he had retreated immediately upon entering the apartment. Without a greeting, even for the boys.

"So Elsa has taken you from me at last, has she?" I said very matter-of-factly. Why should I mince words? Better we all understood our positions.

He turned to look at me, his eyebrows raised in surprise at my remark. Since we arrived in Berlin, I had been clear about my expectations of fidelity, but I never mentioned Elsa outright. I couldn't bear to say her name aloud; I couldn't even fathom what he saw in the vapid, uneducated matron. But after his six-day disappearance—days in which I heard some of his colleagues snickering at me at the local market, as many of our acquaintances in Berlin were part of Elsa's longtime circle—we were past that point.

"Elsa cannot take from you what you do not possess," he answered coldly.

The old Mileva would have crumbled at his icy words, but I did not relent. I remained calm and said, "Please allow me to rephrase. You have abandoned me and your children for Elsa. Am I correct?"

To that, Albert said not a word.

"I suppose it's not the first abandonment, is it? You left us for science long ago, didn't you?" I continued.

Huffing in anger, he yelled, "It's not me who's abandoned you for science and other women but you who has abandoned me with your jealousy and the withdrawal of your affection. You forced me into Elsa's arms."

Shaking my head, I smiled at his infantile worldview. Was he truly so self-focused that he believed I withdrew *my* affections first? That my self-protection and the recent strengthening of my resolve happened *before* he cheated on me and bled me dry of my scientific ambitions? That I pushed him into Elsa's waiting arms? It was so ridiculous that I didn't bother to fashion a response. It would be like arguing with a madman. One made powerful by his popularity, at that.

"Why are you smiling?" he asked angrily.

"Your comment reflects the typical sort of selfish thinking I've grown to expect from you. But which I will tolerate no longer."

"Is that so? I have prepared something that I think will wipe that smile from your face." He thrust his hand out toward me. It held a single piece of paper.

"Oh really?" I asked, taking the paper from his hand.

"Really," he taunted. "Take a look."

"What is this?"

"It is a list of the conditions upon which I will stay in this apartment with you and the boys. This is only so I can maintain a relationship with the boys. As for you and me, I want our relationship to become a business one, with the personal aspects reduced to almost nothing."

"Are you serious?" I asked. Did he think I was chattel for which he could enter a contract? Helene would scream aloud at this demand if she were here, and I couldn't even fathom what Papa would do. Even Mama would not want me to stay in this situation.

"Absolutely. If you cannot agree to these conditions, then I will have no choice but to ask you for a separation."

I glanced down at the sheet of paper. It was covered in Albert's scrawl and resembled nothing so much as the protocols for a physics experiment, the sort Albert and I had written in droves. But the closer I examined it, the more I realized that it was unlike any document Albert had ever written before. It was probably unlike any document *anyone* had ever written before.

It was a contract for my behavior. As I read the barbaric agreement term by term, I grew more outraged. The document enumerated the household duties I *must* perform for Albert: his laundry; the preparation of his meals, to be served in his room; and the cleaning of his bedroom and study, with the requirement that I never touch his desk. Even more incredible was his list of his requirements that I must "obey" in my personal dealings with him. He demanded that I renounce all interaction with him at home; he would control where and when I spoke and what sorts of statements I could make to him and in front of the children. In particular, he mandated that I forgo all physical intimacy with him.

The document would indeed turn me into Albert's chattel.

I felt Helene standing alongside me in solidarity, emboldening me to say, "What on earth makes you think that I would agree to this? That I would sink further down than I've already let you bury me?"

"I will not stay in this apartment with you otherwise," he said with a certain aplomb. I then realized that he won, whether I agreed or not. Whether I stayed or not.

I shoved the paper back into his hands. It saddened me to

think that I already met most of these conditions. How low I had plummeted.

I took a deep breath and calmly announced, "You needn't worry."

He looked incredulous. "You will agree to the terms?"

"Oh no, I would *never* agree to those terms, Albert. You don't have to worry about staying in the apartment with us, because *we* will leave."

CHAPTER 40

July 29, 1914
Berlin, Germany

T HE TRAIN WHISTLE CRIED OUT, AND TETE CLAPPED AT
the sound. He didn't understand the magnitude of this
leave-taking. For him, it was just one more trip to one more
destination. There had been so many.

For me, this train ride back to Zürich was an entirely different
sort of journey. Zürich represented old friends, my years of education, possible work, a healthy climate and steady political situation
for the boys, and the best chance at a happy life without Albert.

Albert stood near us as the train prepared to admit passengers. After hugging Tete, he tried to embrace Hans Albert several
times, but my eldest son wriggled free from his grasp. Hans Albert
was not nearly as unaware—or as forgiving—as his brother.

The train doors opened, and both boys clasped onto my
hands. Albert kneeled down to say one last good-bye to them,
and tears glinted in the corners of his eyes. It was the first sign
of remorse or sadness I'd seen since we arrived in Berlin.

"Why so sad, Papa?" Tete asked, leaning forward to touch
Albert's eyes with his free hand.

The gentle caress unleashed something dammed up in
Albert. He sobbed to the boys, "I will miss you both."

I had only seen Albert cry once before, on the death of his father.

Was Albert finally regretting his actions? Perhaps time apart would make him appreciate us, although I doubted Albert was truly capable of change. *Stop*, I told myself. I couldn't afford to think this way; it opened the door to weakness. And I could no longer accept his tyranny. This was farewell to our marriage.

Tete released my hand and hugged his father. "Don't worry, Papa. We will see you soon."

Hans Albert was unmoved by Albert's rare display of anguish. Instead, he tightened his grip on me. He made no move toward Albert.

"All aboard for Zürich!" The engineer called out from the train window.

"Come, Tete," I said to him. "We must go."

I took him by the hand and, without looking back at Albert, led both boys onto the train. We secured an empty car, and as I settled the boys into their seats with snacks to eat and books to read and the attendant loaded our luggage onto the racks, I saw Albert still standing on the platform. Tears were streaming down his face.

Where had those tears been all this time? I'd spent years without empathy or compassion for myself or the boys or Lieserl. Even in our separation these past weeks, I'd seen no evidence of melancholy over our failed marriage or his parting from his sons. Poor Fritz Haber, a chemistry professor acquaintance of ours, had been enlisted to memorialize the terms of separation we had painfully agreed upon. Custody with me. A yearly sum for the boys' care. Vacations with Albert, but never in Elsa's company.

Household furnishing sent to me in Zürich. Proceeds of any future Nobel Prize to me, an honor that seemed likely, given that he'd been nominated four of the past five years. Negotiating this last term had given rise to the only real show of emotion in our separation, but it was anger, not sadness. Albert had initially resisted the notion of parting with the Nobel Prize monetary proceeds—which he expected from any one of our four 1905 papers—but I insisted. Since he'd unilaterally removed my name from those papers, thereby putting the actual award out of my reach, the least I deserved was the money.

No tears flowed down my cheeks. I was numb.

I smiled over at my anxious boys, trying to assuage their fears. The train car, although brimming with our belongings and ornately decorated in red velvet, felt strangely empty. Was something missing? Our trunks and luggage were stored safely in the racks over our heads, and our handbags and backpacks sat nearby on the benches. It couldn't be the absence of Albert; the boys and I had grown accustomed to traveling without him, to living without him, really. What was the source of this sensation then? Could the missing something be Lieserl? No, she was here with me, the guiding shadow in my life, absent yet somehow always present. Perhaps the something unaccounted for was the old self I was leaving behind. For the first time in a very long time, I felt like Mitza again.

The train's whistle blew, and I peered out the window. There Albert stood. Clacking and roaring, the train began to pick up speed as it exited the station. It sped away faster and faster, making Albert grow smaller and smaller. Like a quanta. Or an atom. Until he disappeared entirely into the ether.

EPILOGUE

August 4, 1948

62 Huttenstrasse
Zürich, Switzerland

Every body continues at rest or in motion in a straight line unless compelled to change by forces impressed upon it. I find this first law of motion, beautiful and profound, an elegant statement of one of God's truths uncovered by man. In my youth, I perceived the tenet as applying solely to objects; only later did I realize that people operate according to this principle too. My childhood path—mathematician, scientist, loner—continued on a straight line until it was acted upon by a force. Albert was the force that impressed upon my straight path.

    Albert's force acted on me in accordance with the second law of motion. I became swept up in his direction and velocity, and his force became my own. As I took on the roles of his lover, the mother of his children, his wife, and his secret scientific partner, I allowed him to trim away all the parts that didn't fit his mold. I expanded others to further his dreams for himself. I suffered silently when my desires did not match his. Like the sacrifice of my professional ambitions for his stellar rise. Like the surrender of my ability to keep Lieserl by my side.

Until I could stand Albert's force no more. The third law of motion triggered, and I exerted a force equal in magnitude and opposite in direction to his. I took back the space that belonged to me. I left him.

Since then, I have stayed still, defying all the laws of motion. I have watched war come to Europe once, then twice, and during those times, I have taken the helping hand of my dear, prescient Helene when I needed it. Even when I had the Nobel Prize money Albert had promised me in our divorce to assist in the raising of my beautiful sons—my brilliant Hans Albert, who went on to become an engineer, and my poor Tete, who succumbed to mental illness—I have reclaimed my intellect and my scientific passion by tutoring promising young female scientists. The sort of girls that Lieserl might have been had she lived. The sort of girl I once was. Perhaps these girls will find the rest of God's patterns in science and, one day, tell my story.

I have witnessed the rise of Albert as a secular saint. But never once have I desired to return to the role of his wife. I have only ever wanted to return to the role of Lieserl's mother.

Which acts should I change to undo the death of Lieserl? Do I begin by altering the path of the innocent young university student? Do I need only return to the days at the Spire with my infant Lieserl when Albert summoned me? To the station where I missed my train? How can I find my way back to her?

Finally, though it is dark, I see. I see the clock. The train. And I understand.

I need not change any act. For I am the train. I am traveling faster than the speed of light, and the hands of the clock are rolling backward. I see my Lieserl.

Mitza

AUTHOR'S NOTE

I confess to beginning this book with only the most common-place understanding of Albert Einstein and hardly any knowledge of his first wife, Mileva Marić. In fact, I had never even heard of Mileva Marić until I helped my son Jack with a report on the wonderful Scholastic children's book *Who Was Albert Einstein?* and it mentioned briefly that Albert Einstein's first wife was also a physicist.

I became intrigued. Who was this unknown woman, a physicist at a time when very few women had university educations? And what role might she have played in the great scientist's discoveries?

When I first began researching Mileva, I learned that rather than being unknown as I had thought, she was the focal point of much debate in the physics community. The part she might have played in the formation of Albert's groundbreaking theories in 1905 was hotly contested, particularly once a cache of letters between the couple from the years 1897 to 1903—when Mileva and Albert were university students together and first married—was discovered in the 1980s. In those letters, Albert and Mileva discussed projects they undertook together, and the letters caused ripples throughout the physics world. Was Mileva simply a sounding board for his brainstorms, as some

scientists insisted? Did she only assist him with the complicated mathematical calculations, as others claimed? Or did she
play a much more critical role, as a few physicists believed?

As I dug into Mileva's history, I discovered that she was
fascinating in her own right, not just as a footnote in Albert
Einstein's story. Her rise from the relative backwater of misogy-
nistic Serbia to the all-male university physics and mathematics
classrooms of Switzerland was nothing short of meteoric. To
my mind, the question of what role she truly played in Albert's
"miracle year" of 1905 became an examination of how Mileva—
after pregnancy, exam failure, and marriage—was forced to sub-
sume her academic ambitions and intellect to Albert's ascent.
Her story was, in many ways, the story of many intelligent,
educated women whose own aspirations were marginalized in
favor of their spouses. I believed it was time that stories such as
these were told.

Given the fresh light this story sheds on the famous Albert,
readers of *The Other Einstein* may be curious as to precisely
how much of the book is truth and how much is speculation.
Whenever possible, in the overarching arc of the story—the
dates, the places, the people—I attempted to stay as close to
the facts as possible, taking necessary liberties for fictional purposes. As one example of these liberties, Mileva did not begin
her residential stint in Zürich at the Engelbrecht Pension but
found her way there through her friendships after staying at
another pension, and thus, the scene with Mileva and her father
meeting the Engelbrechts is entirely fictional, as are many of the
early scenes between Mileva and her pension friends, although
they could have well happened a bit later in her life. And, of

course, there are other instances in which I imagined the details of events about which I knew the barest of facts. In order to make their own assessment about the actual lives of the people depicted in *The Other Einstein*, I invite readers to peruse the collection of papers and letters by and about Albert Einstein and Mileva Marić that are posted online at the marvelous website http://einsteinpapers.press.princeton.edu.

Certainly, speculation exists in *The Other Einstein*—the book is, first and foremost, fiction. For example, the exact fate of Lieserl is mysterious, although not for dint of effort; Michele Zackheim wrote a wonderful book called *Einstein's Daughter: The Search for Lieserl* about her protracted hunt for Lieserl, one that yielded no solution. Was Lieserl given up for adoption? It seems to me quite probable that Lieserl died from the scarlet fever that prompted Mileva to race from Zürich to Serbia.

Similarly, the precise nature of Mileva's contribution to the 1905 theories attributed to Albert is unknown, although no one disputes that, at a minimum, she played the significant part of emotional and intellectual supporter during this critical time. But given how Mileva saw the world and how desperately she must have loved her daughter, isn't it possible that the loss of Lieserl could have inspired Mileva to create the theory of special relativity? Answering through fiction the seemingly unanswerable questions in Mileva's life—exploring the "what ifs"—is what makes writing *The Other Einstein* so interesting to me.

Many books and articles—of the vast library of written material on Albert Einstein, including http://einsteinpapers. press.princeton.edu—assisted me immensely in my research for this book. Of them, I found the following of particular help and inspiration: *Albert Einstein/Mileva Marić: The Love Letters*, edited by Jürgen Renn and Robert Schulmann; *Einstein in Love: A Scientific Romance* by Dennis Overbye; *In Albert's Shadow: The Life and Letters of Mileva Marić, Einstein's First Wife* by Milan Popovic; *Einstein: His Life and Universe* by Walter Isaacson; and *Einstein's Wife: Work and Marriage in the Lives of Five Great Twentieth-Century Women* by Andrea Gabor. These are but a few.

The purpose of *The Other Einstein* is not to diminish Albert Einstein's contribution to humanity and science but to share the humanity behind his scientific contributions. *The Other Einstein* aims to tell the story of a brilliant woman whose light has been lost in Albert's enormous shadow—that of Mileva Marić.

READING GROUP GUIDE

1. Discuss the various ways that gender affects the characters in this novel. Do you think gender would influence Mileva's life in the same way if she lived today?

2. Betrayal is a recurrent motif in the book and an unfortunate reality in Mileva's life. What forms of betrayal does she experience? How does her reaction to those betrayals propel the story forward, for better or worse? Has Mileva engaged in betrayal herself?

3. Discuss the setting of the book, a world on the brink of astounding scientific discoveries, political upheaval, and ultimately horrible World War I atrocities. Does this historical setting affect the characters? What role, if any, does it play in shaping their lives?

4. Over the course of the novel, we learn a great deal about Mileva's childhood and early adult years. What life events led her to math and science? What hurdles did she have to surmount to even get her footing on that path?

5. From a very young age, Mileva assumes that she will never

marry due to her physical disability. How is this disability both a blessing and a curse? How does her limp impact her differently at different life stages?

6. Mileva and Albert are drawn to each other from the beginning of their years together at the Polytechnic. What qualities compel them toward one another?

7. Leaving Lieserl behind with her mother while she awaits Albert in Zürich and Bern is a huge, pivotal moment for Mileva. Do you think she made the right choice? Should she have stayed with Lieserl and disobeyed Albert's request?

8. On several occasions throughout the novel, the characters undergo metamorphoses. What are Mileva's changes, and what instigates them? Do some of them frustrate you or take too long? Does Albert change during the course of the novel? If so, how would you describe his evolution?

9. While Mileva does not form friendships until rather late in her life, the ties she forms are deep. How do her friendships and her acquaintances with other women factor in her ultimate life choices?

10. Albert Einstein is arguably one of the most famous figures of the twentieth century, but *The Other Einstein* shares a story about him that you might not have otherwise heard. Did this novel change your perception of him? About the stories we are told regarding other women in history?

CARNEGIE'S MAID

December 23, 1868
New York, New York

THE GENTLE MELODY OF A CHRISTMAS SONG LIFTED INTO
the air of his study from the street below. The music did
nothing to change his mood or his actions. Ensconced behind
the black walnut desk in his luxuriously appointed St. Nicholas
Hotel suite, fountain pen in hand, Andrew Carnegie wrote like
a madman.

He paused, searching for the correct word. Glancing around
the study, lit by the very latest in gaslights, he saw it as if anew. The
walls were hung with a heavy yellow brocade wallpaper, and dark-
green velvet curtains framed the windows, tied back by heavy gold
cords, affording him a fine view of Broadway. He knew this suite
was superior to any found in America or even Europe. Yet this
fact, which had so pleased him during his earlier visits to New
York, now repulsed him. The curtain's gold cords seemed like
binding ropes, and he felt trapped inside a rarified prison.

He had argued with Mother that they should stay elsewhere,
somewhere less ostentatious. He longed to reside somewhere

that was not haunted by memories of Clara, although he did not say that aloud. It no longer seemed right to stay at the St. Nicholas, not without her. He had spent the better part of a year searching for her, with no success. Not even the detectives, his top security men, or bounty hunters—the best in the business—could locate a hint of her trail.

But Mother would have none of it. *Andra*, she called him in her inimitable brogue, *the trappings of wealth are the Carnegies' right and due, and by God, we will secure our place.* He acquiesced, depleted of the energy to argue. But on their arrival at the St. Nicholas Hotel earlier that day, Andrew took the extraordinary step of banishing his mother to her adjoining suite of rooms and ignoring her pleas that they attend a holiday dinner at the Vanderbilts, an invitation to the near-highest echelon of New York City society that had been hard-won. He needed to be alone with his thoughts of Clara.

Clara. He whispered her name, letting it roll over his tongue like a fine cordial. In the privacy of his study, he let his very first memory of her wash over him. Clara had trailed behind Mother into the parlor of Fairfield, their Pittsburgh home, with a step so light that he barely noticed the tap of her shoes or the swish of her skirts as she crossed the room. Her demure manner and averted gaze did nothing to draw his attention until Mother had barked out some order in Clara's direction. Only then, when Clara lifted her eyes and met his square on, did her presence register. In that fleeting moment, before she quickly lowered her eyes again, he witnessed the sharp intelligence that lay beneath the placid demeanor required for a lady's maid.

Other, more intimate memories of Clara began to take

hold, along with a longing so intense, it caused him physical pain. But then a roar of laughter and the clink of crystal glasses from the Grand Dining Room below his study interrupted his reverie. He wondered who might be celebrating in that gilded room. Could it be one of his steel business colleagues visiting from out of town, or perhaps one of the elusive "upper ten" families deigning to leave their cosseted, insular world of brownstone dinners to peer into the latest in sumptuous New York City dining establishments? Should he go downstairs to see?

Stop, he chastised himself. *This is precisely the sort of status-seeking, greedy thinking that Clara would have loathed.* He had vowed to her that he would carve out a different path from those materialistic industrialists and society folk, and he would keep that vow, even though she was gone. He returned to his mission of honoring her, one he'd attempted countless times as he drafted and redrafted this document. Pressing the tip of the fountain pen so hard that the ink bled through the fragile paper, he wrote:

> *Thirty-three and an income of $50,000 per annum! By this time two years I can so arrange all my business as to secure at least $50,000 per annum. Beyond this never earn—make no effort to increase fortune, but spend the surplus each year for benevolent purposes. Cast aside business forever, except for others.*
>
> *Settle in Oxford and get a thorough education, making the acquaintance of literary men—this will take three years' active work—pay especial attention to speaking in public. Settle then in London and purchase a controlling interest in some newspaper or*

live review and give the general management of it attention, taking a part in public matters, especially those connected with education and improvement of the poorer classes.

Man must have an idol—the amassing of wealth is one of the worst species of idolatry—no idol more debasing than the worship of money. Whatever I engage in I must push inordinately; therefore should I be careful to choose that life which will be the most elevating in its character. To continue much longer overwhelmed by business cares and with most of my thoughts wholly upon the way to make more money in the shortest time, must degrade me beyond hope of permanent recovery. I will resign business at thirty-five, but during the ensuing two years I wish to spend the afternoons in receiving instruction and in reading systematically.

Lifting the pen from the paper, Andrew read. The words were rough and imperfectly formed, but he was satisfied. Although God had willed that he could not have Clara, he would brandish her beliefs like a sword. He would worship the idols of status and money—for their own sake—no longer. Instead, he would amass and utilize reputation and money for one higher purpose only: the betterment of others, particularly the creation of ladders for the immigrants of his adopted land to climb. Through the heavy fog of his despair, Andrew permitted himself the smallest of smiles, the tiniest of appeasements. The letter would have pleased his Clara.

A CONVERSATION
WITH THE AUTHOR

Albert Einstein is such a well-known historical figure. Were you intimidated or afraid to humanize him? What struggles did you have turning him into a round character, not just an "idea" of a person most people have?

I almost didn't write *The Other Einstein* because I found the notion of fictionalizing the iconic Albert Einstein incredibly daunting! Because Albert factors so prominently in Mileva's life, I had to muster my courage to share a side of Albert's personality that wasn't always flattering and that very likely contradicted the more widely held understanding of him, even though my depiction is fictional. Still, I had to remind myself periodically that I was telling an important story about Mileva's life, not Albert's, to reaffirm my commitment to the task.

The Other Einstein relies on a great deal of research. What was that process like?

Researching *The Other Einstein* was both exhilarating and frustrating, especially since I'm an exhaustive researcher who prefers to use original source material. Of course, there is a vast amount of information—both original and secondary—about Albert Einstein, but the research material available about Mileva is more scant, making the process a bit more challenging.

I was fortunate, however, that some letters between Albert and Mileva still exist, as well as some letters between Mileva and Helene. They were invaluable in conjuring up Mileva's voice.

Mitza is a young woman in a man's world, both confident and uncomfortable at the same time. Did you draw on any personal experiences to write those scenes?

I definitely channeled my early years as a very young lawyer at an enormous law firm in New York City when I wrote about Mitza's time at the Polytechnic. When I first started practicing as a commercial litigator in the 1990s, women lawyers were not as prevalent as they are today, and very often, I found myself as the only woman—and the youngest person—in a conference room or courtroom full of men. I remember well summoning my courage to speak or present in those situations, even when I knew that I was the only one with the correct answer. I drew upon those memories and experiences when I wrote about Mitza's own struggles to share her knowledge and insights in similar contexts.

What drew you to the character of Mitza? Why not write the book from Albert's point of view?

I have always been fascinated by the untold tales of history, and Mileva's story had long been hidden from view. Initially, I was drawn to her story because I was interested in viewing this critical period of Albert's life—when most of his revolutionary theories were formed—from a different perspective, one never before explored. But once I learned about Mileva's astounding rise from the relative hinterland of the

Austro-Hungarian Empire to the forward-thinking physics classrooms of fin de siècle Switzerland, I felt honor-bound to write about her own compelling life. As for point of view, the idea of drafting the story from Albert's perspective never really occurred to me; my interest is in unearthing the unknown, and Albert's past has been examined exhaustively. I felt like it was time for a new voice.

How did you start to think about telling the story of this relationship, which is not a love story in the traditional sense?

At the outset, I did have a certain amount of interest in tracking the course of the relationship between Albert and Mileva. Theirs was a passionate affair and magnificent meeting of the minds that devolved rather dramatically over time. But I was also interested in exploring the process of scientific creativity that happened between them—that very moment of insight—and the attribution that happened afterward.

Have you always enjoyed science yourself, or was writing about physics and theory a whole new world for you?

The irony about writing *The Other Einstein* is that I haven't always been a lover of science. In fact, I almost didn't write it because I found the science overwhelming. That said, once I dug into exciting scientific developments of this historical time period, I developed a new appreciation for mathematics and science—physics in particular. Viewed through Mileva's eyes, math and science become a way of discovering divine, universal patterns in our world, a notion I found very intriguing.

ACKNOWLEDGMENTS

Many people were instrumental in helping me bring Mileva Marić out from the shadows of her famous husband, Albert Einstein, and into the light in *The Other Einstein*. My indefatigable agent, Laura Dail, led the charge, and my tremendous Sourcebooks editor, Shana Drehs, took up the torch. The entire Sourcebooks team—Dominique Raccah in the lead, along with the fantastic Valerie Pierce, Heidi Weiland, Heather Moore, Lathea Williams, Stephanie Graham, Heather Hall, Adrienne Krogh, Will Riley, Danielle McNaughton, Travis Hasenour, and so many others—ran with the book from there, becoming unbelievably enthusiastic proponents of *The Other Einstein*.

My wonderful family and friends have been indispensable in their support, including, but definitely not limited to: my Sewickley crew, my Lucky Eight writing ladies, Illana Raia, Kelly Close, and Ponny Conomos Jahn. But, without my boys Jim, Jack, and Ben championing this project, *The Other Einstein* would never have come to light. They have my endless gratitude.